Praise fo

A Christma

‘I adored it! Romanti ...ng and touching, a warm hug of a book’ **Portobello Book Blog**

‘Absolutely beautiful. The whole story has immense warmth and heart’ **Being Anne**

‘Truly magical’ **This Hannah Reads**

‘Completely stole my heart’ **Curled up with a Good Book**

‘A charming and delightful read, gripped me from start to finish’ **Ginger Book Geek**

‘Intriguing, enchanting and whimsical. I loved it’ **Novel Kicks**

‘Completely lived up to my expectations and beyond’ **Herding Cats**

‘Oh my goodness! This book. It was absolutely perfect’ **@Curlygrannylovestoread**

Lottie Cardew

a Christmas Wish on a Carousel

To David,

Thanks for supporting Children in Need!

Happy Christmas & Birthday

Lottie Cardew

Paperback edition first published by
© Cloverdilli House Press 2022
ISBN: 978-1-7397758-0-3

A Christmas Wish on a Carousel

Printed and bound by KDP
A CIP record for this book is available
from the British Library

To the Trendells, for their friendship.
From escape rooms, to shooting stars;
from Murder in the Dark, to treasure hunts by day;
to quizzes and board games via Zoom.

#CircleFamForever
Send

'And though she be but little, she is fierce.'

— WILLIAM SHAKESPEARE

Chapter 1

One of my most vivid memories was of a carousel. The smell of metal on my hands, the candyfloss stuck to my teeth. It would come to me in piercing flashes, against my will. Music, dizziness, joy. My dad's arms tight around me as his laughter mingled with mine; his warm breath in my hair, and the feeling of absolute safety as the world spun around us. A world I thought was kind and fair and full of possibility.

But I wasn't wilfully naïve back then, I was just a little girl.

The carousel in front of me today, though oddly familiar, was different from all the carousels I'd ridden as a child. It wasn't summer, and this wasn't a seaside pleasure park or a travelling fair set up on a village common.

In spite of my layers of thermals, woollens, and wadding, a gusty wind still sneaked through. All my fingers and toes had long since gone numb. Each breath pluming like a feathery mist in front of me, I felt frozen in more ways than one. A statue. Staring up at the merry-go-round lit up in red and green and gold, candy canes rising up from snow-white horses with shimmering, midnight-blue saddles.

For some reason, it was quiet at this end of the Christmas market. I'd managed to slip away from my friends, who seemed intent on sampling every stall that sold alcohol rather than drifting around soaking up the atmosphere. Baileys and hot chocolate, beer in plastic tankards, gluhwein in decorative mugs you could keep as a souvenir.

Having volunteered as driver for the journey home, I'd stuck to plain hot chocolate before eventually detaching myself to look for a loo. A lie; I just needed a moment on my own to breathe again. The weight of expectation (this-is-why-I-hate-blind-dates-with-a-passion) was suffocating. Except it hadn't been sold that way. More a group thing, with no pressure. Cue fake laughter.

The bare branches of the trees around me, intricately strung with fairy lights, suddenly fell still as if the wind had paused a moment to let me take in the carousel in all its strange, gleaming glory.

'You want a turn, Miss?'

The voice jolted me from my thoughts. I looked round.

He was tall; his hair as long, dark, and curly as mine, but pulled back in a pony-tail. Towering over me, he smiled. 'Do you want a turn on the carousel, Miss?'

He probably called every woman under a certain age 'Miss'. Unless it was just a vibe I gave off.

'No, it's all right. Thank you.'

His smile slowly broadened to a grin, with the same empathy my dad would have used on me, as if sensing my apprehension. I trusted him instantly somehow: this swarthy man with tiny stud earrings as bright as stars. Perhaps there was still too much of the little girl left in me.

'There's no one else on it,' I pointed out. Why or how it wasn't overrun, I didn't know. There were still plenty of families milling around the market. The carousel was set slightly apart from the other stalls and attractions, though; more enticing the longer I stood and looked at it.

'That doesn't matter.' He moved towards it, beckoning me to follow. 'I won't even charge you.'

'But I'm an adult.'

'There's no upper age limit.' He laughed, his teeth white and enviably straight. 'What's your name?'

I knew I shouldn't have told him. Ordinarily, I wouldn't have given out my name to every strange man who asked. But nothing about this was ordinary. And this man was more than just strange, he was mesmerising. An astonishing specimen. Dressed in a long black jacket as slick as leather, mulberry coloured jeans, an inky velvet shirt, open at the collar.

'Cara,' I said.

'Hello, Cara.' He scraped a small bow that would have been condescending from anyone else. 'I'm Angelo.'

He held out his hand and, willingly, I took it.

Minutes later, the world was spinning up and down and all around me, as I held on to the candy cane pole rising up from the horse Angelo had steered me to, its peculiar name in gold script across its saddle. 'Heartfelt'.

As a familiar tune from *The Nutcracker* tinkled loudly around me, I laughed, I smiled, I thought of my dad and that long ago day I'd tried to box up and store away, where I couldn't find it. I thought of *all* the happy days boxed up and consigned to dusty shelves in my head. And for the first time in what seemed forever, I felt a sense of possibility bubble inside me.

'Make a wish,' said Angelo, his voice close to my ear. Yet when I turned my head briskly he was standing a few feet away. 'Make a wish,' he repeated, more serious now, his own smile fading. 'You know you want to, Cara.'

I would humour him. There was no harm in it, was there? I closed my eyes.

'Don't tell me,' he added. 'Don't say it aloud. There's no need.'

It wasn't a conventional wish, as wishes went. But it came from the heart – I think. It sprang into my head, fully formed, surprising and desperate.

Nothing happened, of course. Nothing changed. The music and the carousel and the late-November night whirled and dipped around me. It wasn't really that sort of wish.

All too soon, although in other ways it seemed an eternity, the carousel slowed and my turn was over. Angelo helped me down, holding my hand again graciously, at a distance.

'Thank you,' I said. 'That was kind of you. And generous.' Not that my payment, which he still wouldn't accept, would have covered the electricity for even one spin, let alone however many we'd just taken. It could have been twenty spins, it might have been a thousand. My sense of time, of space, of reality, felt warped now.

'Goodbye, Cara.' He bowed again. 'And good luck.'

I walked away without looking round, not wanting the magic to fade, not trusting myself to resist running back. The market swallowed me up with its cacophony of voices; jostle of bodies; blend of smells, both sweet and savoury. My smile felt brittle as I spotted Sallie and the group I'd come into town with, dragged along with them this evening the way I was pulled through life these days.

'There you are!' She raised her sculpted eyebrows at me. 'How long does it take to find a loo?'

'Hope you didn't go too far?' Greg jerked his thumb over his shoulder. 'There's actually a loo just down there.'

'Thanks, I wandered just far enough.' I knew Sallie had meant well, setting me up like this. I still felt like a gooseberry, though. Maybe Greg did, too.

'Here.' My best friend thrust something wrapped in several paper serviettes under my nose. 'Hog roast bap. Extra stuffing and apple sauce. You said you fancied one earlier, and they were about to sell out.'

With an acuteness that took me by surprise, I was suddenly hungrier than I'd been in ages. As if I could feel things more intensely after stepping off that merry-go-round. After holding Angelo's hand.

'Sal, thank you.' I would have hugged her if there wasn't an over-stuffed bap between us.

'You seem to fancy that more than you fancy Greg here.' Sallie's husband Laurence chuckled and wafted beer fumes towards me. I let him off. He would never have said anything like that if he was entirely sober.

My fixed smile met Greg's. Perhaps we shared a flicker of apology and regret. I'm not sure; I'd never been great at reading signals or flirting. Or whatever the opposite of flirting was if you didn't like someone that way. As usual, I was overthinking things.

Just eat, Cara, and let it pass. Eat and remember, tomorrow's a new day.

But that was the problem. Most of my tomorrows were the same as my yesterdays. Little Cara Mia Shaw, stuck in a perpetual rut.

Sallie linked her arm through mine as we headed back towards the car park, sharing jokes with Nushrat and Nushrat's boyfriend Tod over my shoulder. I tuned them out without meaning to, and caught Greg's eye again. He smiled stiffly. He wasn't bad-looking, and it wasn't as if I had a strict physical type I always went for, but the initial chemistry wasn't there.

Would it be worth forcing, though, to see where it might lead? My mum had taught me that. About giving things a chance. She hadn't been drawn to my dad at first, she said. But then a few days later, he'd made her laugh when laughter had felt impossible. And that was it. Enough to tip the scales.

'Love's like that,' Mum had counselled, when I was fifteen and impressionable enough to commit her words to memory. 'Sometimes it can come at you out of nowhere, loud and brash and glorious, and other times it just creeps up from behind and overtakes you. On rare occasions, I think it might somehow manage both, each as miraculous as the other.'

I don't recall how we'd got on to the subject, but I remember we were sharing a slab of lemon drizzle cake, and Mum had been quite lucid and poetic and almost luminous that day, as opposed to dull and grey and lost. I could have listened to her for hours when she was like that; her accent so musical, yet her syntax so precise, as if English was her first language. In a way it was by then, I suppose. The only language she'd spoken in years; studied with a passion since childhood, almost as if she'd known what was going to happen.

What if I missed an opportunity, by not giving Greg a chance? He seemed nice enough. A colleague of Laurence's. Steady income. His own home. A mortgage he could afford. Clean driving licence. Sallie had filled me in on that much. On paper, he was everything a single thirty-one-year-old like me might want in a romantic partner. I couldn't confirm or deny if I was looking for a new relationship, though. To be honest, the whole business of dating and settling down confused me more than ever.

And looping back to that carousel, and my spur of the moment wish… Had I even asked for love, let alone *true* love?

No; not in a conventional, fairy-tale sense. I'd wanted something else that seemed even further away, even less attainable.

As we dropped Greg off, I let him take my number. 'I'll text,' he said. 'Maybe we can go for a drink on our own? Chat properly?'

There were encouraging murmurs from behind me, and I found myself nodding and shrugging. 'Okay, why not?'

I dropped off the others in turn, taking the large, seven-seater SUV back to mine. Sallie or

Laurence would walk over and pick it up the following day. A Saturday. For once, I wasn't working. My time was my own. The entire weekend stretched ahead emptily.

Flopping on to my mattress shortly after arriving home, the metal bedstead creaked, and the darkness and solitude of the countryside all around pressed in on me. Even though I knew I wasn't alone out here, that there was a family of four in the large house next door, I shivered. It might have been down to the fact the radiators had been cold for hours after I'd turned them down when I went out, but I wasn't so sure.

I resisted sleep for as long as I could, scared of dreams that would make no sense but might leave me hollowed out and raw. But by morning, waking up curiously rested, all I could remember dreaming about was a Christmas carousel, a horse called Heartfelt, and a man with stars in his dusky earlobes who'd claimed his name was Angelo.

Chapter 2

Why I'd thought my weekend would be empty, I don't know. I always fell into this trap. There was only so much time I could allot to ploughing through my to-be-read pile before the guilt set in: the nagging feeling that I should be scrubbing and dusting, even though my hovel was so small I'd blitzed through it in less than an hour after work on Wednesday. And then there was my sewing machine and the clothes hanging from the rail, beckoning me over to repair and repurpose. Every item I went on to sell would be a welcome drop in the woeful puddle of my bank account.

I sighed, dithering over what to do first, staring around me as I perched on the bed.

I shouldn't call it a hovel. It was a roof over my head and I was blessed to have it. My two rooms, bathroom included, plus the corridor that doubled as a kitchen, weren't damp or musty. There were no dubious black patches creeping across the ceiling, and when the boiler was on during the day, the heating and hot water could be bliss. Nothing was falling to bits, either, and when I'd first moved in I'd been free to decorate however I wanted. It was a lot more than some people had.

'Bijou,' Sallie and Nushrat called it, at their most magnanimous.

I got on with some sewing, and just before lunch, after Laurence had come over to collect the SUV, and interrogated me briefly on my first impressions of Greg (I knew Sallie wouldn't forgive him if he didn't quiz me), I trudged across the yard to the utility area in the outhouse, to load the washing machine. Although 'outhouse' didn't seem the right term for the huge space; walls and ceilings a matte chalk-white, with skylights and potted palms, and twigs artfully arranged in tall glass vases.

It doubled as a games room, with dartboard, pool and table tennis. There was even one of those air hockey things, and a large TV and sofa for hanging out. Oh, and the small 'foosball' table in the corner which I did my best to ignore, because my dad had loved them so much.

JoJo appeared almost instantly, sleek and resplendent in her kimono-style dressing gown. 'Cara, hun, here you are.' She looked pleased to see me, but it didn't brighten my mood. I knew what was coming. 'You wouldn't mind putting these bits and pieces in with your things, would you? Most of it's darks, like the stuff you wear, so…' She must have been lying in wait, looking out for me from her kitchen.

I don't know why she always acted as if this was a one-off. It was always happening. And she always made me sound like a Goth.

'Sure.' I took the laundry basket from her. It was more than a few bits and pieces, but I couldn't complain. This was JoJo's outhouse. Her washing machine, tumble dryer and heated airer. Even the annexe I called home belonged to her.

'Not got a shift in the café today, then?' she asked airily.

'Not today. I'm back in on Monday.'

'Any plans for the weekend? I noticed you went out yesterday. And Sallie and Laurence's car was in the drive this morning.'

'We went into town for the Christmas market. I drove back, so they could have a drink.'

'Ooh, is the market open now? Any good? Belle and Vicki want to go, though at their age they won't admit it. And Des, of course. He won't admit it, either.' Her laughter bounced off the walls. 'I like the food stalls best, don't you?'

'It was good.' I shrugged. 'There were more stalls than usual, I think. And a Christmas-themed carousel. I haven't seen one of those in town before.'

'Sounds lovely. I like those layered meat pies, you know? From that artisan pie place. Pork and venison and all sorts, with that breadcrumb and cranberry crust.' Her eyes glazed over hungrily. I knew if she ate even one slice of that pie, though, she would fast zealously for days afterwards.

'Mmm.' Most things calling themselves artisan were out of my price range.

'Anyway, Cara, if you're not busy this afternoon, would you mind taking Loki for his walk? Belle has a piano lesson, Vicki's at a friend's, and Des is running errands in town. I'd do it myself, but…'

There was always a 'but'.

'That's fine.' I finished loading the washing machine. 'I'll take him out after lunch.'

Loki the Pomeranian. A ball of ginger fur on legs. I adored him and suspected the feeling was mutual, considering I'd walked him enough times over these last five years since they'd brought him home from the pet rescue. And I always looked after the little dog, and the hefty goldfish Thor and Odin, whenever the Pembroke family were off on one of their regular holidays.

'Cara, you're a star!' JoJo beamed, flicking ruler-straight hair over her shoulder, and trotted out in her ivory satin slipper mules.

I stared at the door she'd left open, marvelling at how she managed to come across as dizzy and vacuous so often when she was anything but. JoJo had been good to me; she was just on another level in terms of income and social status. Her dad, for starters, had been a successful businessman related to some viscount or other.

JoJo had never rested on her laurels, as if to prove she could be every bit as successful. She was the main breadwinner, working her manicured fingers to the bone for all this – the house, the cars, the lifestyle in general. And she was even attempting to go more eco with her brand, although with anti-aging beauty products and cosmetics, it wasn't easy. But I liked that she was making an effort.

After a swift lunch, I bundled myself up for the walk. Dark jeans and jumper, my usual puffy black coat and beanie hat with matching gloves. I slung a crossbody bag around me with a reflective strap, though, easily picked out by passing headlights. Not that I wanted to be dog-walking around these narrow lanes as darkness fell, but it was a gloomy enough day.

Loki spun in gleeful circles when he spotted me letting myself in through the kitchen. The little dog licked my chin as I scooped him up for a brief cuddle before I clipped on his harness and hooked his lead; his bark a series of excited yips, as we let ourselves out. Loki's legs, what you could see of them, might have been short and skinny, but he could have walked for miles if I'd wanted, regardless of the hilly Shropshire countryside.

The pale sun was already dipping towards the horizon and a faint mist creeping in when I turned back for home. As usual I'd warmed up as I'd walked, but when my phone pinged with a text, and I fished it out of my bag, I felt my cheeks flush with heat.

—*Hi Cara. Just wondering if you were free later? I'm at a loose end, so if you are too, would you like to get that drink? BTW this is Greg. Laurence's mate from last night. (The one you fancied marginally less than a hog roast bap.)*

I smiled, approving of people who punctuated their messages, and liking it even more if they made a stab at humour. But did I like Greg enough to go out with him – even casually? On the other hand, if I didn't get to know him, how could I judge with any fairness whether he might grow on me or not?

I texted back before I could change my mind.

—*I'm free too. Where would you like to go?*

Having picked him up yesterday and dropped him off afterwards, I knew he lived in the hamlet of Westerly Sutton, half-way between town and my village. A blink-and-you-might-miss-it sort of place. It didn't even have its own pub.

He messaged back instantly.

—*Anywhere you like in particular?*

I had a quick think.

—*How about the Tarnished Key here in Pebblestow? It doesn't get too busy.*

— *Sounds good. I can pick you up? If it makes you feel safer/more comfortable tell Sallie what's happening. Let me know where and I'll be there at 8?*

He seemed keen. I was out of practice at this,

and even though technically it might be considered a date, it didn't need to be spelled out. I backtracked after typing: *'It's a date'* (pathetic) and changed it to:

— *8 is great with me. I'll see you then.*

And I added directions before sending.

'I guess he must like me, Loki.' I spoke aloud into the crisp air, tangy with the scent of woodsmoke. 'It can't be too obvious that I'm letting myself go, then.' I winked at the dog, trotting loftily at my feet. 'Well, yes, okay, JoJo *does* ply me with tester pots and all sorts, and I do use them, because who doesn't like a freebie that smells like heaven? But maybe I ought to make an effort tonight? Use the stash of make-up she's dumped on me, too. What do you reckon?' I lifted an eyebrow, which probably needed a light pluck, to eliminate any strays. The little dog yipped again, and even gave me one of his classic Pomeranian twirls, mid-walk. 'Right, so that's decided then. Thanks for your feedback. Much appreciated, as always.'

After I'd deposited Loki in an echoey, empty house and fed him dinner while also dusting flakes of goldfish food into Thor and Odin's state-of-the-art tank, I returned to the annexe where I picked out my clothes for later. With the gang all there yesterday for the trip into town, and knowing I would have my coat on most of the time, I hadn't bothered to dress up.

It felt ages since I'd gone out alone with a

man, and I didn't want to dwell too long on my last attempt at maintaining a relationship. It had definitely been a while since I'd contemplated even wearing a skirt and tights instead of my usual jeans or leggings, albeit a pleated vintage skirt and woollen winter tights. At precisely five-foot, I was petite, with curves where I felt they ought to be, but there was no law that said: flaunt it.

'Dainty,' Sallie liked to call me, as if I were some antique china doll, easily broken.

Still, I shaved my legs in the bath after I cobbled together a rushed dinner, although Greg would categorically *not* be seeing them tonight, however the evening went. I was clear with myself on that score. So why bother, I wondered? Because contemporary western culture deemed it the proper thing to do? Because not taking the time would be lazy and 'ew'? I couldn't come up with an answer I was satisfied with.

As I waited for Greg to arrive, the imaginary *tick-tick-tick* of a clock swelling to a crescendo in my head, I sat on my compact two-seater sofa – the only comfy chair in the annexe – and stared at the object I'd just dug out from a cardboard box under my bed. Once upon a time, it had been a large snow-globe sitting proudly on a shelf in my old bedroom. But the globe itself had been smashed years ago, depositing tiny faux snowflakes and shards of plastic in a puddle across a spotty rug and varnished floorboards. It was a miracle no other part of it had broken. I'd sobbed at my clumsiness, and Dad had salvaged what he could, hugging me until I stopped crying.

My parents had bought the snow-globe for me one Christmas, with its detailed depiction of a carousel decked out in green, red and gold, with candy cane poles, and snow-white horses with midnight-blue saddles. I hadn't been wrong to experience a sense of déjà vu yesterday at the market, but up until a few minutes ago, I hadn't been able to place why.

The cardboard box under my bed contained the few Christmas decorations left over from my childhood. The ones I'd wanted to keep; or rather, the ones I couldn't let go. Like the decorations themselves, I was too fragile to put them out on display. They stayed in the box all year round, and I hadn't dared look at them in ages. Tonight probably wasn't the right time to torment myself, but curiosity had got the better of me.

I was in a strange, wild sort of mood when I heard Greg's car and saw the flash of headlights through my curtains as I sprang to my feet. I slammed and locked the front door before he could catch a glimpse of the hovel's interior. Like most people, though, he was distracted by the massive modern house it was attached to, with its pristine cream façade. The fact I lived in a tiny annexe seemed to pass people by, as if the Pembrokes' wealth must have rubbed off on me and I was far more intriguing because of it.

As I slid into his car, Greg whistled – not at me, thankfully – and peered over his steering wheel at the house. The car smelled clean and fresh, which was a plus. I caught a trace of aftershave, too. 'Nice place,' he commented appreciatively.

'It is.' I buckled myself in. 'But I'm no relation of theirs. The Pembrokes. They're the family who own it. Have you heard of JoJo Pem? It's a high-end beauty brand?'

He screwed up his brow. 'Vaguely… I think.'

'Well, it's her house. I used to work for them.' I explained it all as succinctly as I could, while Greg cautiously navigated Swallowtail Lane down the hill towards the village, his headlights the only illumination apart from a silvery moon veiled by clouds. 'We lived in Manchester at first. I was their nanny when JoJo and Des's kids were little. Two girls: Belle and Vicki. When they bought this place, JoJo asked if I was willing to move to the countryside, too. I didn't have anything keeping me in the city, so I moved with them.'

'How old are the kids now?'

'Fifteen and fourteen. I haven't been their nanny in a long while. I used to live in the house with them; had my own room and en suite. I planned to leave, when the time came. Find another position – back in Manchester, if I had to – but…' I hesitated.

It was too soon to get into the nitty-gritty

of why I'd stayed; the reasons I'd moved into the annexe. I barely knew this man, his chunky arms confidently gripping the steering wheel as he glanced at me every so often, spurring me on, willing me to open up. He seemed genuinely curious and interested. And he really wasn't too bad on the eyes.

But I'd felt so odd minutes ago, so disorientated – staring down at the carousel on my coffee table, almost a miniature of the carousel at the Christmas market – I didn't know how I felt now, beyond ruffled. As if something had reached inside and stirred up my emotions, until they whirled dizzily like the snowflakes that had once danced in my snow-globe. I badly needed them to settle.

'I think JoJo likes having someone around if they're not there,' I said. It wasn't a lie. 'And I still help her out a lot.' Another *not*-lie; in fact, that was definitely a big fat truth.

We drove through the village and around Market Square, already decked out for Christmas, a zigzag of coloured lights overhead. The Tarnished Key was at the far end. A blast of warmth from the inglenook fireplace made my face flush almost as soon as we walked in, both of us momentarily dazzled by the flashing lights and glittery baubles obscuring a fat, sprawling Christmas tree.

The pub was busier than I'd expected, but Greg steered me with calm efficiency towards a small table at the back, away from the crowded bar and the stifling heat from the fire. It seemed to exist in its own little hushed bubble, and I sank appreciatively on to the padded bench.

'Is this okay?' There was a dent in his brow I recognised as concern. 'We can go someplace else if you want? Find another pub? Somewhere quieter...?'

'It's a Saturday night. I don't think "quieter" exists.'

After filling Sallie in on what was happening tonight, I'd also begged her and the others to stay away, not bump into us here accidentally on purpose. I needed to chat to Greg on my own. I knew my being here with him might generate gossip in the village, and the pub landlady had already raised her eyebrows, and given me a subtle wink, but I let it skim over me. There was a price to living in a place like Pebblestow.

Greg snorted grimly. 'I'm getting too old for this, then.'

'How old are you?' I should have framed that better, but I didn't always see the point in dawdling.

'Sallie didn't tell you? I'd have thought that was the first thing you'd ask when someone's trying to set you up. Didn't you want to know?'

I bit my lip, though now I possibly had lipstick on my teeth. 'Sorry, she probably did say. I might not have been listening. To be truthful, I was a bit sceptical about the whole thing.'

He hesitated a moment. 'So was I, if we're being honest. And I'm sorry if I seemed… distant, yesterday. I've never had much success when mates suggest I meet someone they know. Anyway,' he sighed, 'I'm thirty-three. I've been working with Laurence a few months now, but I'm not an IT geek like him. I'm in sales. More into the psychology of selling, though, rather than bullying folk into buying stuff, so don't worry. I'm fairly bland, as blokes go.' He gave me a watery smile as if apologising.

It irked me, that he felt ashamed of it. But I wasn't annoyed at him, just society again.

'Good,' I said. 'Because I'm not into toxic masculinity or mansplaining. I like to pay my own way, too, so on that note…' I pulled out my purse.

'Listen, Cara, let me get the first round and you get the second. How does that sound? I'm not trying to be all alpha, or—'

'Okay,' I cut in, before he apologised again. Was it always like this, these days? Dating? Would we tiptoe around each other all evening, microscopically analysing everything we said? I was seriously rusty, although it hadn't been as long as it felt. 'The next round's on me.'

'So then…? What can I get you?'

'Oh, right. Of course.' Attempting a polite chuckle, I might have sounded as if I were being strangled; but Greg didn't look at me weirdly, so I seemed to get away with it. 'You can't buy me a drink if you don't know what I want,' I added unnecessarily.

Screw it. My nerves were frazzled. I needed to loosen up while still keeping my wits about me. Alcohol would definitely have to be involved, but nothing too potent.

'Medium white wine spritzer, please. With soda water, not lemonade. And ice is fine.'

'Very specific. I like that.' Greg grinned, and wove his way towards the bar.

I stared at his retreating back, and wondered if perhaps I might fancy him a little bit, after all.

Chapter 3

It was the 'may' that did it for me.

The 'May I kiss you, Cara?' that came at the end of the evening when Greg dropped me home. He'd only had half a lager shandy and then stuck to pints of Coke. Very restrained, I'd thought, while unashamedly downing my white wine spritzers. Alongside the fact he was driving, he'd seemed more relaxed than me, so I evidently needed them more than he did.

I didn't drink that often. I preferred to keep a clear head. Like last night, when I'd been happy to designate myself as driver; I was insured on the SUV and drove it regularly enough. But going out on my own with Greg was different – I'd wanted just enough of a buzz to get by without crossing the line into slapstick or silly.

Greg and I had a good time, from where I was sitting, finding myself mildly surprised and a little excited by the notion. We each carried a proportionate share of the conversation, and I kept my history well within my comfort zone. Greg had lived with someone for a few years, but it hadn't worked out. Obviously. He was currently single, after all. (I didn't say that, of course, and neither did he; it just hovered between us, a pathetic unspoken quip.) Anyway, that was the most serious relationship he'd had, and it was a while back. But now dating seemed to be getting harder, not easier.

I knew what he meant. I'd had boyfriends, I explained to him, but below the average if Sallie was to be believed. None of those relationships had ever translated to anything long-term. What I didn't go on to say was that perhaps the blokes weren't entirely at fault.

Sallie and Nushrat had listened to my laments often enough, and their advice never wavered. At some point in every relationship, it seemed, a part of me would back off. My friends claimed they could see it, even though I denied having any idea what they meant. Were they implying I deliberately botched things? Because anything I might have done was unconscious, not intentional.

It was fair to say, though, I didn't have a clear vision for what I wanted. I couldn't picture myself living a life I might deserve with someone who cared about me. Either that, or I didn't *want* to visualise it. Every time I tried, I saw my parents. I saw how much they'd loved each other and couldn't bear to be apart, and that daunted and diminished me, because of how it all ended.

So that night, when Greg said, 'May I?', I tilted my head to his and forced myself to live in the moment. Not the potentially heart-throbbing moments to come, or the ones I might eventually run away from without realising, but that moment with him in his car. A brief few seconds, over far too quickly.

The kiss was soft and undemanding, and all the sweeter and more potent because of it.

We confirmed we wanted to see each other again, and then I let myself into the hovel and locked the door behind me. At the sound of Greg's car fading into the night, I closed my eyes and leaned against the nearest patch of free wall. I knew I'd go over all this again tomorrow, with a clearer head, but I couldn't help scanning the events of the evening anyway in case I forgot some vital element. Something that might have seemed trivial at the time. It streamed through my head like a movie, and to my relief, there were very few awkward silences compared to healthy bursts of laughter and long spells of flowing conversation.

He'd been so polite, so chivalrous in a way that didn't set my teeth on edge. And at the end, so grammatically correct. Too many people would have said, 'Can I…?' or just pounced without even asking. But that quiet, earnest 'May I?' had been a revelation.

I sighed, unzipping my coat and hanging it up. What was left of my old snow-globe caught my eye, on the coffee table surrounded by stacks of books, some my own, others from the library. In the absence of a bookshelf, even a small one, I had to make every available surface count. I sat down and ran my hand over the nearest paperback. A small town American romance. Enemies to lovers. I couldn't say Greg had been my enemy when we'd first met, but I'd felt no spark, no chemistry. And yet, only twenty-four hours later, I'd let him kiss me and enjoyed it.

Why?

I blinked at the miniature carousel. Was it something to do with what I'd asked for? Was that it? I couldn't see a connection. But still, I'd made a wish last night, there was no denying it. Like the child I'd once been, blowing out candles on a birthday cake and obstinately asking for the same thing each time; except this wish was different from my childhood plea. Nevertheless, I'd sent my heart out into the frostbitten universe, and perhaps that simple act was magic enough.

I'd taken a first step.

Other thoughts crept in later, though, as I brushed my teeth and got ready for bed. I wondered if perhaps Sallie and Laurence had picked out Greg for another reason, aside from his availability, common decency and socioeconomic status. Did Sallie suspect he was the kind of man who would put up a fight, not throw in the towel the second I messed up? My best friend liked to tease, but she was ferociously protective of me, too. She wouldn't push me towards anyone she didn't feel was worthy, and Nushrat wouldn't have gone along with it if she didn't approve either.

For their sake, to keep them happy – and off my back – I probably needed to make a go of this. However much they loved me, there was only so much self-sabotage they could possibly bear to watch before throwing in the towel themselves.

I woke up at ten the next morning to my phone lighting up with a string of iMessages from JoJo. It was also emitting the urgent, annoying siren I'd assigned to her profile the other day. No one's fault but mine, for thinking it would be funny.

With a groan, I sat up in bed and pushed back my hair, which insisted on falling forward until I scrabbled for a scrunchie and scooped it all back. My alarm at nine clearly hadn't gone off; or if it had, its dulcet tones hadn't been enough to rouse me. Through bleary eyes, I scrolled through JoJo's messages, getting the gist of what she wanted. I messaged back, hoping autocorrect wouldn't rephrase me too drastically.

—Sorry, I overslept. Yes, I'm free and happy to help. I'll be over after breakfast. Give me 20 mins.

I washed, dressed, gobbled down a toasted bagel, and hurried next door.

'I know it's not an emergency,' said JoJo, greeting me with a mug of strong, foamy cappuccino from her own barista machine; at least she knew how to reward me. 'But right this minute, it feels like one. The girls desperately want all the trees up already. I swear it gets earlier every year. And Des has gone off to play golf with an old friend – at least it's the weather for it today – so I'm stuck here trying to get the boxes down on my own.'

I already knew Belle and Vicki were 'busy' from the messages JoJo had sent me. 'Homework' was a noisy affair these days, judging by the laughter and music blasting from the family lounge.

Loki came bounding from the bowels of the large house, no doubt having stirred himself from one of the many luxury dog beds scattered around the downstairs. He leapt up, pawing my knees. I made a fuss of him till he was satisfied.

'Now wait down here, there's a good boy,' JoJo said with a frown, clicking the concertina stair-gate behind us as we went upstairs. Loki wasn't allowed up in the bedrooms. His fluffy tail stilled, and drooped in disappointment.

The numerous, neatly labelled boxes with all the Pembrokes' Christmas paraphernalia, were stored in the loft. This wasn't the first time I'd come to JoJo's aid. Not a single year had gone by since I'd known her that I hadn't been involved to some degree in this ritual. And not a year went by that she didn't add to her collection. JoJo professed to hate the hassle of the festive season, but never seemed to make it easier for herself.

I knew I'd be the one climbing into the loft and lugging the plastic storage boxes down. For a start, even climbing a couple of 'rungs' of the mechanically operated loft ladder – essentially a staircase that descended from the huge vault in the roof – supposedly triggered her vertigo. And secondly, she never dressed appropriately for the task. Today she was in a multi-layered linen outfit. The top floated around her romantically, with its long butterfly sleeves, and the flared trousers flapped around her endless legs, the effect almost skirt-like. Gold and silver bangles rattled on both wrists as she took each crate from me.

A while later, the boxes were all in the appropriate rooms.

The Pembrokes could never have a real tree. Apparently, Des was allergic to them, and JoJo didn't like the prickliness of pine needles anyway, which was just as well. Their main tree, an immense thing, always went in the hall, where there was a large open space created by the curving staircase. The tree was too tall for a normal room.

The shorter, jet-black Christmas tree, with contrasting white ornaments, went in a corner of the open-plan kitchen and dining area, the pink one in the family lounge, and Belle and Vicki had smaller tinselly ones in each of their bedrooms.

'You're a good friend, you know that, Cara?' JoJo announced, a couple of hours later as we added the finishing touches to the tree in the hall, Loki watching suspiciously. The laughter and music had migrated upstairs as the girls decorated their own trees; whatever solo artist or band they'd been listening to earlier now substituted for cheesy Christmas hits that never seemed to grow old, each generation claiming them for their own. Or maybe I was too nostalgic, and didn't know anything. Perhaps Belle and Vicki were just being ironic.

They were hard to fathom these days compared to the cherubic twosome who'd flitted around the old house in sparkly tutus with coordinating wings and wands. They'd loved me once, and told me so frequently. I'd actually been someone to look up to. But they were on the brink of womanhood now, as willowy and stunning as their mum. I was probably just the sad frump who happened to live next door. Old-fashioned and past it, by their standards.

How had that happened? When had things changed?

I looked across at JoJo now. She'd called me her friend. She'd never said that before. That wasn't our dynamic. JoJo might not mean to, but she still treated me like an employee. All the Pembrokes did. I could never be on their level.

JoJo sighed raggedly. 'They weren't in short supply once. Friends,' she said, when I gave her a blank look. 'Somewhere along the line, the more successful I got, the fewer I had… Except for you, Cara. You've always been here.' She looked across at me, lips flattened, eyes heavy.

I didn't know what to say, so I concentrated on moving a delicate transparent angel made of hand-blown glass, up out of reach, safe from accidental knocks.

Of course I'd always been *here*. For over a third of my life I hadn't known where else to go. And at this rate, I'd never leave until I was pushed out. Treading water, while holding on to the life preserver this family had thrown me.

I was a minion, though, not a friend. That was the territory I was familiar with.

'This Christmas already feels different,' JoJo continued, her mood growing bleaker, as she fiddled distractedly with her bangles. 'What with Des…' she tailed off, glanced away distantly, then back again. 'And I feel even more stressed with Wilfred coming to stay. Although I love him to bits, it's not great timing. Then again, we can't always choose what happens to us… can we?' She looked straight at me, then seemed to realise what she'd said. 'Cara, I'm sorry. I didn't mean—'

'It's okay.' I straightened up. All that remained in the box at my feet was the bubble wrap and tissue paper the decorations had been so carefully swaddled in – by me, last January. 'You're right. We don't always get to choose.'

'I guess Wilfred's been down that road himself recently. Which is why I want to make it up to him this Christmas. See to it that he doesn't get all mopey. I might even throw a party, what do you think?'

'Er, yeah. Parties are always good.' JoJo didn't usually need much of an excuse. And I had lots of practice clearing up afterwards. 'So, how long is Des's brother staying then?'

She stared at me, puckering her brow as if mildly affronted. 'Do you mean Wilfred...? Cara – he's *my* brother. Well, half-brother. I'm always talking about him. My dad's mistress's son. Remember?'

I poked my tongue into my cheek. She wasn't *always* talking about him. The girls and Des seemed to mention him more. Uncle Wilf. It had to be the same person, surely.

JoJo Pembroke, public figure, consistently kept a tight lid on her life beyond her immediate family unit, and even Des and the girls rarely featured in the images she shared online. I felt as if she'd only shared the bare minimum with me, too. Her father – the businessman related to a viscount – had died just before I'd started working for her, and JoJo's mum had remarried soon after, settling down with her new husband in a huge pile in Guernsey and seldom returning to the mainland.

'I'm sorry. Why did I think he was Des's brother?' My apology sounded garbled. 'You all visit him in Canada, don't you, when you've been over there on holiday?'

I couldn't honestly say JoJo had ever claimed him as her own sibling in front of me, and as I'd never had to meet the guy, I hadn't paid much attention. But he wasn't even her full-blown brother, if that was the right way of putting it (I was an only child, how was I supposed to know these things?) and he was their dad's *mistress's* son? What on earth...?

'That's right.' JoJo stood back a few feet to look at the tree, eyes narrowed, surveying it critically. 'He's been living in Canada since his late teens. Sixteen years now since they left; Wilfred and his mum. Steph was Canadian but Wilfred's got dual citizenship. Because of Dad, I suppose; who knows? Plus he was born in Cheshire, like me. How does the tree look, Cara?'

'Er...' I stood back to study it myself. 'Lovely.' As usual. JoJo had a good eye. But I wasn't bad at it, either. 'Doesn't it feel weird, though – the fact he's your dad's... well, you know?'

JoJo smiled, as if I were ten years old and didn't know much about adults and their curious ways. 'The fact my only sibling is the product of an extramarital affair? Dad was with Steph for years, and my mum was aware of it for part of that time. They all agreed Wilfred and I should grow up knowing each other; we shouldn't be lied to, or kept apart. I was only four when he was born; I didn't know any better. Being around Steph was almost like having a second mum.'

I stared at her. 'That was... noble of them.'

'Virtuous of my mother, most of all – don't you think?'

'I guess. Yes.' I was struggling to wrap my head around the whole thing.

'When Dad and Steph split up, though, she went back to Canada and Wilfred went with her. My parents stayed together, till Dad passed away, of course.'

'Right... I see.' I really didn't. The complexity of it all was bizarre; the sort of thing I read about in the gossip mags at my rare trips to the hairdresser's. 'So Wilfred's just here to spend Christmas with you?'

'Not exactly. It's not a holiday, as such.' She sighed. 'Do you fancy another coffee?'

I wasn't about to say no. Besides, JoJo opening up like this was riveting. I sat in an armchair near the vast granite-topped island that dominated the kitchen, watching her play barista, while Loki demanded I rub his belly.

'Wilfred might be coming back to stay, for good.' JoJo finally placed the Emma Bridgewater mugs on a low table between us. 'You see, Steph's dead now. Turns out she had undiagnosed cardiac issues. And then earlier this year, Wilfred's fiancé, well... she ditched him. On Valentine's

Day.'

I pulled a sympathetic face. 'Harsh.'

'Very. He's been spiralling ever since. Quit his job. He was a university lecturer. English and linguistics. Something like that. Don't repeat this, but I've always zoned out when he's gone on about it.'

I could picture this Wilfred clearly now. Tall and fair like JoJo, but without her self-confidence or flair for fashion. A stale tweed jacket and round, wire-framed glasses were added to the vision, although I backtracked on the balding head and bushy whiskers when I remembered he could only be in his mid-thirties. But even his name made him sound ancient and professorial.

The Pembrokes might bring me back generous gifts from their sojourns abroad, but thankfully they never bragged about their fantastic vacations by splashing photos all over the socials. There might be a few posed shots of JoJo in glam locations, but she was strict with the girls and Des's own output. If Wilfred had been in the few pictures I'd seen, he'd never stood out.

'So would you mind?' JoJo was saying, and I realised I'd been miles away.

'Mind?'

'Picking him up from the airport on Thursday? I already checked with Sallie, and you're not working. And of course, you can take my car. Des is busy, and I've got back-to-back meetings all day. I'd go myself, if I could.'

I let this sink in. JoJo had the disconcerting habit of phoning the café to check on my shifts, and Sallie was too much in awe of the highly coveted JoJo Pem brand, and the free stuff that regularly came her way, to deny her this information. In fact Sallie couldn't get over the fact they breathed the same air in the same village, although technically the Pembrokes lived outside it, their house set flamboyantly on the apex of Swallowtail Lane.

'You want me to collect your half-brother from the airport?'

'Manchester, yes. Not Birmingham. He hates flights that aren't direct. And it's easier just to call him my brother. We're honestly that close.' JoJo clasped her hands together. 'I knew you wouldn't mind. You're such a good person, Cara. I'll never regret the day I hired you. Anyway, I'll make sure the car's all fuelled up for you; you're always saying how much you love to drive it. If you weren't around, I would have organised a taxi for poor Wilfred, but it doesn't seem right. Much nicer to have the personal touch; he's quite a reserved, private person at heart. I really want to make this Christmas as special as I can for him, despite everything. He needs family around. Now more than ever.'

I didn't see what was so personal about having a complete stranger meet you at the airport, especially after spending however many hours on a plane. He would no doubt feel all grubby and exhausted, and wouldn't want to make small-talk anyway. Even less so if he was as timid or shy as JoJo was making out. In his shoes (scuffed tan leather brogues, if I went along with the image in my head) I'd have much preferred the anonymity of a taxi ride or equivalent.

But it was too late. Somehow I'd agreed to it, and JoJo had moved on. She was breezily asking if I minded taking Loki for his walk now. But to drink my cappuccino first, 'Cara, you absolute star,' while it was still nice and hot.

Chapter 4

'So, it went well, then?' Sallie grinned at me as she sifted icing sugar over one of her famous 'Granny's recipe' mince pies. 'Your date with Greg? I knew you'd like him if you gave him a chance.'

'It wasn't a date,' I muttered, trying to decipher my writing on the order for Table Four.

'Did you kiss at the end?'

'What?' I squinted at the notepad, deliberately vague with my response. 'Kiss?'

'You do remember what one of those is, don't you? It hasn't been that long. Lips smacking together. Tongues—'

'There were no tongues,' I cut in sharply, and realised too late she'd been aiming to catch me out.

I swore under my breath, while Sallie laughed in triumph. 'But locking lips was involved? So it sounds like a date, to me.'

I glared at her across the small industrial kitchen, shiny and hygienic in stainless steel and chrome. 'Look, it was a good evening, I won't deny that. And we're meant to be going out again this Saturday for dinner, in town.'

Sallie's flaxen bob bounced as she pumped the air. 'I knew you were a good match. You just needed time to ignite that spark, away from the rest of us.'

'Look, he's nice. But it's really early days, so don't go buying a new hat or anything.'

'Marriage talk already!' My so-called BFF made an 'o' shape with her mouth. 'Wow.'

'The opposite of marriage talk. I told you *not* to buy a new hat. No way am I biddable little wifey material, anyway.' I stared off out of the window into the backyard for a moment. 'A bit like Belle, I suppose.'

Sallie's brow wrinkled. 'Belle Pembroke?'

'Belle as in Beauty.' But she still looked confused. 'And the Beast?'

'Oh, right. Her. Get your nose out of your books, and go pop out a bunch of babies for Gaston – that kind of thing?' Sallie slipped one of my hand-made crocheted cosies over a teapot for one. 'But you're hardly a career girl, Cara. The ambitious sort, I mean.'

I didn't say anything, just stared at the striped tea cosy, one of many I'd made for Sallie's café.

'I'm sorry, hun,' she rushed on. 'I didn't mean it that way. It's not that you don't work hard. You put in the graft as much as anyone around here.

It's just... you're not the entrepreneurial type, are you? Never dreamed of your own business empire like JoJo, for instance. Though I don't blame you, business loans are a bugger, and don't get me started on payroll. I hate the account side of things.'

'Just as well Laurence likes it then.'

I didn't want to talk about me and my lack of direction or initiative. My modest online shops on two sites, sparsely stocked with crocheted and knitted items, and the vintage clothes I mended and repurposed, hardly amounted to an enterprise.

I hadn't always been lacking in ambition, though. Or motivation.

'Thank God for Laurence,' Sallie agreed, but I knew she would have managed well enough if he hadn't been willing to help. She had the right mentality to just plough on. Resilience, they called it. And Sallie had it in spades.

'I'm happy, and that's the main thing,' I said, although I don't know why I bothered. She looked across the kitchen as if she could see straight through me.

'If you want to know what "happy" really is, go take this tea and mince pie to Table Nine. The old dear hasn't stopped smiling. She's a proper ray of sunshine.'

'But—'

Sallie snatched the notepad from my grasp. 'Let *me* handle this. You just take this tray to

Table Nine. And don't hurry back – she likes to chat.'

Great. One of those. Sallie always palmed them off on me; or on Polly, one of the other waitresses, who wasn't here today but had more sweetness and charm in her little finger than I had in my whole body.

Sallie's café wasn't large, the most coveted spot undoubtedly the table for two set in a large bow window at the front, where you could watch the world – or at least the village – go by through the leaded glass. But Table Nine was in a nook of its own at the back, away from the toilet door, counter, and the other patrons. I liked this spot most of all. It had the best view of the entire café and anyone who sat there could be as nosy as they liked, and people-watch to their heart's content, often without anyone else realising.

It was the pink beret I noticed first. *Hot* pink, in a soft, fluffy knit. Not the sort of thing you tended to see on little old ladies around here. And there was no disputing that the customer waiting at Table Nine was little and definitely old. I was terrible at guessing people's ages, but she might have been in her late eighties or even nineties. Attempting to match the beret was a bright pink scarf, in a less fluffy yarn; bobbly and well-cherished.

As she spotted me coming towards her with the tray, the woman sat as straight as her bony shoulders would allow and her face lit up with obvious delight. I hoped Sallie hadn't kept her waiting long.

'I believe this order is for you.' I forced myself to sound cheerful. A smile like hers didn't deserve my glumness.

'It is, it is.' She rubbed her gnarled, liver-spotted hands together and looked on with pleasure through silver-rimmed glasses as I gingerly transferred the milk jug, teapot, cup and saucer, and the mince pie on its own fancy scalloped plate, from the tray to the table.

'There's sugar right here.' I gestured to the bowl of sugar cubes beside a vase with a single silk flower poking out of it. 'Be careful, the tea's very hot. In fact, would you like me to pour? And do you need hot water, on the side?'

Up close, the woman was just a wisp of a thing really, as if she might blow away with the slightest gust of wind. Her dogtooth-checked coat hung over the back of her chair, and she wore a pale blue jumper with a swirly metallic pattern, which clung to every bone. There was no flesh on the poor thing. I wondered how she had the strength to even tilt her head and beam up at me.

'That's very kind, but I don't need extra water, although I'll ask if I change my mind. And I can manage the pouring well enough. But I'll let it brew a bit longer first. I like my tea strong. Like my men.' She winked at me from a lightly powdered crepe-paper face. There was a grace and ease about her. A casual confidence you didn't tend to see on many of the older residents around here, her frizzy white hair smoothed back and tucked under the beret.

'Cheeky.' I feigned a laugh. 'I suppose I like my men strong, too.'

'In spirit most of all, I hope,' said the woman. 'My husband, God rest him, might not have been the most physically robust of men at the end, but his spirit never wavered.'

'Oh, I'm sorry.' It was an automatic response, the café was a stamping ground for widows and widowers, there was nothing new about that.

'Don't be sorry, my dear. We had a wonderful life together. Well over fifty years. He only passed away in March, and it was peaceful, in his sleep. The doctor said he didn't suffer. We'd all choose that way, wouldn't we, if we could?'

I didn't say anything, just stared at the gingham tablecloth.

'I'm sorry,' said the old lady, her voice nowhere near as feeble as I'd expected it to be when I'd first set eyes on her. 'I've hit a nerve – haven't I?'

'What?' I jerked my head up. 'No… Not at all. I just…'

'What's your name? You're such a pretty thing. I'm guessing you have a lovely name to match.'

'Oh… er, it's Cara. My name's Cara.'

'Ah, I was right. Italian for 'beloved' or 'darling', isn't it?'

'Something like that,' I muttered.

'Well, it's a pleasure to meet you, Cara. I'm Perdita.'

'Really? I studied *The Winter's Tale* in school. The play, I mean.'

'William Shakespeare.' I watched as she stroked the tea cosy, a brittle fingernail tracing each stripe. 'Yes, I suppose I was like Perdita in *The Winter's Tale* once. The "lost" one. Although I'm not as lost these days. And I'm extremely glad to be here, Cara.'

'Have you just moved to the village?' I was curious now.

'I'm only here for a few weeks, till just before Christmas. My family owns Riverside, up off the north road. Do you know it?'

'Riverside?' I couldn't say I'd heard of the place.

'It's just outside the village. You can't see the actual house from the road, it's on a private lane. We rent it out to holidaymakers nowadays, but I wanted to come alone for a few weeks myself, to get away before the chaos of Christmas and New Year. The festive season's rather noisy in my family; too many little ones scampering around, for a start. And it'll be the first one without my husband since…' She sighed, then bucked up. 'But he always said, if he went first, I shouldn't get depressed and shut myself away. I've always been at my best doing something useful, and I've never broken a promise to him yet. I'm not about to start now. Plus, my children and nieces, and their own offspring – they all still need me.'

A pin unexpectedly jabbed my heart. 'But you're staying at this Riverside on your own?'

'I am. Don't look so surprised, Cara. I'm old but I'm not decrepit.'

'I know, I didn't mean… Anyway, you should try the mince pie while it's still warm. They're famous around here, from an old family recipe. Not my family. I don't have any. Sallie's. She owns the café. Though you might have guessed that from its name—'

Amazingly nimble, Perdita stretched out and patted my arm. It felt warm and reassuring. 'Calm down, Cara, dear. It's fine. Don't put on an act for me, trying to be bright and breezy. I've lived too long not to see through it. I'll be leaving you a large tip, regardless.'

'Oh, I didn't… You don't have to.'

'But I will. And now those young mums on Table Five seem to be trying to get your attention, so you ought to find out what they want. I'll see you again soon. I've a feeling that Sallie's is going to be a favourite haunt of mine.' Perdita flapped her hand, as if dismissing me, but nicely.

I gave her one last smile – a genuine one, this time – before turning and hurrying away.

Chapter 5

Self-consciously twiddling my hair, though it was curly enough, I stood by the barrier and attempted to hold up the rectangle of cardboard, with 'Wilfred Brooks' Sharpie-d across it, as discreetly as possible. I wanted to melt into the floor. This wasn't my thing at all. I hated drawing attention to myself.

JoJo had sent me a photo of her brother last night. Well, a photo of them both, taken at Niagara Falls, by the look of it, a cagoule hood obscuring half his face, while JoJo somehow managed to look windswept and gorgeous.

I'd messaged back:

—Don't you have anything clearer?

Although spontaneous family snaps and JoJo probably didn't gel. Between the carefully staged social media shots, and the countless studio portraits around her home of her stunning daughters – either with her and Des, or just the girls alone – I'd speculated if JoJo could bring herself to store anything that wasn't aesthetically pleasing on her iPhone if she couldn't put up with it anywhere else.

A minute later, the siren on my own, much older model of iPhone, had gone off and, lo and behold, there was another photo. I'd sighed. Okay, an improvement, but still. I'd messaged back. Again.

—Why is he dressed like Sherlock Holmes?

—It was a fancy dress party. I cropped out Zoe his ex. She went as Doctor Watson. I didn't have many recent pics of Wilfred without her in them too and I deleted the ones I couldn't crop easily. Can't stand the sight of her any more.

I'd tried to zoom in, but the picture had been taken with a flash in low light. Under the deerstalker cap, JoJo's brother had red eyes and looked a bit pixelated. I still wasn't sure how I was meant to recognise him, which was why I'd made the sign to hold up, after asking JoJo for his surname, and to help him locate me, too.

Brooks. He'd kept his mother's name. But it had been futile googling him; he seemed as private as JoJo had made out.

So, here I was, scanning the endless stream of people at Arrivals while trying to remain inconspicuous. I hadn't realised there would be such a crowd, and I berated myself – and JoJo – for the oversight that I didn't have her brother's number, in case we missed each other.

Suddenly, though, I straightened, and stepped back from the barrier. A broad-shouldered man was striding menacingly towards me, wheeling the largest of Samsonite cases with another huge bag slung at his side. Distressed suede-effect jacket, slate-grey shirt, slim-fitting dark jeans merging at the bottom with classic Doc Martens. No sensible brogues. No tweed, or owlish spectacles. And no cagoule hood or deer-stalker cap.

His chestnut hair was an unruly mop of curls, not quite as spirally as mine, and a thick layer of stubble shadowed his jaw. I couldn't say he wasn't aesthetically pleasing. I wouldn't have deleted photos of him from my phone, put it that way, regardless of who was with him in the shot. Then again, he wasn't my brother. Also, to be finicky about it, I wasn't keen on the pissed-off and exhausted look.

'Just as well you're holding that.' His gruff, rumbling voice had less of a Canadian accent to it than I'd expected. 'You look nothing like your picture.'

'Picture?'

The man – Wilfred Brooks, I deduced – slid out his phone, swiped it a couple of times, then thrust it at me.

What on earth had JoJo sent him? When had she even taken that? It was true that every now and again, in the absence of other victims, she would give me a makeover to experiment with new products and techniques; and she'd often forward me the photos she took, promising she wouldn't share them without my permission. In this particular picture, which I couldn't even remember seeing before, I was wearing JoJo's spare kimono dressing gown, and aside from the fake lashes and contouring and goodness knew what else, I looked completely airbrushed and not like me at all. My hair was piled high on my head, casual and tousled and slightly come-hither.

I dared to lift my gaze again. Wilfred Brooks was still frowning in a disgruntled fashion, the lashes around his clear hazel eyes so dark, he looked as if he was wearing eyeliner himself. Not exactly like his photos, either.

Narkiness flared through me, as I folded up the rectangle of cardboard bearing his name. 'Sorry to disappoint.'

'Hell,' he said, 'I'm relieved. The picture's terrifying. I thought my sister was trying to set me up.'

'Oh.' Somewhere in all that, there was a compliment wrapped up in an insult. Or the other way around. My brow furrowed as I tried to work out how I felt about it.

'I think that came out wrong. But I'm knackered. I hate flying,' Wilfred went on. 'What I mean is, you look… harmless. What's your name again? It's in this thread with JoJo somewhere.' He consulted his phone again. 'Sorry, but my memory's not great.'

'I'm Cara.'

'And you work for my sister? Her PA or something?'

I snorted. 'Ha! No. Alyson's her PA. I'm much lower down the pecking order.'

'Cara...' He seemed to be testing the name out on his tongue, or working out a puzzle. Then abruptly his face cleared. 'Right, okay. I know you. You're the ex-nanny they can't get rid of.'

A flood of something cold coursed through me, followed by a hot flush of embarrassment.

'I'm sorry.' His hand was on my shoulder now, but only briefly. I don't know how he'd got round to my side of the barrier so fast, though. There was no way he could have ducked underneath it, but maybe I'd been standing motionless and mortified for longer than I'd realised.

'I didn't mean that to come out how it sounded, either,' he continued, while I wondered what exactly he could see in my face that made him feel the need to comfort me. 'I should just shut up, at least till the jetlag wears off.'

I muttered something vague, sweary but indecipherable, then: 'Do you need me to carry anything, or wheel that case for you?'

'Er—'

'I'm stronger than I look.'

'I don't doubt it, it's just... I'm capable of transporting my own luggage to the car.'

'Fine. Come on, then. This way.'

Like some paranormal presence I couldn't shake off, I was eerily cognisant of him right behind me. In the lift, I became even more aware, as we shuffled closer together to make room for other travellers and their baggage. Most disturbingly of all, I was more than merely conscious of his breadth and height as we eventually climbed into JoJo's car, the cabin a sleek, sumptuous cocoon – I was *overwhelmed* by it. There was just too much of him, and too little of me.

Ordinarily, I loved driving, but not today. Today I'd been stressed enough by the sat nav, and the bewildering signs dotted around the airport (they bewildered me, at least), and now I had to drive back with a man who, in spite of his huffy attitude, had already detonated my ovaries.

'Apologies if I stink,' said Wilfred Brooks, cutting into my rampant thoughts. 'I did put on extra deodorant and aftershave, and brush my teeth on the plane, but you know what long haul flights are like.'

'Um, I've never been on one, actually. And don't worry, Mr Brooks, you don't stink.' Unless it was possible to stink of nice things, like spices and bergamot and vanilla…

Sheesh. Stop it, Cara.

'Listen, you don't call my sister Mrs Pembroke any more – do you?'

'What?' I needed to stop sniffing the air, but the car was filling up with his scent. 'I – I never called her that. She never wanted me to.'

'Good. So don't call me Mr Brooks. I'm just Wilf. JoJo's the only person left who still calls me

Wilfred, and the only one I'd let get away with it.'

'Right.' I started the car up. 'Listen, not to be rude or anything, but maybe you should shut your eyes and try to get some rest on the way back.'

'I'm not convinced that's the best thing for jetlag.'

'Screw jetlag. You've always got tomorrow to get over it, or are you in some kind of hurry?'

'True. And it's probably wise if I don't insult you again, or you might just kick me out at the next service centre.'

'You mean, service station.'

He tossed his hand dismissively. 'Whatever. It's been a while since I've been back here.'

'I'd call it more than a while, or we would have met before now.'

'And it's a crying shame that we haven't – don't you think? We seem to have such a rapport already.'

I was all too aware of his stiff smile now. Surreally, I was more comfortable with the menacing look. 'Please go to sleep, *Wilf*.'

His laugh was weary and guttural. 'I'll do my best to oblige, Cara.'

'Thank you.' I directed my gaze forward. 'And I'll do my best to get us home in one piece.'

Safely on my own again, I collapsed with relief on my bed.

JoJo's brother had crashed out, just as I'd hoped, his head thankfully drooping towards the window and not flopping towards me, but my senses had still been heightened all the way back.

It felt ages since I'd been alone with a sleeping man beside me. My last boyfriend, effectively. Sid Atkinson, the gym owner. Before he'd ditched me for that Liz from the Wayfarer Inn in town. They were engaged now, a child on the way. Nushrat had imparted the news reluctantly, but I'd seen them not that long ago, anyway, in Town Hall Square. Sid looking brawny as he carried their shopping; Liz rubbing her baby-bump, smiling as if she knew some secret no one else did. I'd envied them for their sense of purpose, but nothing else. My feelings for Sid had long since flittered away, if they were ever really there.

I'm not saying it hadn't been a knife to my heart when he'd announced it was over. I was vulnerable and human, and being spurned was seldom good. I'd languished around for days, hiding my humiliation, because I'd only ever been the dumpee, not the dumper. When that happened repeatedly, it was easy to start wondering what was wrong with me. And that was without the benefit of Sallie and Nushrat piling in, conjecturing that maybe I'd brought it on myself because I hadn't been willing to bare my soul to him, even if I had bared other things.

I doubted very much that Sid had left me for Liz's soul. But my friends wouldn't be deterred. Not to say they didn't call him a bastard or an effing scumbag, and other words to that effect, just that they never laid the blame entirely at his door.

Anyway, my present clarity concerning Sid had only come with the benefit of hindsight. And armed with that knowledge, I knew exactly what I needed to do going forward.

Guard myself from pretty men. Stomp on, and stamp out, the first flicker of dangerous attraction. If I couldn't be trusted to keep my weaknesses in check, then I shouldn't get involved in anything I knew (from the outset) would end badly. Rejection hurt too much, and I was tired of hurting.

I closed my eyes and made myself think of Greg.

Great on paper Greg.

A while later, my phone pinged. A nice sound, not a JoJo alert. I sat up again, groggy but glad of the interruption. If I slept now, I wouldn't sleep when it was actually bedtime. I needed to keep moving, eat something, stop moping about. I had no reason to be in such a funk.

I reached for my phone. Spooky! Had he sensed me thinking about him?

—*Looking forward to our meal on Saturday. I've reserved a table at Aqua Vitae for 7.30. If I pick you up at 6.30, we can have a drink at the bar beforehand?*

Ooh, Aqua Vitae. Good choice.

I eyed the clothes rail to one side of my bedroom/living-room/dining-room. My own apparel hung at one end, ordinary, safe and meek; at the other end was the stuff I bought from charity shops or the vintage clothes store in town, and spruced up with the aim of reselling. If I'd acquired it in a charity shop, I always gave them a percentage of my profits, to ease my conscience. There was a navy crushed velvet dress I'd had for a while, after mending a split seam, but couldn't bring myself to list on Depop. It fitted me perfectly, and I'd envisioned that one day, if all the stars aligned, I might have the opportunity to wear it.

Greg was my opportunity. Aqua Vitae – its front window twinkling with a curtain of fairy lights all year round, not just at Christmas – the perfect backdrop. I'd only ever been there once, in a group for Sallie's thirtieth, a couple of years ago. But I could remember thinking at the time how romantic a setting it would be for a date, and that if a man I liked ever invited me for dinner there, I ought to take it as *A Sign*.

Which meant I had to do everything in my power not to mess this up.

Chapter 6

I was working until two on Saturday. Sallie gave me one last job at half-one, to drive up to the Northridge estate and deliver a cake for a children's birthday party. Northridge was a cluster of Tudor-style, new-build homes tacked to the northern end of the village, overrun by TV-ad families with TV-ad lives – imprinted in my memory from the days I used to watch TV with ads. I never liked having to go there. However much I told myself I didn't crave or covet what they had, I always left the place feeling like a failure.

Society's expectations, that was all. A need to fit in, ingrained over time. Or maybe a safety mechanism most of us were born with. Safety in numbers, that sort of thing. Maybe Greg would know, if he liked psychology so much. I made a mental note to discuss it with him tonight. It would make me sound intelligent, and boost my prospects of becoming Miss Right-With-Long-Term-Potential, not just Miss Right-Till-The-

Guy-Gets-Bored-Or-I-Screw-Up.

I was mulling over what 'long-term potential' might actually entail, and if I would be any good at it, when I turned a corner on to the north road and spotted a familiar, jaunty, fuchsia-pink beret.

I slowed the SUV alongside the old lady and pressed the button to open the passenger window. 'Perdita?' I spoke softly, worried I might scare her.

She stopped with a judder, turning to blink into the SUV's dark interior. 'Oh... Hello, dear.' The same radiant smile as the other day. 'Cara – isn't it? From Sallie's café.'

'Are you walking home?'

'To Riverside, yes. Slow and steady wins the race. I haven't been able to drive for a few years now. My doctors had to wrestle me for the car keys, though. I wouldn't give them up without a fight.'

I hoped I could laugh about stuff like that if I made it to her age. She looked as if she was about to keel over; her gait had seemed so unsteady. And she only had a multicoloured walking stick for support, not a frame or any of those other contraptions I saw folk use around the village.

'You weren't in the café today,' I said.

'No, not today. I just popped to the general store for a few bits and pieces. It's an excuse to get out. Most of my supplies are being delivered.' She held up a macramé shopping bag, and winked. 'Please don't tell my children I'm sneaking around. They think I'm safely tucked up at Riverside for the duration of my stay.'

The fact I didn't know her children made this straightforward enough, but I didn't point that out. 'Listen, can I give you a lift up there? It can't be an easy walk. I have to make a delivery along the way, but it won't take long.'

She regarded me for a moment, as if weighing it up. 'That would be lovely. But you have to let me repay your kindness, Cara.'

I made a 'pfft' sound and flapped my hand. 'It's no hassle, honestly. Sallie said I could drop the SUV back any time this afternoon. Now and again I borrow it to go to the retail park just outside town.'

'I know the one. Were you planning on going there today?'

'Not today, no.' I jumped out to open the passenger door for Perdita, and helped her climb inside. As I suspected, she was feather-light. 'I've got a date tonight,' I went on, the words flowing when ordinarily I might have been more cagey with a stranger, 'and I don't want to be late getting ready. Time-keeping isn't always my forte when I'm stressed.'

'A date!' Her eyes widened as she let me buckle her in. 'That sounds exciting. But then again, anything along those lines sounds exciting from my perspective. Why would you be stressed about it, though? Dates were supposed to be fun when I was your age.'

'They're still meant to be. I just get nervous and tense sometimes when I don't know the man in question that well yet.'

'Ah, this boy of yours – you've only just met?'

'Mutual friends set us up. It might be working, it might not. Early days, but I want to make my best effort. And he's in his thirties; not really a boy.'

'At my age, I call any man under fifty a boy.'

'And I'm sure the patriarchy appreciate it, Perdita. Are you OK?' I checked, as she burst into a coughing fit.

'I am, I am. Don't worry, my dear, I won't die on you, I'm sure of it. Now where do we have to go for this delivery of yours?'

'Just up here.' I indicated left and turned into the Northridge estate, only to be greeted with inflatable snowmen and white wicker reindeer like clones on every lawn. As we drove slowly along the narrow, winding street, the snowmen and reindeer seemed to get bigger, along with the houses and cars.

Perdita sighed. 'They'll be putting up decorations in August, at this rate. It gets earlier every year, doesn't it? Still, I have a few bits and pieces out myself, so I can't talk.'

'I don't mind seeing all the decorations up already. It's just, on this estate, they seem to have to outdo each other all year round about everything. Like it's some unofficial competition. I don't see what the prize is, though.'

Perdita gazed around at the neat houses with their matching gardens. 'Unfortunately, Cara, there's a lot of pressure on people. And we can't judge what goes on behind closed doors. A happy exterior might not mean everything's rosy indoors. You shouldn't get caught up thinking you're doing something wrong, if you're only comparing yourself to an imaginary life. Which is all any of us are doing when we judge ourselves that way. We're not walking in their shoes, and they're not walking in ours.'

'True. But we're still all throwing stones while living in our glass houses. I'm not sure that'll ever stop.' I might as well add to the platitudes, although I was probably confusing matters. I spotted Number Eleven and braked gently. I had precious cargo, and I wasn't just referring to my delivery. 'You don't mind waiting here, do you? I won't be long.'

'What are you dropping off?' Perdita asked, as I slid back the door. I let her peek inside the tall white box. 'A fairy-tale castle! That's beautiful. Sallie's very talented.'

'She is,' I said. 'I'm useless at baking.'

'Practice might change that, and I'm sure you're excellent at other things.'

'I wouldn't say "excellent"...' A sigh escaped me. 'Anyway – back in a minute.'

'I won't run off, don't worry.' Her eyes twinkled, and I tried to twinkle back at her, but I wasn't the twinkly sort.

Fifteen minutes later (the birthday girl's mum had kept me talking) I was apologising to Perdita while she brushed it nonchalantly aside with 'I'm not in any hurry, Cara, dear. Not yet.' And she gave me directions, because I'd never heard of Willow Lane or the house that was supposedly at the end of it.

'Oh,' I said, noticing a gap in the high hedgerow, and the sign indicating it was the entrance to a private road. 'I've probably driven past a hundred times and never noticed.'

'People do,' said Perdita. 'It's one of the reasons my husband and I fell in love with the place. The sense of privacy. The aloneness. I don't think either of us were keen on the idea of having neighbours in close proximity. I mean, I *like* people, don't think badly of me. We weren't one of those annoying snobby couples who thought ourselves better than anyone else; we just liked having our own space, without being overlooked. And we were fortunate to have the opportunity. We so narrowly missed out on a life together when we first started out, we never took anything for granted after that.'

I wondered if she might have been referring to the last world war. But was she old enough to have had her sweetheart go off back then, to fight for King and Country? I'm not even sure why that was the scenario my brain leapt to first. Either way, I would have to do the maths later. On the spot mental calisthenics made me freeze up. I needed pen and paper, or my phone doubling as a calculator.

'It's beautiful,' I said, eyes widening. 'A place like this, I mean.'

The narrow lane, lined with hedgerow, had opened abruptly on to a sweep of gravel, and a large red-brick house – more than worthy of a score of Instagram hashtags – loomed ahead. A sign on a low wall confirmed this was indeed Riverside. I braked gently again, parking close to the mustard-yellow front door with a holly wreath hanging beneath a small square pane of blue glass. Ivy, recently trimmed by the look of it, curved obediently around the doorframe.

I assisted Perdita out of the car. 'Riverside didn't always look like this,' she explained, taking my arm. 'It had been standing empty for a long while when my husband bought it, as an investment, in part; although we weren't married yet then. You can imagine the state it was in. But we had a vision for it and we followed it faithfully. We couldn't bear to see it standing sad and neglected; there'd been some sort of dispute over the inheritance after the previous owner passed away. Anyway, it took us years to restore it completely, doing work as and when we could afford to, but it was more than habitable when the children came along, even if it might not have looked all that pretty yet. A labour of love, they call it – don't they?'

‘It’s beautiful,’ I said again, utterly entranced. This place was ten times more appealing to me than the Pembrokes’ immaculate, modern house. ‘Didn’t you say it was a holiday home now?’

‘Well remembered, Cara. Yes. Which is one of the reasons I go in and out round the back. As well as struggling with *those* now, although I loved them once…’ She gestured with her walking stick toward the stone steps leading up to the front door. ‘There’s no one staying here right now, but I like to keep my own private space anyway. The bit that holidaymakers and the rental agency can’t access.’

‘Sneaky.’ I smiled, holding her arm and her shopping bag, as she opened a gate and guided me along a crazy-paved path down the side of the house to a small, enclosed garden.

‘It’s extra income, and I like the fact other families can come here and enjoy it, the way my husband and I used to. My children and grandchildren share the place for a few weeks in the summer, but they’ve got busy schedules. Much as my brood might have wanted to stay here forever, it wasn’t realistic. It comforts me to think of Riverside full of life and fun again, even if the people enjoying it most of the time are strangers. And I love reading the visitor’s book; they leave such wonderful comments.’ I watched as Perdita let herself in through a low back door. ‘The times my husband almost banged his head…’ She chuckled at the memory as she ushered me inside. 'Come along, dear. You're more than welcome.'

I followed her into a huge kitchen, with a high ceiling compared to the doorway. A long, scrubbed pine table stood in the centre, and a window-seat scattered with vibrant, patterned cushions took up all the space to my right. Straight ahead, in pride of place, there was a distinctive tiled alcove housing the largest, and most modern, range cooker I'd ever seen.

Although it wasn't a particularly sunny day, the room seemed to draw in what light it could and bounce it back at us. Perdita slid her walking stick into an umbrella stand, before slipping off her coat. Taken aback by the loveliness around us, the mix of old and new, I looked on as the old woman unwound her scarf, and hung her beret beside it on the row of coat-pegs by the back door.

She indicated for me to put her shopping on the table. 'I know the rustic look isn't for everyone, so there's a smaller, newer kitchen at the front, which the guests use. It's perfectly functional, with all the latest gadgets. But this room was always the heart of the house, my family's favourite spot, and – selfishly perhaps – I can't bear to share it. Like the little garden out there; it's private, too. The guests can use the larger one behind it, though, so I don't feel too guilty. Would you like a cup of tea, dear? Something to eat perhaps? Have you had lunch yet?'

'I haven't, no. I was going to have it when I got home. But, please, don't go to any trouble—'

'It's no trouble,' Perdita cut in, 'if you kindly give me a hand, and put the kettle on. Just hang your coat up next to mine, and make yourself at home. It would be a pleasure to entertain, I have to admit; it's been quiet around here. Do you like quiche?' She took a box out of the fridge, and lifted the lid for me to peer inside. 'Sautéed green peppers, red onions, sundried tomatoes… One of my husband's recipes.'

It looked delicious, the eggy filling bursting with colour. My mouth watered just looking at it. 'Was he a cook or a chef or… actually, what's the difference?'

'I don't think there's much of one. And he wasn't a professional. But the kitchen was more his domain than mine, in an experimenting-with-food sort of way.'

'Very enlightened.' I nodded approvingly, as I filled the kettle and put it on to boil. A row of tin caddies, neatly labelled, made it easy for me to find the tea bags, although it looked as if she kept a selection of loose leaf tea, too. 'Do you want normal tea, Perdita, or one of the fancy ones?'

'I'll just have normal. And don't worry about making it in a pot. Just put the bags straight in the mugs. They're in the cupboard above your head.'

'Any particular one?' None of them seemed

from the same range, and they were all different shapes and sizes. Not like the kitchen from my childhood, where the crockery always had to match and Mum literally wept when something smashed, because the pattern she loved had long since been discontinued. Dad had always managed to source an exact replacement, though. I dreaded to think how much he'd spent over the years. 'Do you have a favourite mug?'

'Any of those will do,' said Perdita. 'I'm fond of them all. Unfortunately my favourites broke a long time ago. Occasionally, I might pair one to my mood, but I'm relatively mood-free today, so…' She smiled as she dished up quiche and salad on to mismatched plates. 'Actually, that's not true. I can honestly say my mood is euphoric right now.'

'That's a powerful word.'

'But it's true. It's so wonderful to have you here. To be able to sit down to share a meal and chat with you.'

The poor woman must be lonelier than she made out. As I set the tea down on the table a few minutes later though, I wondered, with a little wrench, if she was confusing me with someone else. An old friend, perhaps? Someone she'd been close to in her youth? Yet, in a way, I couldn't deny that I felt happy, too. Perhaps it was down to the fact I was so comfortable in Perdita's presence. But what if I was welcoming her company, because, subconsciously, I felt I'd missed out when it came to my own grandparents?

Both my grandfathers had died before I was even born. As for my grandmothers… My dad's mum had lived in a nursing home till she passed away when I was nine, having never remembered my name from one visit to the next, through no fault of her own. In contrast to my mum's mother, who'd lived far away in an ancient house on the outskirts of Verona (I'd seen an old photograph once) nursing her grudges and refusing to acknowledge my existence, let alone accept my mum's marriage to my dad.

On second thoughts, Perdita couldn't be anything like that woman Sophia Constanza Russo. I couldn't imagine her going to her grave estranged from any of her children. Perdita spoke about them so warmly, brimming with pride and affection.

My mum had named me Cara Mia, alluding to her Italian heritage, in the hope it might soften her own mother's heart towards me perhaps, but as far as I was aware, it hadn't. As the years went on, she'd stopped talking about her family, and Dad had advised me never to press her on the subject. But I'd already worked out my mother's past seemed to be impacting her present and her future, contributing to the sadness that always followed her around, like a sin she could never be absolved from. I knew better than to risk making things worse.

'You seem very lost in thought,' observed Perdita gently.

I looked up from my plate. 'I was just thinking about my grandmother. The one I never knew.'

'Oh? What about her?'

'Just *why* I never knew her. How families can break apart like that, over stuff that doesn't end up mattering in the grand scheme of things.'

'And yet, so many do. What troubles you most about yours, dear?'

I blew out my cheeks, considering the question. Would it matter if I told Perdita? If I poured my heart out? There was nothing she could do except listen, and maybe offer a word or two of comfort. There was no threat in that.

And so, I found myself explaining to this elderly woman, still a stranger in many ways, how my mother had met my father when he was an exchange student in Italy. How they'd kept up a correspondence after he'd returned to England, and managed to keep the flame of their young love alive, fanning it in spite of my mother's strict, old-fashioned, authoritarian upbringing. Yet eventually they'd had no choice but to run away together 'in disgrace'. My mother had been pregnant with me by that point, after my dad secretly returned to Verona the following summer.

Mum had risked the anger of her family, hoping for years that they might come around, particularly her own mother. But Sophia had never given in, never softened; carrying her resentment to the grave a year before Mum died herself. My only aunt, who I'd also never met, had written a brief, cold letter to my mother, to inform her.

'But your parents never stopped loving each other?' Perdita prompted, when I finally lapsed into silence. Perhaps she was mining for a vein of positivity, in a sad old story that must have repeated itself through the ages, all around the world, and would probably go on repeating itself because we never seemed to learn from our mistakes. 'I'm sorry, Cara. I'm assuming they're no longer with you, from the way you referred to them in the past tense...?'

'They both died when I was eighteen.'

Perdita tilted her head; frizzy white hair scraped back in an elaborate chignon, but wispy spirals had escaped and were curling around her ears, Regency heroine style.

'So young,' she murmured, then louder: 'That must have been an incredibly difficult time for you.'

'It was,' I admitted. 'A lot changed.'

More than a lot. My entire life had shifted course.

'And this time of year... it must be hard without them.' I could feel her empathy washing over me.

I pushed aside my plate. I'd managed quite a bit though, I realised, even as I'd spilled my soul. 'I was lucky to make good friends when I moved to Pebblestow, and they keep me going at this time of year. Make sure I don't have too many chances to wallow. And JoJo and her family – that's another story – they've always insisted I spend Christmas Day with them.'

Even if it did involve organising the cooking to make sure it all ran smoothly (JoJo liked to cook, but was useless with her timings), as well as clearing up afterwards, once JoJo crashed out.

'Well, I'm intrigued to hear all about this "JoJo", when we've got more time,' said Perdita. 'I'd love for you to come back another day.'

I reached across and patted her hand. Somehow, I felt instinctively that she wouldn't mind. Her skin felt dry and fragile, as if she might crack if I held on to her too tightly. 'I'd like that. You'll be coming into the café again, though, won't you?'

'Of course I will.'

'Good. You cheer the place up, Perdita. I'm not saying it's dull. Just that, most of the time, it's… predictable. And, if I can, I'll give you a lift any time you want. Even if I'm working, I can pop out if we're not too rushed off our feet. I don't have my own car, but Sallie always lets me borrow hers, if I need to. And I'm insured on JoJo's, too. So if she's not using it…'

'That's kind and generous of you, considering your time's precious, Cara.'

'Not really. Shall I leave you my number?' She pushed a pad and pen towards me, which had been lying beside a fruit bowl, and I wrote down my details. 'It's not as if I'm a heart surgeon or anything.' I scraped back my chair. 'Shall I clear up the lunch things for you?'

'No, it's fine, please leave it. I insist. And lots of people lead significant, fulfilling lives without being heart surgeons. My children, for instance… But that's also another story. What I mean is, time is so very important. You mustn't waste too much of it on the wrong things.'

I stared at her, every line on her face that had probably been hard earned, every bump and twist of her crooked fingers, which had no doubt grafted to make this idyllic home a reality.

'But how do you know what the wrong things are?' I said.

Perdita regarded me for a moment, eyes filling with fresh sorrow. 'We should swap our names, my dear. You seem lost, compared to me. And I've been so very loved.'

I offered her a wry look as I slipped on my coat. 'Maybe we should.' With a quick dab at a sudden stray tear, taking me aback, I turned to her from the door. 'Thanks for lunch, anyway. It made a nice change for me, too.'

'And thank you for the lift. Would you like me to see you out?'

'I can find my way back round to the front. Please, you stay here and rest.'

'Enjoy your date tonight,' she called out after me. 'Make sure he makes your heart sing, Cara!'

Whatever that meant.

But I couldn't help my watery smile as I followed the path hugging the side of the house. I'm not sure my heart had ever played a tune or burst into song for any man. Other parts of me might have burst into flame a bit, but that was a separate topic. I sensed Perdita would know all about that, too. I had an inkling she'd enjoyed a healthy, fruitful marriage. She hadn't said exactly how many children she had, but it sounded like a lot. And even when she spoke about her husband now, I could sense a spark of passion tangled up with the grief and love.

As I climbed back into the SUV, I reminded myself I might never have anything close to that – if I decided I wanted it, after all – without giving it a fair chance.

Chapter 7

The meal went amazingly. Greg and I talked non-stop. Everything easy again. Flowing. Like the Pinot Grigio I consumed. Just as well the three courses of Mediterranean cuisine soaked up much of the alcohol. There was even a tiny frisson of something electric when his hand crept across the table and my fingers interlocked with his. And when his thumb rhythmically stroked the inside of my wrist as our conversation grazed over psychology – yes, I'd got that in – and even world affairs and politics, I sighed. Not just because I hadn't been touched like this in so long, but because we were so *compatible*. Such an easy fit. Sallie and Nushrat – and Laurence, bless him – had been right. And I'd so nearly cast Greg aside, because I hadn't felt an instant attraction.

Afterwards, we walked along the river, still holding hands. Enjoying the rare sense of contentment, mesmerised by the embankment's festive lights reflected in the rippling water, I let him take over the conversation, his words washing over me.

We ended up at the Christmas market again, the quieter end, but this time there was just an empty space where the carousel had stood last week. With a sharp tug, it pulled me out of my dream-like state.

'It's gone.' I stared at the dark gap between the trees.

I must have said it out loud, although I hadn't meant to. Greg turned to me. 'What's gone?'

'The carousel. The merry-go-round.'

'What?'

'Last time, when we were here with the others, I had a ride on it, on my own.' I stopped short of telling him about the wish I'd made. It seemed childish now, when it hadn't felt like that before.

'I didn't see it. Then again, the rest of us didn't make it down this far.'

I let go of Greg's hand to pull my coat tighter around me. The night felt colder than it had a moment earlier.

'Do you want to head back?' His tone was conscientious, concerned. 'Or wander through the market?'

I looked up into his brown eyes, not quite as dark as mine, and my gaze traced the shape of his cleanshaven jaw and cheekbones, up to where his hair spiked out naturally from his now-furrowed brow. The sum of all parts was appealing. Not a pretty, artificial male, like Sid, but dangerous territory still. I had to be careful.

'Cara, are you all right?'

'Yes,' I muttered, spurring myself on, because if I treaded *too* carefully I'd be at a standstill. There had to be some safe-ish middle ground, surely. 'Greg, I don't really feel like hanging around the market, but when you drop me off at home would you like to come in for a coffee? I know we had one in the restaurant, but there's nothing to stop us having another.'

He blinked down at me for a long moment, his brow still creased. 'Okay,' he said slowly, 'but for the sake of clarity, you do mean coffee and not something else? Because, like I said the last time, I'm seriously out of practice at all this.'

'I wasn't being euphemistic,' I said hastily. 'I really did mean coffee. I have decaf. It's only instant, but…'

'Okay,' he nodded, 'that sounds good. If you're not too tired?'

We turned and headed back towards the car park.

'I'm not that tired,' I said.

'Neither am I. In fact, I hate that this evening has to end. I've really enjoyed myself.' He reached for my hand again. 'I like you, Cara. You make this all seem a lot less… complicated.'

'I know. I feel the same.'

'So – coffee then?'

'Fairtrade decaf.'

'Sounds amazing.'

And as Greg stroked my wrist, I speculated if we'd tipped over into euphemism now, after all.

By the time we made it back to Pebblestow, my inhibitions – loosened a little by the wine earlier – had tightened up again. My stomach was tense as I scrambled out of the car, remembering the state I'd left the hovel in earlier. I hadn't expected to be inviting him in tonight. An idea popped into my head.

'Greg, would you mind waiting here a minute? I just need to check something.'

He looked at me quizzically as he blipped his car closed. 'Sure. Take your time.'

I hurried around the side of the annexe, security lights flashing on overhead. To my relief, I found the outbuilding in darkness. A final security light flashed on and I let myself in using the key on my fob. I spoke aloud, commanding the softer wall lights to come on rather than the spotlights recessed in the ceiling. I hurried back to where Greg was waiting.

'Follow me.' I held out my hand encouragingly. 'I want to show you something.'

'Wow.' His eyebrows shot up when I led him into the games room, as I'd guessed they would. 'This is some set-up...'

'Thought you might appreciate it. None of it's mine, of course.' Aside from the laundry hanging behind a screen in the utility area, which I didn't draw attention to. 'But it's fine for me to use it socially. If the Pembrokes aren't around.' I led him between the tables, glad of the diversion. 'Fancy a game of pool? I promise not to hustle you.'

'What happened to the decaf coffee?'

I hesitated. 'I can run to mine and make some, if you still want it?'

Greg stared at me. At length, he grimaced. 'I should have realised it would get complicated. Too good to last, I guess.'

'What?' My own brow creased. 'I'm not... I'm sorry, Greg. I really did mean to invite you in when I brought up the subject of coffee. And I literally did mean coffee. At least, at first. I'm not sure what I meant after that. I don't want the evening to end either, it's just...'

'Look' – he stepped closer, the luscious remnants of his aftershave musky and enticing – 'Cara, I don't want to sound as if I'm pressuring you. I'm sorry. I'm just not sure how to read you right now. That's all. You have every right to change your mind about whatever it was you did, or didn't, expect.'

'Right. Good.' I twiddled my hair, blinking up at him. 'Thank you.'

The more I thought about it, I'd expected a kiss at the very least. A swoonier one, effectively, than the one we'd shared the other day. It would be a natural progression, wouldn't it? So it wasn't particularly random of me to shrink the gap between us and tilt my face up to his.

Greg gazed down, and then slowly his mouth met mine for the second time. Heat bled through me. With no restraint now, and more than likely springing from some suppressed need, I slid my arms around him. Suddenly, reciprocally, his arms were around me, too, drawing me against him; his kiss, this time, far from soft and tentative.

It was only when the coughing grew louder that I registered it properly. Before that, the sound had only seemed a fuzzy thing, on the periphery of my senses. Greg and I pulled back from our embrace, slightly dazed, looking towards the door.

'Sorry to interrupt what seemed a really genuine and enthusiastic display of affection,' said Wilf Brooks, filling the doorframe, hands in pockets, shoulders back. 'But I need to borrow Cara. If that's okay?'

He crooked an eyebrow at Greg, who failed to respond fast enough. The eyebrow grew more crooked.

'Er… Yeah,' said Greg. 'Sure. Um…'

I snapped out of my daze with a frown directed at Wilf. 'Why do you need his permission?'

And why was Greg giving it?!

'I thought it was polite to ask your guest if he could spare you.' Barely a hint of a smile.

'Wilf is JoJo's brother, from Canada,' I explained to Greg, before frowning at Wilf again. 'And Greg's a friend of mine.'

'Not sure "friend" is the word I'd use,' said Wilf, 'unless "benefits" is somewhere in the sentence.'

'What—'

'Cara said she's allowed in here,' Greg cut in. 'If no one else is using it.'

A strange thing to come out with, as if that was fazing him the most, not the fact we'd been caught in an 'enthusiastic' clinch by someone who was being an arse about it. We had every right to be clinching, if we wanted.

'I never implied she wasn't,' said Wilf. 'I believe she's also allowed to use the swimming pool in the summer, but I still need to borrow her, if that's all right with you both? I've been waiting for her to come home. I'd like her help with something.'

Greg turned to me, smiling nervously. 'It's fine. I'll call you during the week, okay? I really enjoyed myself this evening.'

He was leaving – just like that? Didn't he want to hear what was going on? Why Wilf wanted my help? Wasn't he curious? I knew I was, in spite of myself. But no. He just air-kissed me, and nodded at Wilf, who stepped aside to let him pass.

Frustrated, I bit on the inside of my cheek, and twiddled my hair again, loose over one shoulder. I couldn't stand the silence, which Wilf didn't seem in a hurry to break. He didn't seem in *any* sort of hurry now that Greg was gone.

'So?' I had to prompt.

He looked me up and down. 'Nice dress. Not convinced about the shoes, though.'

What the…?

'Listen,' he sighed, and seemed to soften, 'sorry to ruin your plans for the rest of the evening.'

'You didn't.'

'It didn't look that way.'

'Wherever you think it was going to end up, it wasn't.' A lie of sorts, because I couldn't be sure what might have happened.

'It seemed pretty obvious where it was heading. But that's between you and your boyfriend, although next time I'd stick to your place. And make sure you use these things called a lock and a key. I'm happy to demonstrate how they work.'

I swore inwardly, and crossed my arms over my chest, aware the crushed velvet dress was a little more low cut than I normally wore, though why that hadn't bothered me earlier in the evening I didn't know.

'Greg's not my boyfriend. We've only been out a couple of times.'

Wilf appeared to take a moment to register this, before turning towards the door. 'Again, not really my business. I'd just like your help with something, if you don't mind?'

'I don't mind.' My voice was flinty. I hoped my glare was, too, as I followed him across the yard into the house. Admittedly, I was glaring at his back, but that was better than nothing; there was enough of it between his shoulders to aim at.

Loki came running and I scooped him up. I'd missed him the last couple of days. Apparently 'Uncle Wilf' had taken him for his walk on Friday, Vicki had explained, when she'd been hanging out in the games room with a friend this afternoon and I'd been shoving JoJo's towels into the tumble dryer.

'Glad he's over his jetlag,' I'd mumbled, and stalked out.

'She's in here,' Wilf said now, pointing to the family lounge.

'Who?' I looked at him vacantly. 'What's going on?'

'Something to do with Des.' Wilf turned back to me, a gravelly plea overriding the sardonic tone. 'To be entirely honest, I'm out of my depth. And not up to speed with what's been going on around here.'

'I... What do you mean? What's been going on?'

He hesitated, narrowing his eyes. 'I thought... The way JoJo talks about you... You're her friend, aren't you?'

'No. Well, yes. But not really.'

How could you be a friend to someone you were so beholden to? Someone who continued to treat you like an employee, even without a contract? And I couldn't lay the blame entirely on JoJo, because I still acted like staff. However relaxed the arrangement, the annexe was my home without my paying a penny in rent, and I had to earn my keep somehow.

'Look, I don't know *what* I am exactly,' I admitted, as Loki squirmed in my arms. I put him down again, and instantly the little Pom ran back to his bed in the kitchen. I turned to Wilf, frowning up into his impatient, perplexed face – no less distracting than a couple of days ago – and tried to sound as if I hadn't touched a drop of wine that night and was perfectly lucid and competent. 'But I'm always happy to help, if I can.'

Chapter 8

'Cara?' JoJo glanced up as we entered, and stopped her pacing of the ivory, shaggy rug with its flecks of silver. If she wasn't careful she'd trip. That rug was a health hazard, however much it had set her back. I'd been caught out by it myself in the past. 'What are you doing here?'

'Wilf thought you might need me.' I could sense him behind me again, as I had the other day: an intimidating, vampirish presence I seemed horribly aware of, as if every nerve was on red alert around him.

She stared over my shoulder. I couldn't see the look her brother gave her. Some non-verbal exchange took place, though, because he never spoke, yet JoJo's face seemed to change. Even the tiniest of muscles tightened.

'He shouldn't have bothered you, Cara. I'm fine.'

She didn't look it. Her hair, usually so flawless, was mussed up and tangled as if she'd been trailing her fingers through it in agitation. The same fingers that were now interlocked as she wrung her hands and resumed her pacing.

I turned back to Wilf, asking quietly, 'Where are the girls?'

'Upstairs in their rooms. They haven't been down since she started like this.'

Lowering my voice further: 'And Des?'

Wilf gave a small shrug. 'Who knows? I've barely seen him since I got here on Thursday. I get on well with him normally, but… It's not like him, to act so… apathetic. Not the Des I know. Then again, I've never seen him on his home turf. He went out this morning and hasn't been back. And now he won't answer JoJo's calls. Which is what set this off.' He gestured towards his sister.

'Okay. Right.' I massaged my temples with my fingertips, desperate for a clear head. 'Could you get her a drink? One of her herbal teas. Camomile's probably best. Or a brandy, perhaps? That's medicinal, isn't it?'

Wilf hesitated, narrowing his eyes again, as if he couldn't fathom me out. 'I'll make a tea. Alcohol isn't a good idea. You know that – don't you?'

Was I meant to? It wasn't as if she never over-indulged, but…

'She isn't an alcoholic,' I muttered. If Wilf wasn't so tall, his ear not so far out of range, I could have been more discreet about it.

'I never said she was, I just…' He stopped,

shook his head. 'Look, I'll go make the tea. You stay here with Jo.'

It was the first time I'd heard anyone call her that. She'd stated categorically at my interview, all those years ago, that she was JoJo – nothing more, nothing less.

Wilf left, shutting the door behind him, and I went over to his sister and steered her towards the cream leather couch.

'Come and sit down,' I coaxed. 'Wilf's making you a camomile tea.'

JoJo sat down as instructed but flashed me a scowl. 'It's *Wilfred*.'

I touched her arm, trying to still it. She was scratching the back of her hand now; if she wasn't careful, she'd make it red raw. 'He asked me to call him Wilf, though.'

'Well, he shouldn't. Zoe called him Wilf. Steph and my parents always used his proper name. Wilfred Arthur. Our grandad's name, too.' JoJo blinked at me, her lashes – fake, as usual – fluttered over tear-stained cheeks. 'But why would you need to know all this?' she said acerbically. 'It's not like I ever wanted to tell you before. You're not family.'

I'd been crouched in front of her, but I rocked back as if she'd slapped me.

'I'm sorry,' she added quickly, snatching at my hand, 'I didn't mean it that way. It was just hearing you call him Wilf, the way *she* did… Zoe hurt him so much. You don't know how awful it was to see him like that.'

It came back to me now, how JoJo had flown to Toronto on her own for a couple of weeks, back in February. At the time she'd claimed it was a business trip, but now I mused if it was to visit her brother, to make sure he was okay. She could have said that, though – couldn't she? Why all the secrecy?

Then again, maybe we were designed that way; curating events in our lives and exposing only what we wanted. As a humble nanny, I'd kept so much back from JoJo once, although she'd found out a lot on her own. It was only later, at another crossroads in my life, that I'd shared nearly everything with her.

I'd never once felt she might hold that against me. Or over me, even – like a dagger she could drive into my back if I set a foot wrong. But now, for the first time, I felt a prickle of trepidation in my gut.

'I'm not Zoe, though,' I reminded her, as unthreateningly as I could. 'And I think it's only fair he decides what people should call him, don't you? Besides, he told me you were the only one who could get away with calling him Wilfred. I suppose, now that his mum's gone, you're all he has left – aside from the girls. And you're obviously very close. You're really lucky to have each other.'

'I'm all he has left…' Her words were an echo of mine to some extent; the ones that must have mattered most to her. 'The girls have always called him Uncle Wilf. He likes that. It's just, the way you said it... it upset me more than it should. Reminded me of Zoe.' JoJo held my gaze. 'And you're not like her, Cara. You're nice. Safe. I know you wouldn't do anything to hurt me or my family. I wouldn't have trusted Wilfred with anyone else. Not Alyson, for a start. She offered, you know, to pick him up last Thursday. Ha, right. She would have been on his radar straight away,' JoJo hissed. 'Alyson's the sort he's always gone for, but he's just too vulnerable for anything like that right now.'

I pictured JoJo's PA, who came to the house often enough, purring into the driveway in her sleek, smoky-grey sports car. Tall and athletic (I think she was a runner). Titian red hair sliced in a sharp bob. Legs up to her armpits. While JoJo tried to work from home as much as possible these days, Alyson was the physical go-between with the rest of the team in JoJo Pem's headquarters, over an hour away in Chester.

'You could have sent him a less OTT photo of me, in that case.' I tried to smile, to lighten the mood.

'What?' JoJo failed to smile back. 'Oh, the photo I sent Wilfred? It wasn't over the top!' She reeled back on the sofa, as if insulted. 'I just don't have that many of you looking your best, Cara. And I'd never want to shame a woman by circulating a bad picture. You know my philosophy.

Natural inner beauty, made visibly better.'

I pursed my lips. I don't know why Wilf would have thought his sister was trying to set him up when I so evidently wasn't his type. But I could see why JoJo hadn't wanted Alyson to fetch him from the airport, and I didn't blame her. It was intriguing, yet nice, that she was so protective of her brother, in spite of their unconventional family ties.

'Anyway, I'm sorry he bothered you tonight,' JoJo went on, 'because I'm fine. Just a little anxious about Des. I can't get hold of him.'

'I'm sure he's okay. His phone's out of charge, probably. Or he's lost track of time.' All the trite excuses I could think of came barrelling out as I rubbed her hand soothingly. I'd never known her to be so fidgety and hard to divert.

Wilf reappeared. 'I'm not sure if I've brewed it long enough.' He looked at me as I knelt in front of his sister now, and I think gratitude or something close to it might have passed across his face before he came forward and set the mug down on a low table. I nodded at him.

'Thank you,' said JoJo, then lifted her head. 'Is that a car? Can you hear a car?'

'I'll go look.' Wilf walked out again, returning a few moments later. 'It's him. It's Des.'

'Oh, thank God.' JoJo sprang up, pushing past me in her hurry to get to the door.

I unfolded myself stiffly, clambering to my feet, but my wedged heel caught on the edge of the rug: the infernal, shaggy death-trap. If Wilf hadn't reached out, with impeccable reflexes, to grab me, I might have toppled into one of the glass tables on either side of the couch. I almost laughed, as he released me. But then he spoiled it by opening his mouth.

'I knew there was a good reason I wasn't keen on those shoes.'

And the laughter soured in my throat.

'It isn't your place to comment, though.' I should have just thanked him, but a shot of adrenaline had pulsed through me at my near-fall, and now it had nowhere to go.

'Only stating my opinion.'

'But I never asked for it. And that's the problem, these days. Too many people strutting around spouting their views all the time, thinking everyone wants to hear them.'

'Technically speaking,' he went on smoothly, 'that's *your* opinion, so... pot – kettle – black? Anyway, more crucially, aren't you going to thank me? I saved you a trip to the ER.'

'A&E. A *potential* trip. And I would have happily thanked you, but then you had to insult my shoes. They're my favourite pair.'

He shrugged. So laid-back, he was virtually horizontal. 'As long as Gary likes them.'

'Greg.' I glared.

'Knew it was some four letter name that began with G.'

Under my breath, I muttered a different four

letter word, which began (and ended) with 't'. 'Are you always like this?' I added, louder.

'Like what?'

'So... confrontational.'

'Frequently. But not always.'

I flounced past him to the door, trying not to wobble. These shoes had cost me enough when I'd saved up for them a couple of years ago. Now, though, exasperated and confused, I felt like an infant learning to walk for the first time. And I'd intentionally avoided wasting my cherished savings on higher, more lethal, heels, because I knew I would have broken my neck if I wore the sort of shoes JoJo favoured.

It annoyed me that I was acting like this. I'd always been irritated by people who ought to have the intelligence to know better than to pick pointless fights. But despite my fists balled up at my sides, I didn't want to pile on the hate and lump Wilf into that category precipitously. Or myself, because I wasn't behaving much better. It wouldn't be fair when I barely knew him. Who was he *really*? This Wilfred Arthur Brooks, son of Steph Brooks, half-brother to JoJo Pembroke, and heartbroken ex-fiancé of Zoe Something.

In spite of my bruised ego, I paused to consider that Wilf might not always have been this way. Scar tissue was sometimes thick and hard, and ugly in the eye of the wrong beholder, particularly the emotional variety. His ex could be to blame for this, if the break-up had been as devastating as JoJo made out.

Through the wide archway to the hall, I saw JoJo now, holding on to her husband as if she'd never let go again. Des was rubbing her back, his chin resting on her shoulder. A wiry man, with dirty blond splashed through his hair to disguise the grey, and charismatic baby blue eyes. He caught my discomforted gaze, then looked at Wilf, the briefest hint of acknowledgment as he steered his wife to the foot of the stairs. 'Come along, JoJo, darling. It's all right, I'm here now.'

I turned away, something about the scene that hit me almost viscerally, as if a woman of her calibre shouldn't be reduced to that. The JoJo Pembroke I knew was strong-willed and accomplished and if, on occasion, she was prone to histrionics, she usually had her reasons. Her cleverness was well disguised. Time and again I'd witnessed people caught off guard. And she could twist me round her finger without much effort. But tonight had taken me by surprise in an altogether different way. I hadn't seen her quite like this before.

I didn't like it.

If JoJo Pembroke could be so affected by a man, what hope was there for the rest of us?

'Coffee?' said a voice close by. 'I think I'm still in a different time zone. I'm not tired enough to go to bed.'

I blinked, untangling myself from my thoughts to take in the fact that Wilf was now staring at me from across the granite-topped island in the kitchen area, waiting for my response.

'Do you want to join me for a coffee?' He spoke slowly – patronisingly? – before turning to rummage in a cupboard and changing tack; speeding up, sounding almost conciliatory. 'I swear I saw a jar of some instant decaf just now, when I was looking for the tea. And I'll try to be less combative for the next twenty minutes, if you're enough of a sucker to risk it.'

'Decaf?' I snorted, and found myself clambering with my usual lack of sophistication on to one of the swivelling bar stools.

'What's so funny?' He shot me a look as he continued to rummage. 'And I'll take that you've sat down as a "thanks, Wilf, I'll have a coffee with you."'

'Nothing's funny.' I remembered my evening with Greg, which felt so distant now, even though it couldn't have been more than a half hour since we'd pulled into the driveway. 'You had to be there.'

'Oh. One of those. Don't bother trying to explain.'

'I hadn't planned to. Do you not know how to work that thing?' I pointed to JoJo's gleaming coffee machine, which wouldn't have looked out of place in the café.

'I've never been employed as a barista, so, no. I don't see why she can't have a standard coffee maker, like I had.'

'Well, I don't know how to use it, either. She won't let me near it. It's her "precious."' I imitated Gollum, in voice and gesture.

It was Wilf's turn to snort. 'What makes you think she'd let *me* near it, then?'

'Your tight sibling bond? I don't know. There isn't much rivalry, as far as I can tell.'

'No.' A frown slashed his brow. 'I guess not, considering.'

'Considering what?' I might as well be nosy; what harm could it do?

He found the jar, at last, and put it down heavily on the worktop. Not so laid-back now. 'This place. Her story.' Wilf gestured around him. 'She's achieved this from basically nothing. I know Dad left her money, which meant she didn't have to resort to loans or investors, like other people might, but... he left me an equal amount, and I haven't done anything with it. Nothing on this scale. And yeah, I've used some. My salary wasn't exactly up to...' he stopped abruptly, and in my head I inserted 'Zoe's standards' because it seemed a feasible way to end the sentence. 'Anyway,' the frown hardened on his brow, 'I've saved the rest. Which sounds boring, I know, compared to what my sister did with her share, but—'

'No, it doesn't. I mean, we're not all cut out to be business moguls like JoJo.' I ran a finger across the glittery flecks in the granite worktop, wondering what might have happened if I'd been left with something to invest thirteen years ago. Would it have made much difference? 'Your sister's worked hard, but she's got the mindset for it, too. The vision. You can't do anything on the scale of JoJo Pem without that.'

'No… I guess. But she hasn't managed all this alone. She's had help behind the scenes.' He looked at me again. 'How old were you when you first started working for her?'

'How old…?' I shrugged. 'I'd just turned nineteen. I was lucky to get the job. I suppose I must have seemed desperate.' I tried to weave humour into my voice, but wasn't sure I pulled it off.

'Do you like your coffee strong?' he asked. 'Sugar? Sweetener?'

I shook my head. 'Just average strength, with a splash of milk.'

A minute or so later, he slid a mug across the island towards me and perched on a bar stool opposite, to nurse his own mug. 'You know, Cara, I think it was JoJo who was desperate. Des was supposed to be this perfect house husband. And he wasn't living up to her expectations, if my mum and I were reading between the lines correctly, which is hard from afar. You can only piece things together with the information you have.'

I tried to think back, to those early days in that house in Didsbury, Manchester. I'd found it awkward at first, with Des around more than

JoJo. She'd been out of the house much of the time back then, focussing on her business. And I couldn't say I hadn't fretted just a little that Des might step over some line. But he'd behaved faultlessly towards me, and I wondered if I'd fallen into the trap of believing a tired cliché. Not that I was a tall, nubile, Scandinavian blonde, sashaying around in cropped top and hot-pants; effortlessly beautiful; temptation on legs. I wasn't an au pair, for a start. And I'd never been employed by the Pembrokes through an agency, either, so my role had always seemed less straightforward than perhaps it should have been, less defined. Some ever-shifting hybrid between nanny and housekeeper.

Maybe the lack of temptation was one of the things JoJo had liked about me, sucked in by the cliché herself. Next to her, in the looks department, I was inconsequential. She'd more or less insinuated something along those lines this evening, hadn't she? I wasn't a threat to her brother. Not like Zoe or Alyson. I was safety on legs, apparently, and she could easily trust his heart and his other vital organs around me.

It was just as well Greg found me attractive. I still had the warm glow of our evening together like an ember in my chest, however long ago it might seem now; otherwise I might have gone back to the hovel and slumped miserably on my bed, potentially devouring the entire tin of mince pies Sallie had sent home with me yesterday. JoJo couldn't have been plainer. I was lucky to have even caught Greg's eye. My self-esteem was taking a battering.

'You have dog hair on you,' said Wilf, gesturing to my top half. 'On your dress. From Loki.'

'Oh.' I glanced down past my pert cleavage, which I'd achieved with a little assistance from a push-up bra. My cheeks heated up, but Wilf had hardly been complimenting me. 'It's nothing, just a bit of fuzz, that's all. I've got a lint roller somewhere; I'll sort it out later.'

'I can't believe JoJo got a dog like that when everything around here is so pristine and pale.'

'The girls had something to do with it. And you've got to admit: Loki's cute.' I gazed at the fluffball, asleep face-up in his bed, legs crooked in the air and head at a ludicrous angle.

'Oh, he's cute. And a fast worker. Got me eating out of his hand already.'

I blew softly into my coffee to cool it down, and deliberately didn't meet Wilf's intense gaze. This was a far cry from how I'd imagined my evening would go when I'd been getting ready earlier. How could it have crossed my mind that I'd end up sitting in JoJo's kitchen, talking about dog hair with her unpredictable, half-Canadian half-brother? I didn't want to examine why I hadn't said it was late and left the minute Des got home, but my mind trotted off, attempting to analyse it anyway.

Surely it was irrelevant that Wilf was hot,

in a different way from my coffee. He was out of bounds, if I'd interpreted JoJo correctly. Also, I wasn't even his type; and, personality-wise, he definitely wasn't mine. He confounded me, though. Intimidating and sweat-inducing at the same time, even in faded sweatshirt and jeans. I wanted to run from his presence as much as I wanted to stay.

But I wasn't about to do anything that would risk JoJo's wrath. Unofficially, I was still that nineteen-year-old she'd rescued, and I could never repay her for the opportunity she'd given me to start over, not just once but twice.

I would have to keep reminding myself that Wilf Brooks was an extension of the Pembrokes. Not some separate unit, existing in isolation, but a family member who'd returned to the fold in need of their help. A brother and an uncle, seeking solace and a place to stay while he stitched his life back together. I had to treat him the way I treated the rest of them.

So, when we lapsed into silence, I allowed it to get awkward and uncomfortable, and wouldn't give him the satisfaction of the verbal sparring we'd exchanged earlier, although I sensed he might be waiting. It wasn't exactly how I would have behaved around the others, but it was the best I could manage right now. I was relieved when Wilf failed to suppress a succession of yawns, and I pointed out that maybe he'd finally synced to Greenwich Mean Time and ought to get some rest.

'You might be right.' He detached himself from the bar stool easily, while I slithered off mine, holding on to the island for support.

At the door that led to the yard, I turned and thanked him for the coffee, not that I'd had much.

'Thank *you*,' he said. 'For the company. And I'm sorry if I messed up your plans – with Greg. I really thought you might be able to help.'

'You didn't mess up anything,' I lied. 'I'm only sorry I wasn't as useful as you thought I'd be.'

His eyes held mine. 'You were, Cara. I think you've always been helping her. More than you know. And I'm grateful for that.'

I wrenched my gaze away, a heat low in my belly unnervingly eclipsing the ember in my chest. After a mumbled, 'See you around, I guess,' I scurried back to the hovel, kicked off my shoes and changed into my thickest pyjamas before brushing my teeth. I went on to commit the ultimate offence, in JoJo Pem's eyes, of not removing my make-up before climbing into bed and burrowing under the duvet. But it was better than the offences my head was committing as it hit the pillow, which would have horrified JoJo Pembroke, the devoted sister.

Chapter 9

I normally enjoyed Christmas shopping with Sallie and Nushrat, especially as we always started early in December, to avoid the last minute rush. Sallie had shut the café ahead of time – it was empty, anyway – and we'd met Nushrat in town after she'd finished work at the library.

It was late-night closing, and in the buzzy, wintry darkness shop windows glittered with tinsel and sparkly fake snow and lavish gift ideas. Everywhere we looked, we were being enticed to spend as if there was no tomorrow. Except I was all too aware a couple of direct debits were coming out of my bank account the next day, so I had a small finite amount to splurge with, compared to my friends. Unlike them, I'd never had a credit card. I worried how much trouble I'd find myself in if I did.

This year wasn't turning out to be as fun as other times, anyway. Sallie and Nushrat seemed to be expecting me to buy Greg a gift, and kept plying me with suggestions.

'I've only been out with him twice,' I reminded them, when we stopped for hot chocolate in the market. We'd already walked the length of it and to my relief the carousel wasn't there this time, either. Like a secret I carried alone and didn't want to share, in case whoever I told went on to spoil the magic, the sense of possibility growing inside me. It was silly, I knew, to be nurturing such thoughts each time my mind went back to that night, but I couldn't help myself.

'Three times,' I continued, 'if you count when we all went out as a group, and I wasn't even sure I liked him then.'

'But you must do, now?' Sallie winked, and puckered her lips.

'You didn't let that first impression get in the way, which was good,' said Nushrat, more sensibly. 'And if he's called you twice this week already, he must really like you, too.' She swept back her waist-length brown hair with its silky, tawny streaks, as I watched with a jab of envy. I'd pulled my unmanageable curls back in a scrunchie today, but they kept escaping and tickling my face. 'He's a catch, Cara, compared to the sort you normally go for.'

'Very attentive,' agreed Sallie. 'I'm pretty sure he'll be getting you something, so you can't be empty-handed when he gives you one. A gift, I mean.' She batted innocent eyelashes at me, as I glared at her over the froth in my hot chocolate.

'It's not as if we're spending Christmas Day together, though. I'm at JoJo's, as usual—'

'Cinderella to her wicked stepmother.' Sallie coughed, as my glare intensified. '*Joke*.'

'Greg's going to his brother and sister-in-law's, in Preston,' I went on. 'He mentioned it over dinner at Aqua Vitae. He's got nephews or nieces he's godfather to, and he enjoys spending as much time as he can with them.'

'Aw,' sighed Nushrat, 'he likes kids. That's another box ticked.'

'Maybe I don't, though. Like kids,' I said, more stubborn and wound-up by the second. 'I haven't decided if I want any. So the last thing I need is a man hounding me, desperate to pollinate my eggs.'

'Are you perhaps taking the birds and bees a bit too literally?' said Sallie.

'You know what I'm talking about.'

'But you worked as a nanny.' Nushrat was the broody one out of my friends. Her brow wrinkled in consternation. 'How can you not love children?'

'*Precisely* because. I have too much experience.'

'But it's different when it's your own.'

'And it's a scary responsibility even when they're not. I was petrified of getting something wrong or failing them, pretty much every day. Anyway,' I had to get Nushrat off the subject of how I'd handled Belle and Vicki when they were younger, because, if I was truthful, it hadn't always been mess and stress, 'what I mean is, Greg and I might not even be together by the time Christmas comes around, so—'

'Damn, Cara.' Sallie shook her head. 'You can't talk like this already. It's too soon to start doubting yourself, or him. Just enjoy this part while you can. Make the most of it and have fun. It's not called the honeymoon period for nothing.'

'It's not called that, at all.'

'Yes, it is.'

'Greg and I aren't married. I hardly know him.'

'So get to know him,' urged Sallie. 'Properly. Spend as much time as you can together. Get to the point where you're so wrapped up in him that you won't be tempted to run, or mess it up. He's a good bloke, trust me. He must be. Laurence wouldn't have suggested setting you up if he had even the slightest concern about Greg.'

I didn't doubt that; I'd known Laurence as long as I'd known Sallie. 'You can't force me to fall in love, Sal. And who knows, maybe I'm ultimately meant to be on my own? And that wouldn't be the worst thing. I think I could be okay with it.'

But I was preaching to the unconverted. Sallie and Nushrat were too loved-up to imagine someone could be content to spend their life without a partner or family. And perhaps

I was being contrary and… confrontational, for another reason. I wriggled uncomfortably inside my coat.

'It helps if you get to know him better, like Sallie says, so you can see how sweet he is.' Nushrat wasn't going to let up, either. 'Does he want to take you out somewhere nice again?'

I rolled my eyes. They were determined to shove me into Greg's waiting arms. Yet the more they pushed, the more I felt myself resist. I wanted to make them both happy, but why couldn't I do it some other way, without all the hassle?

'It's my turn to pay next time round. So I offered to cook him dinner. I can't afford anywhere as nice as Aqua Vitae.'

Nushrat screwed up her nose. 'Dinner at your place?'

'It's perfectly adequate,' I said snippily. 'And I'll tidy first.'

Sallie was shaking her head. 'Adequate for the likes of Sid Atkinson, maybe. But Greg's in a different league. You can't cook a gourmet meal there, hun. You can barely cook anything.'

'You can't even call it a kitchen,' said Nushrat. 'It's a corridor.'

'Use the café,' Sallie suggested. 'I don't mind. You can make it all sexy and romantic, with candles and fairy lights and the lamps turned low. Just make sure the blinds are down. And don't infringe any hygiene regulations.'

I looked at her, slightly open mouthed. 'I can honestly say, Sal, I've never thought of your café as "sexy". Cinnamon swirls and gingerbread men have never featured in any of my fantasies.'

'You're fantasising wrong then, my love.' Sallie laughed and Nushrat giggled, and I held back from asking how old they were.

But they had a point. I was deluding myself if I thought I could attempt the sort of meal I had planned with my limited resources at the hovel.

'Okay,' I muttered, then more clearly: 'thanks, Sal. That's kind of you.'

'Oh, it's not kind,' she said, pinning me with a sharp look. 'From what Laurence says, Greg seems to deserve better than he's had in the past, too. I just want you to get this right. You could be good for each other. And I need to see you happy. We both do, don't we?' She looked at Nushrat, who nodded and tucked her arm through mine.

'You're overdue some happiness, Cara, love,' my other friend agreed. 'Now come on, I'm going numb. Let's keep shopping. You don't have to rush to buy Greg anything today. It might be better to wait, you're right. Get an idea of what he'd like.'

I sighed inwardly. 'Maybe you can help me pick out something for each of the Pembrokes, then.'

I always gave out individual (modest) gifts, considering I was at theirs for Christmas Day.

'And you've got that brother of JoJo's to add

to the list this year,' said Nushrat, pulling a face, 'if you're keeping to tradition. Have you got any idea what to give him yet?'

I shrugged, and tried to sound nonchalant. 'Not a clue.'

As if it was the least of my worries, when the reverse was probably closer to the truth.

Perdita had returned, her beret and her smile lighting up the café as I took my break early so I could sit with her at the table she preferred, at the back.

'How did your date go with your young man?' She'd remembered all about it, and was eager to know more. 'I'll try my best not to call him a boy again.'

'Oh, the meal was great.'

'And the company?'

'Great, too. We never stopped talking, and we've loads in common. Likes and dislikes, that kind of thing. My mates all think it's a match made in heaven.'

With her usual twinkle, Perdita leaned over her teacup. 'And the song in your heart when he's around – I hope it's the most beautiful tune, Cara. It ought to be.'

Unable to help myself, I let out a less-than-tuneful laugh. 'I was never any good in music class. I don't know what it's supposed to sound like, Perdita, so I can't comment on that.'

Her eyes narrowed. 'You've never been in love?'

I stared over her shoulder for a long moment, sinking into my memories like quicksand. 'I don't think so... no. Not properly. That's not to say I've been a nun or shut myself away. I've had my share of crushes. And I've fallen in lust, I guess.' I blinked at her, refocussing. 'Sorry. Too much info?'

'Not at my age. I've seen it all. Well, not all.' She emitted a crackly, girlish laugh that warmed my stomach. 'But I know the difference between real love and the other sort.'

'So do I,' I admitted. 'Just not personally. I've seen what love that deep can do, and it's terrifying.'

'You're frightened?'

I glanced over my shoulder briefly, but no one else was in earshot. Not the other café-goers, or Sallie behind the counter. Not if I kept my voice low. 'I think what I'm scared of most is being dependent on someone to that extent. To give every part of myself, knowing how easily it might work against me.'

This was true, if I was brutally frank. I could faff around my feelings and my reasons for being cautious as much as I liked, but the truth followed me around like a shadow.

'Oh, my dear.' Perdita shook her head. 'You're

too young to speak like that.'

I shook my head back at her. 'I'm not that young. But I saw how my mum couldn't live without my dad. How it affected her, after what happened to him.'

'Do you mind me asking, Cara…' she hesitated, but eventually went on: 'what *did* happen?'

I spread out my fingers on the table, my stubby nails shining turquoise with my favourite polish, the only splash of upbeat colour aside from the candy stripe apron Sallie made me wear. The rest of me was in monochrome black leggings and grey chenille jumper, my dark hair twisted into a large and (very) messy bun.

'He died,' I said simply, staring at my blue-green fingernails, keeping the details to a bare minimum, 'and my mum died soon after, because she couldn't handle being apart from him.' I lifted my hesitant gaze to Perdita's. 'So you see, love *is* scary. I have every right to think of it like that.'

She stared at me across the table, that same empathy I'd felt last time washing over me in a giant wave. 'I'm so sorry, my dear. That you had to go through that. And at such a young age, too. To be left alone in the world…'

'I wanted to go, too,' I confessed, my voice barely above a whisper. 'I didn't want to be left behind. I was eighteen. They classed me as an adult: everyone who got involved afterwards. I was left to get on with it. To cope.'

'But you were just a child still! A child who'd lost both her parents. Couldn't they see that?' Perdita tilted her head, blinking at me with damp eyes as she put her hand out across the table.

I allowed myself to take it, to feel the dry, papery skin and the bulging veins; the knuckles deformed by work and age. As if she was the grandmother I'd never known. Never had the opportunity to care about.

'What happened next?' she prompted kindly; not curious for the sake of it, I suspected, but because she wanted to help, even if that simply meant listening. And so I opened up further, to an extent that was rare for me.

'I dropped out of university,' I said. 'Even with the loans and a part-time job, I couldn't afford it – the shortfall. Maybe I could have got help from other sources, but I couldn't think straight. I didn't want to. I hadn't realised how little money there was at home. My dad had kept his financial troubles so well hidden. I guess he was trying to give Mum and me the life he felt we ought to have, but without insuring any of it, if something happened to him. Everything was sold to pay off debts. The house, nearly everything in it. And after all that… my heart wasn't in my degree any more. It was only my second term. They'd given me some kind of compassionate leave, an extension or whatever. I never went back, though, except to pack up my things.'

'So, what then? You went out to work full-time?'

'I sofa-surfed for a while, with old school friends and their parents. But I couldn't stand all the pity, so I acted out. Stayed out too late, too often. Came back in a bad way. I soon outstayed my welcome everywhere, so...' With a rueful sigh, I checked my watch. My break was nearly over.

'What did you do next?' urged Perdita.

'I somehow managed to get work with the Pembrokes. My old art teacher from school, she'd heard what had happened to me, my situation; she helped knock me into shape before I applied. Miss Wells,' I reminisced fondly. 'She was nice. My favourite teacher. She knew a friend of JoJo's. That's how I wangled an interview when they were looking for a live-in childminder and someone to help around the house.'

'Did you have experience with children?'

'I had a bit. I'd done some babysitting for neighbours when I was about fifteen, sixteen. I wasn't a complete novice. But it was a steep learning curve, taking on Belle and Vicki full-time. A huge step, compared to just putting a kid to bed, reading them a story, and watching TV while I waited for their parents to get home. But JoJo's husband was around, too, so I wasn't entirely alone with them. Not at first. And JoJo was great. I did some courses: childcare and first aid, that sort of thing; she paid for them all. She even paid for my driving lessons. I owe her a lot, and I don't just mean money-wise.'

'Did you ever feel that she treated you like a charity case, though?'

'What?' I twitched in my chair.

'As if you were her good deed for the day? Or her lifetime, by the sound of it. She seems intent on keeping you around.'

I shrugged in discomfort. 'Who knows what I am to her? I'm used to pity by now, though. Other people deserve it a lot more than me, but I get it anyway. There was a point, when Belle and Vicki were older, that I thought I might be "superfluous to requirements."' I made speech marks with my fingers. 'So I started to make plans to leave, go back to Manchester, but it was hard just even thinking about it. I'd made friends here in Pebblestow. I felt... at home.'

'So you stayed on?'

I checked my watch again. I could hear the noise level in the café rising behind me. New customers had arrived, and I couldn't leave Sallie to deal with them singlehandedly. There was no other staff around yet today.

'Perdita, I'm sorry, I'd better go help Sal. Before she docks my wages, or fires me. Seriously, though, it was good to chat.' I had to admit that talking like this had been therapeutic. Yet I'd shied away from it too often in the past with people who weren't being paid to listen, more than likely to my own detriment. 'Are you rushing off?' I added.

Her lips widened into her characteristic smile, like sunshine breaking through cloud. 'I'm not "rushing" anywhere these days, Cara. But I'm not in a hurry to head back to Riverside yet, if that's what you meant. I'd be quite content for you to bring me another tea after I finish this one, if that's all right? And maybe another mince pie…'

I laughed. My emotions always seemed to be on a rollercoaster around her. 'Happy to oblige. And if you can stretch out your time here for another forty minutes or so, Polly starts her shift and I can quickly run you back home again.'

'But you'll be busy here.'

'I'll charm Sal, don't worry. She'll have Polly to shout at, too. And it'll only take ten minutes. I'll just make sure you get into the house okay. It's one thing walking down here and taking your time, especially if the weather's good, but you don't want to trek all the way back up that hill if you don't have to.'

I still marvelled at how she managed to get down into the village on her own, in the first place, relying only on her walking stick and stacks of gritty determination. I could understand why her children might worry. I would, too, in their shoes. In fact, I did worry about her, I realised, as I wove towards the counter. In the short time I'd known her, she'd somehow sneaked under my skin, with her defiant pink beret and her mischievous twinkle and the huge heart in that skeletal little body.

But was it wrong of Perdita to put her family through that? The people who cared about her, anxious and torn over what she might do next. It was one thing, the right to free will and independence, but another to be obstinate, foolhardy or selfish. How could you tell the difference, though? How could you decide what was reckless and wrong, when sometimes it felt like the most natural thing in the world just to follow your instincts?

Chapter 10

'Blame Loki, not me. This is his fault.'

'Sorry?' I blinked a few times, trying to clear my vision as I stood at the rear door that gave on to the yard, having answered an urgent, ominous knock.

My eyes were blurry. I'd been reading for ages without a break and without noticing how much time had passed. I was supposed to be packing up a couple of items I'd sold online, before taking them to the general store in the village to arrange a courier delivery. But the minutes and hours had run away with me, lost to the latest thriller Nushrat had recommended from the library.

It struck me, with a stomach-sinking thud, that I was wearing a blanket. Okay, so I had a vest top and pyjama bottoms on, too, and slippers shaped like duck's feet, but over the top of it all was a crocheted throw draped around my shoulders, made up of about eighty granny squares.

It wasn't my best look.

As my vision grew less bleary, I noted that

Wilf was smiling, rather than looking menacing. Meanwhile, Loki had pushed past my legs and darted into the hovel behind me.

'I thought you might be JoJo,' I said, while I swivelled to see where the little dog had disappeared to. 'And what did you mean about Loki? What's his fault?'

'This. The fact he escaped while I was trying to get him ready for his walk. I got as far as putting on his harness when he bolted. Came straight here, to your door. Vicki says you often took him out? Maybe he's missing that.'

'Oh. I *used* to walk him...'

'Before I turned up?'

'Only when everyone else was busy. I'd hardly call it a routine.' I didn't want to make Wilf feel bad for usurping a role I hadn't realised I'd enjoyed so much.

Clutching my blanket, I shuffled as hurriedly as I could in my slippers towards the main living area, suddenly worried I might have left chocolate reindeer lying around. Poisoning Loki hadn't been on my agenda today. The little dog had merely leapt up on to my compact sofa, though, and seemed to be trying to make himself comfortable among the cushions. I was about to shrug off the blanket and grab him, when I realised Wilf was behind me. Disconcerted, I turned to face him again. Instead of waiting at the door, he'd walked in uninvited and was now poking around, surveying the space in all its bijou, bohemian glory.

His smile vanished, replaced by something I couldn't define.

Inside me, shame clashed with wounded pride. I might call it a hovel, but it was my home. Small, but cosy most of the time. Cluttered, but with *my* things; possessions I'd either thrifted and upcycled, or coveted and saved up for. More importantly, it was decorated to my taste. Which was so far from JoJo's minimalist, coordinated style that I think she got a migraine just coming in here. Wilf probably hated it, too, judging by his inscrutable expression. But why should I care what he thought?

Except I did. Too much. Then again, I was always defensive when a stranger saw the hovel for the first time.

'How long have you lived here, Cara?' he asked, in a low voice that seemed to rumble right through me.

I gripped the blanket tighter around my shoulders. 'A few years.'

He took in the clothes rail and the sofa; the coffee table with its piles of books; the drop-leaf table where my sewing machine lived and the trolley beside it stuffed with yarn and haberdashery; and finally his gaze landed on the bed, which was the double JoJo had insisted I transfer from next door, because apparently I couldn't survive without the top-of-the-range, memory foam mattress she'd bought for me when we'd moved to Pebblestow. The bed took up too much room, and as I'd been sprawled on it, reading, it was a rumpled mass of chartreuse satin pillows and berry-red velour duvet. I was suddenly reminded of a harem. A dozen chiffony scarves draped and entwined around the metal headboard did nothing to dispel the illusion.

Wilf turned away from it sharply and walked back to the 'kitchen', where he continued his appraisal as if he was some sniffy estate agent. He took it all in without saying a word. The small fridge-freezer next to the built-in cupboard with sink and draining board; the portable two-ring induction hob, which stood on a slimline butcher's block table by my kettle and toaster; another trolley, full of food items this time; and my microwave on a shelf at eye level. I saw it afresh through his eyes, and hated myself for cringing. Yes, it was packed into the corridor that led to the bathroom, but it was more than sufficient for my needs.

Wilf turned to face me again. 'It's very... colourful.'

'Oh.' I paused to absorb this. 'You sound surprised.'

'I am. You're not a colourful person.' He looked me over, taking in the blanket in every rainbow hue. 'Normally.'

'You haven't known me long enough to say what's normal. And you shouldn't have just barged in like this.'

'But Loki—'

'You could have waited outside while I fetched him for you.'

'I could,' Wilf conceded, 'but I was curious. JoJo said you don't pay rent or contribute much to running costs. You're basically still live-in staff, but without a salary.'

I was aware of my voice rising, and the fact I was now hot and sweaty under the blanket. 'How I exist, and what I do to earn my place here, is nothing to do with you.'

He looked away, a frown crossing his face before he looked back at me. 'I just know what JoJo can be like sometimes, that's all.' His voice and expression grew more neutral, as he added, 'Listen… do you want to walk with Loki and me today? If you're not busy? I think Loki's missing you. And between you and me, I could do with a guide. I ended up in the middle of some field with a bunch of hostile-looking cows yesterday.'

'The cows in this part of Shropshire are perfectly sociable, provided you don't antagonise them.' I bit my lip, wondering why I did this around him, or he did this around me. Rotated from belligerent and surly to something else entirely.

'Maybe I'm reading them all wrong, then.'

'Canadian cows might be different.'

'It's likely I need a translator, if I'm going to be mixing with the UK variety.' His smile returned, slow and oddly tentative this time. 'So, how about it? Will you volunteer?'

'To translate? To steer you away from fields with cows in the first place, which would be the advisable thing to do? Or stop you endangering Loki's life by letting him run around, unattended?'

'All of the above. Although, for the record, I never let Loki off the lead around livestock. And he was never in any danger just now.'

'Crap. The chocolate reindeer...' I almost tripped in my slippers as I rushed back to the Pomeranian. He was curled up between two cushions, though, eyes fluttering drowsily.

'Lazy devil.' Wilf was towering behind me again. 'I'll take him outside and let you get changed. How long do you need?'

'Five minutes?'

He picked up the little dog. 'I'll give you four.'

My gaze followed him as he strode out. Wilf had filled the place so utterly, his height and breadth packed into a high-performance anorak and slim-fitting blue jeans, now that he was gone there was suddenly more space and air in here than ever.

I dressed quickly, and tried not to fixate on it.

The walk was longer than I'd usually take on my own. Light was already leaching from the sky as we turned back for home. I don't know why we'd dragged it out. The conversation was hardly easy. We seemed to endure brooding silences that left me jittery and flushed, or the other extreme of stumbling over each other verbally to get the jokes out.

I fancied him too much, I told myself, his gloved hand taking mine to help me over a stile and keeping hold of it a moment longer than necessary. I could skirt around the issue in my own head, or just confront it and try to move on. Wilf stirred something in me that hadn't been disturbed to this extent in a long while, if ever. But I had to weigh up the repercussions scrupulously – or else.

Like Greg, he wasn't as conventionally pretty as men I'd gravitated towards in the past, nor as charming. Although charm could be misleading, I'd learned; and false. There was a capricious energy simmering beneath the exterior that disturbed me, though. A reserve, at times, that intrigued. Wilf was an enigma wrapped up in a luscious outer shell, and I usually avoided his sort. They were too emotionally draining.

But it wasn't my emotions he was piquing most right now, and I hated myself for that. Hated the way I couldn't keep Greg pinned to my thoughts for longer than a few seconds, however hard I tried. And I wondered how much of my inner turmoil Wilf could sense, and whether I was just an easy target. A female in the right age bracket who couldn't hide her attraction to him as well as she wanted. Was he homing in on me because he was lonely and bored and a bit lost in his life right now, and I was simply there, in his line of vision, making it too obvious that I'd toppled heavily into insta-lust the second I saw him striding through the airport towards me?

According to his half-sister, I wasn't the sort *he* usually went for. So if he could sense I was drawn to him, what did he want with me? A quick fling, to alleviate the boredom? Someone who was unlikely to rebuff him if he felt the need to bridge the gap between his ex, Zoe, and his next high-stakes relationship? But I couldn't see inside his head, and maybe I was reading too much into it.

What I had to prioritise, above all else, was my loyalty to JoJo.

JoJo and the rest of her family.

Liking Wilf this way felt almost incestuous after my history with the Pembrokes. I had so much more to lose than he did. If he couldn't see that, or was intending to ignore it, then I ought to steer well clear.

Also – he'd met Greg. Wouldn't it transgress some unwritten rule if he made a move on me now? But codes like that were so sexist, so proprietorial. I could make decisions about my life without their input.

Damn, Cara. Why is your brain so feral? Why can't you just see this for a dog walk with another human being – plus the aforementioned dog – instead of turning it into some massive drama?

'Are you okay?' As the Pembrokes' house loomed ahead, ghostly against the dusk sky, Wilf slowed his pace. 'You seem… weird.'

'What?'

'The last few minutes. I don't know… It's usually me who does the zoning out.' He was about to say more, I thought, but his jaw clamped shut.

I zipped up my coat the last couple of inches, even though I felt throttled enough right this second. 'No, I'm okay. Sorry. Had you been talking to me?'

Wilf looked away and then back again, latching on to my gaze. 'I was just asking if you wanted to do this again another day? Walk Loki with me? When you're not working.'

I swallowed. He was a bad man. A *very* bad man. He shouldn't be tempting me like this.

'At least some of us have a job,' I heard myself mutter, loud enough for him to hear.

What the hell, Cara? Dismayed, I wondered if I'd spoken out of self-defence. A pre-emptive attack.

Wilf's eyes flared with surprise. I saw him gulp, his Adam's apple bobbing where the collar of his own coat opened.

'I'm sorry,' I tried to backtrack. 'But… JoJo said you weren't exactly here on holiday…'

'Job or not, I'm paying my way,' he said, after an excruciatingly long pause. 'And I'm not insolvent, or anywhere close. My mum as well as my dad saw to that; though I'd rather have them both still around, rather than their money. But when I figure out which of my plans I want to pursue, I'll either be looking for a place of my own around here, or moving down to Bristol.'

It should have felt like bragging, the way he threw in how healthy his finances were at present, but he seemed almost ashamed again, as if he'd failed at something. Or let people down.

'So you're definitely not going back to Canada?' I said.

'I wasn't aiming to, no.'

'What's in Bristol, though?'

This sounded like an interrogation now. I wasn't acting like myself at all.

'An old friend, from way back. He's starting a new tutoring business and he's looking for a partner. He'd deal with the maths side of things, I'd handle the English.'

'That sounds... promising.'

'Maybe,' said Wilf, 'but I'm not sure I want to go down the teaching or tutoring route again. I have ideas of my own taking up headspace. Too many, probably.'

'And these ideas – they'd involve you being more local, would they? To Pebblestow?'

'Potentially. After so many years away, I'm keen on the idea of staying close to JoJo and the girls. Family's important. Especially after my mum...' Wilf tailed off, shuffling his feet. Loki pressed against him, as if in sympathy.

I was a bad woman. A *very* bad woman. Certainly no better than this man. 'I'm sorry… again. I shouldn't have said what I did. I'm too impulsive sometimes, but that's no excuse.'

Wilf bent down, scooped up the little dog, held him close as Loki licked his hand. 'Sometimes there is an excuse, though. Or a reason, rather. For acting on impulse. That doesn't mean we should.'

'No.' I wasn't sure what we were talking about. If I ought to be reading between the lines.

'Don't let me get too impulsive, Cara.' His eyes locked with mine again, his face dark in the dim light. 'I'm not on the rebound, I dealt with the break-up ages ago; I want you to believe that. But it's not good for me – to leap into things too fast. I need someone to hold me back. Stop me making a fool of myself, or of them.'

'Right,' I said slowly, unable to tear my gaze away. 'It sounds like you still have a lot of thinking to do, anyway – about your life, your future.'

He nodded, sighed. 'Yeah. Yeah, I do. I don't really need… distractions.' He was still looking at me as he said it.

Damn him. Was that all I'd be? Was he actually being this brutally honest? Or was I misreading the conversation entirely?

'Even very appealing ones,' he went on, 'who just happen to be in close proximity.'

I wasn't misreading anything. My face heated

up. I prayed it wasn't visible in the quickening darkness. Wilf was well aware I fancied him; he was making that plain enough even to me. But he seemed to be testing the waters, to see how shallow they were, or how deep. How much I might be willing to respond to my attraction.

I was such a fool to have been so transparent in the first place. Unless he was primed, from experience, to notice immediately when a woman had the hots for him.

'I'm going to be very busy the next few days, at the café.' I forced the words out. 'So I won't be able to walk Loki with you, I'm sorry. But I'm sure you'll manage fine on your own.'

After another protracted pause, he inclined his head, his curls flopping low over his brow. 'Understood. And probably for the best… all things considered.'

'Definitely.'

We hesitated a moment, while he shuffled his Doc Martens a bit more and I turned the air inside me blue. Then together, but a world apart, we walked the last stretch up to the house in silence.

Chapter 11

I slid my phone back in my pocket after checking the time, and drummed my fingers on the steering wheel, too twitchy to look for consolation in the paperback I'd brought with me. Besides, I'd forgotten to pick up the little clip-light I attached to books to read in the dark. I didn't want to use the car's interior light, worried it might drain the battery, though that was probably irrational. I dug in my pocket and pulled out my phone again, to send Greg a text, not unlike other texts I'd been sending him in an effort to be mutually attentive.

—Am bored and cold. What about you? What are you up to?

A minute later, I got a reply.

—Loading the dishwasher. Is it OK to ask why you're bored and cold??

—Picking up JoJo's daughters from dance class. Everyone else busy.

Even Wilf hadn't been around, although I was doing my best to avoid him, and I suspected he was keeping out of my way, too. I felt as if I'd dreamt the exchange during our dog walk the other day. It seemed so surreal looking back, and left me feeling crumply and weak. And angry. But with myself, most of all. I was trying not to dwell on why that was.

I frowned at my phone again and picked up where I'd left off.

—The class is dragging on. I think they're rehearsing for something. Fun. Not.

—I bet you went to dance classes when you were their age.

I grunted at the notion.

—Me?!! I'm as graceful as an elephant on ice skates with four left feet.

—I might take you dancing one day and judge for myself. I bet you're not that bad.

A sweet thought, but Greg was deluding himself. I was terrible.

—What? To some tea dance? I don't think they have those for our age group.

—We could go to a ballroom dancing class? They have one in town. Maybe try it in the New Year?

My thumbs hesitated over the screen. He'd mentioned the future, quite nonchalantly, in a text. And admittedly, not the future as in years from now but only January, which was just next month. The intention was plain, though – Greg wanted to keep seeing me.

Right now, Christmas seemed like the pinnacle of some mountain we needed to conquer, and after that there would be a different, clearer view ahead. An easy glide down into spring and the long, warm days of summer. Except winter was bumpy, wasn't it? We had to get through that first. Therefore we wouldn't be gliding. And why was I being so metaphorical and oblique and strange, when effectively all he'd suggested was going to a ballroom dancing class? There was no reason for me to feel as if he'd stealthily slid a noose around my neck. We were just having fun. Getting to know each other, which is what Sallie and Nushrat had prescribed. Going to this class might be a laugh; an easy way of interacting without it getting too heavy, too soon.

Nevertheless, I was non-committal in my reply.

—Maybe. We'll see. Ask me again when I've had a few drinks.

—And when will that be? I need to make a note of the date.

—JoJo's party, maybe. The Saturday before Christmas.

I'd hesitated over asking him, but screw it, why not?

Do you want to come? It's just at her house, but her parties can be wild. Lavish wild. Not call the police wild.

—I can imagine. And OK. Sounds great, count me in.

I smiled, relieved to have an arm to dangle from. I typed back, self-consciously:

—Yay. And I'm looking forward to seeing you this Saturday at the café. I promise not to give you food poisoning.

Greg took a moment to respond, while I stared unseeingly out of the misted window.

—It was good of Sallie to offer, but I wanted to eat at yours. I hoped to see you in your natural environment.

This was flirting, right? So how far should I go? I chewed contemplatively on my bottom lip, which was already chapped enough from the cold weather.

—The café's home for me too. It'll be just as romantic. You'll see.

I'd vacillated over saying 'romantic' or 'good', but riskily left it at the former and hit send. His reply came seconds later.

—See you soon. Can't wait. xx

Two kisses? Was that intentional?

—Me neither. Got to go, the girls are coming out.

An excuse, but I felt queasy and light-headed, as if I'd stood up too fast after crouching. I honestly did like Greg. He seemed a good person, a good man. I wanted to be sure I deserved someone of his ilk, but recently – with all the stray, less-than-chaste thoughts in my head, unrelated to him – I wasn't certain I deserved anyone.

A burst of light, of noise. I glanced up.

The doors to the dance studio had opened, and a blur of teenagers spilled into the car park. I rubbed at the window, only to see a gaggle of fluffy bomber jackets and leg warmers. Belle and Vicki ran straight to the car, waving to their friends before opening the rear doors and slinging in their dance bags.

I started the engine, waiting for the windscreen to demist, and consulted the sisters in the rear-view mirror. 'You know, one of you can sit up front. I'm house-trained, and I don't bite.'

A memory popped into my head of strapping them into their booster seats. It only seemed like yesterday, and made me feel old and slightly panicky, as if life was racing by and I was lagging behind.

'Yeah, but TikTok,' said Vicki, waving her phone at me. 'I need to show Belle something. Where's Uncle Wilf, he's been picking us up from everything lately?'

'How am I supposed to know?' I snapped, instantly regretting it.

'He was going somewhere,' Belle told her sister, 'remember? Mum was taking him to the station this morning.'

'Oh, yeah. Bath.'

'No...' Belle shook her head, then waggled a finger at Vicki. '*Bristol.*'

'Same difference. Aren't they next to each other or something?'

The car still in neutral, I frowned at the girls in the mirror. 'He went to Bristol?'

'To see some friend of his, I think.' Vicki was enthralled by her phone now, her heart-shaped face illuminated by the screen. 'I think he's back tomorrow, or the weekend. I don't know.'

I was surprised I hadn't been asked to walk the dog in Wilf's absence today; then again, I'd been at work all afternoon.

'Last time he picked us up, we pretended he was our chauffeur,' said Belle, leaning forwards, as if to confide a secret.

She was the eldest in age, but the younger in other ways. There had always been a sweetness to her that Vicki lacked. A thread of charm and innocence, inevitably growing thinner. I was sure I hadn't been as worldly as these two when I'd been their age.

'Uncle Wilf was okay with it,' Belle added hastily. 'He thinks it's funny.'

'Yeah. He said we should buy him a uniform for Christmas.' Vicki rolled her eyes.

Right. Enough. The thought of Wilf in a uniform, even a chauffeur's one, had made my palms clammy. And that was no good for my grip on the steering wheel, or the chances of keeping my thoughts and libido safely centred on Greg.

'Okay, let's get you home.' I grimaced, sliding the car out of neutral. 'Your mum'll be wondering where you are.'

The library in town was a haven of warmth and

light, luring me out of the cold, dark wetness of the square, not that it took much persuasion. I shook my brolly outside the door before closing it and stuffing it into a shopping bag with food supplies. I needed to collect a few books I'd requested, one for myself and a couple for Perdita, who'd asked if I wouldn't mind taking them out on my card. My pick. As long as they were modern romances, preferably set around the festive season.

Nushrat was at the circular counter. She pulled out the books from a shelf underneath the desk as soon as she saw me approaching. 'Are you sure they're going to be suitable for an old lady?' Her brow wrinkled as she stacked them on the counter. 'Not too racy?' She lowered her voice. 'They've got "bedroom scenes."'

'You mean, sex?'

Her eyes widened, and she looked around, checking no one had overheard. 'Keep your voice down. You're in a library.'

'And you're a prude,' I said in a stage whisper.

'No, I just get loads of complaints from people her age, telling me that sort of thing didn't go on in their day.'

'They're lying to you, Nushrat. Anyway, Perdita seems to have a ton of kids. I bet she knows what ought to go into a bedroom scene better than we do. The main thing is, she asked for romantic, contemporary and Christmassy, so do these fit the criteria? She can skip any bits she doesn't like.'

'Yes,' said Nushrat. 'Romance galore. Couples gallivanting in the snow. One misunderstanding after another, because people still can't communicate properly, even with a plethora of electronic devices at their disposal. Oh, and Christmas trees everywhere, and crackling log fires, et cetera. You get the gist.'

I sighed. 'All I've got is a crackling radiator.'

'You're such a pessimist. Listen, I don't know if he's got a real fire, but I'm sure you could have a lovely, romantic time with Greg, if you wanted. I know you go to the Pembrokes' on the Twenty-fifth, and Greg's away in Preston, but I'm sure he'd love to see you when he's back, and—'

'Crap.' I stared behind Nushrat into the heart of the library.

'What?' She swung round.

Walking towards us, a couple of primary-coloured books under his arm and a large overnight bag slung over his shoulder, was Wilf. I was the proverbial deer caught in headlights as he looked at me unsmilingly before slapping the books on the counter.

'Hello, Cara.' High spots of colour flared on his cheekbones. Could he possibly be embarrassed?

'Hey.' I think it was a whimper. Whatever it was, it deserved zero points for effort.

Nushrat looked at me, then back at Wilf. Her eyelashes started doing that involuntary fluttery thing they always seemed to do around good-looking men.

I felt a stab of annoyance. We shouldn't be going gaga like this at our age, even over men like Wilf.

So why did we? An evolutionary thing, I hypothesised crossly. A merciless, primal instinct buried deep in our reproductive cells, that needed any potential offspring – whether we wanted children, or not – to be attractive and strong. With mischievous eyes, and silken mops of curly chestnut hair. I could picture them now... two or maybe three... a couple of girls perhaps, and a boy, sitting around a Christmas tree, laughing with delight as their dad walked in dressed as Santa, a puppy in his arms—

What in heaven's name...?

Not my kids. Not mine, by any *stretch of the imagination. Not my puppy, not my Christmas tree. Most definitely not my life.*

'Cara are you okay?' Nushrat was asking, and I used all my mental energy to drag myself back to the library. 'Do you two know each other?' she went on. An innocent enough question. I'm not sure how she made it sound so loaded.

'This is Wilf,' I said, my voice in the wrong octave.

'JoJo's *brother*, Wilf? *Really*? Cara, you never mentioned—' She stopped herself, but I knew what she was going to say.

I'd never confided in Nushrat or Sallie that he

might exceed their expectations in real life. And I'd been right not to, because that would have been shallow, I reminded myself now, knowing full well that wasn't the reason I hadn't said anything.

'Cara never mentioned what?' Wilf hooked an eyebrow in my direction.

I ignored the question, praying Nushrat would, too.

'This is my good friend, Nushrat,' I said instead. 'She's a librarian here.'

'I'd hope so, seeing as she's on the other side of that counter.' He looked at her and spread his mouth into a dazzling smile, which he'd never used on me. It was natural and spontaneous and charming, and I was instantly jealous. 'Hi, Nushrat. It's good to meet you.'

'Likewise,' she sighed, her eyelashes working overtime.

'You might be able to help,' said Wilf, effortlessly suave. 'Would it be okay to borrow these books on my sister's card? I have no idea when she last used it. I don't think she has much time to read these days; I'm amazed she ever did. She dug it out for me a few days ago.'

'I can sort you out,' said Nushrat. 'With a card of your own. If you've got ID and some proof of address—'

'I don't. Have proof of address. And I'm not sure if I'm going to be sticking around in the area after New Year, so…' He shrugged, as if in apology, and I caught him looking at me out of the corner of his eye. 'Don't worry if the card's expired or—'

Nushrat smiled. 'No, it's fine. I just need the books, too.' She dragged them across the counter towards her. I flicked my gaze over them while pretending not to.

They were both non-fiction. One was about entrepreneurship, the other was about having a business mindset and the 'will to succeed', or something along those lines. I loathed stuff like that. People setting themselves up as gurus and spouting any old rubbish to tap into other people's insecurities. Only on rare occasions did they actually have the experience and authority to know what they were talking about.

Nushrat started scanning my own books. Wilf looked at them openly, without hiding what he was doing.

'Interesting reading material. I never had you down as a hopeless romantic, Cara.'

'I'm not,' I said, quickly sliding the more serious historical novel towards me, thankful I hadn't gone for something more salacious. 'This is mine. The others are for Perdita.'

'Perdita?'

'This old woman who's staying in the village,' said Nushrat.

'Just outside the village,' I clarified. 'She lived in Pebblestow most of her life, from what I can gather, but she's just back now for December.'

'Cara's been helping her out.' Nushrat passed the books to me again, and I piled them carefully into a spare shopping bag.

'I'm not helping that much. She's just here on her own.'

Wilf turned to me, leaning against the counter. 'You feel sorry for her?'

'No.' I frowned. 'No... I don't think I do. Not any more. Perdita's not the sort of person you end up feeling sorry for, once you get to know her. I think I'm more... *inspired* by her, than anything else.'

'I'd like to meet her,' said Nushrat, 'if I ever get the chance.'

'I wouldn't mind meeting her, too,' said Wilf. 'She sounds fascinating if she's managed to inspire Cara so much, although I'd like to hear what exactly she's inspired in her.'

I pushed a stray curl out of my eyes. I'd tried to clip some of them back earlier, but the squalls of wind and rain as I'd walked through town had clawed at my hair, as if for fun. 'I just meant that Perdita seems to have lived an interesting life, that's all. Anyway, Nushrat,' I turned back to her, 'are you still all right giving me a lift home when you finish?' I'd arranged it with her earlier, when I said I'd drop in to collect the books. 'I don't fancy having to take the bus back. Not with all these bags.'

'If you don't mind waiting half-an-hour?'

'You could always share a taxi with me right

now, if you like?' Wilf butted in again. 'I walked down here from the station an hour ago, but I don't want to bother JoJo or Des for a ride back.'

'Oh…' I was whimpering again, damn it. No, no, *no*. I didn't want to be alone with him again, even with a cabby present. 'That's very kind of you, but—'

'Look,' said Nushrat, 'if you can wait thirty minutes, forty tops, I can take you both home. Save your money.'

Wilf flashed that smile at her again. There was something so unaffected about it. As if this was the real Wilf Brooks and all I'd encountered up to now was some strange clone who didn't know how to behave like a simple human. 'Are you sure?'

'Of course,' said Nushrat. Flutter, flutter.

'You have to let us cover the petrol, at least,' said Wilf.

'Don't be daft.' She flapped her hand at him.

'A coffee, then? Cara and I will wait for you next door, in the coffee house I saw. I'll get you something for the journey home. Do you have a cup holder?'

'In my car?' Although Nushrat's lashes weren't fake, they were still in danger of flying off at any moment. 'Well, yes. I do…'

'I know what she likes.' I sighed weakly, resigning myself to my fate. Unless I could think of some excuse fast, I was stuck in Wilf's company for the next hour or so. But my mind was treacherously blank. 'I'll order for her. And look,' I turned to him, 'you'd better put your books in here with mine. They'll get wet if it's still raining out there.'

'Let me carry it, then.' Wilf took the bag from me. He tried to take my other shopping bag, too, but I wouldn't let go.

I felt Nushrat's eyes on us as we headed for the door. Wilf held it open while I wrestled with my brolly.

'Do you really need that,' he said, 'seeing as we're only going next door?'

'I – er – might walk around a bit instead. Meet you and Nushrat there in a little while. You can order her an eggnog latte. She loves those, and you only get them this time of year.'

'Cara…' Wilf took my arm, easing me away from the glass doors of the library, out of Nushrat's eyeline. 'Please don't do this.'

'Do what?' I struggled with the umbrella as the wind tried to blow it out of my grasp.

'You can't walk around aimlessly in this weather. Just come have a coffee. I'm not going to say or do anything to make you uncomfortable again. I'm sorry about the other day. I should never…' He shook his head, his hand still on my arm. He seemed to realise he hadn't let go yet, and stepped back as he did so. 'I can only apologise. I can't rewind what I said, or what I implied.' The high spots of colour were back in his cheeks. 'I *like* you, Cara, and I thought… maybe… you might like me, too.'

I stopped battling with the umbrella and fought with myself instead, frowning into the enticing amber depths of the coffee shop, because I couldn't look at him when I said what I had to say.

'Look, Wilf, you don't know me. And I really don't know you. So this "liking" business – it isn't the most accurate word, is it? I think we both know what is.' There was no way I was going to utter it to his face, though. 'I know I'm living right next door, and it would be so convenient to just think: what the hell, let's have a bit of fun for a while, till we get bored or you disappear down south. And I guess we could come to some mutual arrangement, or whatever. But I'm not in the market for that, and I'm sorry if I've given off vibes that I am. The truth is... I'm still seeing Greg, and I want to make a proper go of it, because I've made too much of a pig's ear of that kind of thing in the past. And then there's JoJo... she'd absolutely *hate* it. Hate us creeping around behind her back. Neither of us owe her that. The fallout just wouldn't be worth it.'

I stopped to take a breath and because I didn't know what else I could say. A tendril of damp hair lashed across my face, and I swept it back with equal ferocity. Had I totally humiliated myself?

'Reset, then,' said Wilf, his own hair flattening wetly.

'What?'

'I'm pressing the reset button, and we're going to start again. I'm going to pretend the first thing I thought when I saw you at the airport wasn't that you look so much lovelier in real life than in your photo. And I'm going to ignore the fact I want to laugh when I'm around you, even though I haven't laughed properly in months. Or that you make me tongue-tied sometimes when I haven't felt that in years. And I'm going to pretend I wouldn't get completely soaked out here in the rain while I explain the difference between "like" and "*like*". Because I get it, Cara. You have a life, and I can't barge in and expect you to drop everything just because I feel a connection with you.'

Oh. My. God. Had he really said all that? I felt as if I might have hallucinated the whole thing. I had no idea how to respond.

'Look,' pleaded Wilf, 'before we both catch pneumonia, please can we go inside and grab a hot drink? For JoJo's sake, for *everyone's* sake, I think we ought to at least try to be friends. Keep it straightforward – and maybe not so honest? Would that be okay with you? Do you think we could manage that, Cara?'

He reached for the door handle, looking at me over his shoulder.

Stunned and mute, my insides turning to liquid, I nodded.

Chapter 12

'Of course, they'll never be as good as Sallie's in the café,' Perdita sighed, 'and my hands aren't as steady as they used to be, but with so much time at my disposal I suppose it was inevitable I'd take this up as a hobby. All those baking shows have a lot to answer for. Their popularity never wanes.'

She'd invited me to Riverside for afternoon tea, and I'd been glad of the distraction. It was becoming increasingly difficult to steer my mind down the safe route I needed it to travel, which was elevating my stress levels by the day. Yet I always felt soothed by the time I left Perdita's side. Revitalised and a little more focused.

I boggled at the tiny sandwiches, fondant fancies and pastries she'd laid out on an antique, three-tier cake stand, and lavished her with compliments. Without a hint of smugness, Perdita explained how she'd made them. We sat in her kitchen for over an hour, in a halo of easy companionship, and after tea she insisted she wanted to show me the reason the house was called Riverside. And I was curious to know, already calmer than I'd been in days, as if she'd put a potion in my tea.

We wrapped ourselves up in our outdoor gear, and she plucked a blanket from a wicker basket by the window-seat. Jangling her set of keys, Perdita led the way through the private garden to a wooden door set in the wall, and, just like that, as if stepping into a childhood storybook, I found myself in another world.

'You can appreciate the view from upstairs,' Perdita explained, 'but not from the kitchen. I wanted you to see it in the flesh, though, as it were. Not through glass.'

My jaw dropped, stunned by the landscape in front of me. JoJo's house was on a hill, too, but the view was nothing like this.

'Let's sit for a while, till we get too cold.' Perdita led me to a wooden bench, where we huddled together, sharing the blanket, the brick wall of the enclosed garden behind us and lush undulating hills all the way to the horizon in front. The main garden was on a gentle incline; a sweep of green lawn dotted with fruit trees and bordered on both sides by an abundance of shrubs. I didn't know one tree from another unless it was obvious, especially when their branches were bare, so Perdita pointed each one out.

'You should see them in blossom. It was always my favourite time of year here.' She sighed, and pulled the blanket a few inches higher.

Beyond the lawn was another wall and a set of steps leading down a sharper incline to the river beyond. Through a scrolled metal gate, I could make out a wooden jetty jutting out into the water.

'My husband and I used to have a rowing boat,' Perdita explained. 'When we first got married. It was so dreamy – and fun. But we had the wall built once the children came along. The gate's still locked now, so holidaymakers can't stray down there, either.'

'I'm guessing that's the River Pebble?'

She nodded. 'There's a kink just past that willow,' Perdita pointed, 'and then it curves round the hill and flows through the east of the village.'

'It's all so beautiful… I can't get over it. Was this house always called Riverside, then?'

A wistful smile hovered on her lips for a few seconds, tearing at my heart. 'It was on a weathered sign on that low wall out front when my husband and I first came to this place together. It didn't feel right to call it anything else. Of course, as I've said before, we weren't actually married then. We'd barely even started out. But we knew, at that moment, how much we wanted all this to be ours, however neglected it was. That was also the day we realised how destined we were to be together, in spite of everything.'

I studied Perdita beside me, so grateful I'd met her, my eyes misting over till I had to look away. Such an air of confidence and determination. I envied her family for the life they'd enjoyed, this house that must have been straining at the seams with love and laughter. And I envied Perdita, too. She was magical. Entrancing. Yet despite my jealousy, I didn't want to be anywhere else right now than sitting on this bench with her, on this bright, dry December day.

'Hard to imagine the forecasters are predicting we might have a white Christmas, isn't it?' She changed the subject. 'On an afternoon like this.'

'I'll only believe it when I see it.'

I felt her gaze on me as I turned to take in the magnificence of the garden and the view again. 'You seem like the kind of person who doesn't set a lot of store by pure faith, Cara. We can't always see something before we believe in it, though.'

'You mean, heaven, hell, that sort of thing...?' The life after this one, if such a place or state existed.

I kept my eyes fixed on the river, trying not to think about my parents, although unsurprisingly I did. They weren't just ashes I'd scattered on the wind. They *couldn't* be. For their sake I wanted to imagine there was so much more out there. Mum had endured enough of hell while she was alive, and I couldn't pretend my dad hadn't needed to go there enough times, too, in an attempt to drag her back. Surely they were at peace now. It made no sense otherwise.

'I *want* to believe the universe knows what it's doing, Perdita.'

'Oh well, I'm sure it does, in some unfathomable way. But I'm not talking in a spiritual sense, as such. I mean, feelings – those intangible things inside us we can't see. For instance, I have a suspicion that you're very confused today. You haven't been quite yourself since you got here.'

'Ha!' I let out a grim laugh. 'I'm always confused, remember? You told me your name suited me best, because I seemed more lost than you.'

'Are you trying to catch me out?' She laughed back, the whispery sound swiftly snatched up by the breeze. 'I remember saying it, my dear. But you're even more lost than usual. Has something happened with your young man?'

I wrapped my arms around myself under the blanket. 'No,' I said, wriggling on the bench, 'I can't fault Greg so far. It's just… there's another "young man" on the scene now, too.'

There was no reason to hold back. I had no one else to discuss it with and I badly needed to articulate the situation out loud. Being here at Riverside with Perdita was the closest I'd come to some kind of no man's land.

After Wilf's declaration outside the library, he'd been true to his word, slipping into a cool, platonic mode that ironically fazed me more than his previous behaviour. All he'd talked about in the coffee shop was his old friend in Bristol, the plans for the new business venture, how much this friend wanted Wilf on board. It sounded like a done deal, and I hadn't known what Wilf wanted me to say in response, so I'd said very little.

In the car on the way back to Pebblestow, he'd sat up front where there was more legroom, and chatted to Nushrat, asking polite questions that weren't overly personal but would still reassure her he was interested in what she had to say. And I believed he genuinely was. Not because he was attempting to flirt – he was nothing short of respectful – but because he wanted to hear her story. So I'd sat miserably in the back while they'd shared a comfortable, relaxed conversation. The sort he hadn't been able to share with me. Which had to be my fault, too, not just his. After Nushrat dropped us off, I'd let myself into the hovel with only a mumbled, 'See you,' over my shoulder, as Wilf headed for the door of the main house, mumbling something equally generic back at me.

Later, though, he'd knocked on the rear door of the annexe, and barely making eye contact had asked for his books, which were in the bag I hadn't unpacked yet.

'Enjoy,' I'd said, handing them over. Strangely, it felt as if I'd also been handing over permission for Wilf to leave Pebblestow and erase himself from my life, even though he'd barely been in it to start with.

'A lot still to consider…' An echo from the

other day. Our dog walk together. 'I'm thinking these books might help.'

'I hope they bring you lots of clarity.'

'And yours, too,' he'd said, without even a hint of sarcasm. 'I hope you enjoy escaping to wherever they take you.'

'Mine? They really are for Perdita; the lady staying in the village,' I'd protested. 'I don't read romances like that myself.'

A lie. I read most genres. My tastes had always been eclectic.

'Pity.' Wilf had lifted his eyes to mine, almost daring me to protest, before heading back across the yard as I heard JoJo call his name.

To compound my troubles, at my next shift at the café I'd been grilled by Sallie about Wilf, after Nushrat had gushed all about him. Sal was too astute not to notice me squirming, even though I'd played it down. I'd had to listen to a lecture about not getting side-tracked by a handsome face and a body to match, particularly when said face and body belonged to someone who might not be in the area long.

Dutifully, I'd nodded in all the right places, and emphasised that Wilf and I were just acquaintances and Greg had nothing to worry about. Although it smarted that I had to tag that on. This was my life, not Greg's. And we weren't serious enough to have discussed whether or not we were exclusive. Unfortunately, I'd made the mistake of adding that, too, and Sallie had snapped back that exclusivity was implied in this situation, and if I did anything rash she'd never talk to me again.

She hadn't meant that.

I don't think.

'So, let me get this straight,' Perdita said now, turning towards me, wearing a frown for once, 'your friends don't approve of this new boy?'

I'd definitely spilled more beans than I'd meant to. It had been so easy, though. So effortless to share my woes with her.

'Man,' I corrected, automatically heating up under the blanket. 'Very much a man. And I don't think it's disapproval, as such. I think Nushrat really liked him as a person. It's just the circumstances; I'm supposed to be going out with Greg. And I do like him. Greg, I mean. And crucially, for my friends, so do they. On paper he's the best candidate. He ticks all the right boxes.'

The creases multiplied in Perdita's brow. 'Love isn't about boxes, Cara! I should know. This Greg of yours – I keep waiting for you to tell me that he makes your heart sing. That's what I need to hear. Even if you haven't seen him in person since I last spoke to you, you should be calling each other whenever you can. Sharing messages that make you smile like you've never smiled before, because they're reaching secret places deep inside you. Otherwise, I'm really not surprised if someone is trying to steal you away. Greg should be trying his best, not his second-best.'

Perdita seemed to have been overdosing on romance novels before she'd even had a chance to read the ones I'd brought.

And I was more guilty of not 'trying' than Greg.

To divert away from that, I said, 'I bet it was more romantic when you were young, though. People used to send love letters dabbed with cologne, and you could tie them up with a ribbon and hide them under the floorboards.'

Perdita emitted a crackly laugh. 'You make me sound positively Victorian.'

'I'm sorry. I wasn't implying you wrote them with a quill or anything. Maybe a gold-nib fountain pen.'

She smiled. 'Don't try to steer the subject on to me. We were talking about you.'

'Yes… So… Anyway…' I took a deep breath. 'Greg and I text a bit, and sometimes he calls me. But, frankly, neither of the "young men" are managing a song in my heart right now. In fact, my heart isn't doing much of anything except pumping blood around, and having palpitations every now and again. But that's all right. I don't know Greg or Wilf well enough. I'm just attracted to them both. Or maybe one more than the other, currently. But the wrong one, because it looks like he'll be leaving Pebblestow soon enough. And when you think he hasn't been back in the UK in years, I wouldn't be surprised if he doesn't get tired of Bristol, too, sooner or later, and head off somewhere else. Like Dubai. They always need English tutors in Dubai, don't they? And then, even if he did stay around here, I can't do anything about it because JoJo would string me up by the balls – if I had balls – just for looking at Wilf that way. I don't think any woman would be worthy, in JoJo's eyes, after what Zoe did to him. Least of all "staff" like me. I need to know my place, Perdita. And I need to stay there.'

'Goodness.' She stretched across and tremulously patted the blanket over my knees. 'Have you finished? That's a lot of words strung together, Cara. But that's all they sound like to me. Just words. I'm not sure how much you're convinced by them.'

Did it matter? And which words exactly weren't swaying Perdita? Or me?

I fell silent, accepting I'd gone off on a verbal ramble and the poor woman had been forced to sit through it.

'Anyway,' she said, 'it also sounds as if you're focusing too much on one aspect of your life and forgetting about the others. I admit to remembering: romance can do that. But you shouldn't let it eclipse everything else for too long, or it can seem very bleak if things aren't going well. A man in your life won't miraculously fix everything that's wrong. It's good to have a partner if you want one, of course. My husband's moral support meant the world to me, and when that's mutual, it's a wonderful thing. But you need to be able to believe in yourself first.'

I laughed histrionically inside. Or maybe it was more of a scream.

'What other aspects of life do you mean?' I said. 'Work? Hobbies?'

'Dreams. Aspirations.'

The laugh/scream grew louder. I had long since put my aspirations away, nothing but a moth beating its wings against a light bulb.

'I don't have dreams like that.'

'Never?' said Perdita. 'Or just not now?'

With a shrug, I picked at a loose thread on my scarf. 'Things might have been different once, when I was younger.'

'You're still young, Cara!'

'Yes, but… It's not the same. Maybe I'm more cynical.'

'Less hopeful?'

I tipped my head back, blinking up at the opalescent sky for a moment. 'Do you remember how I told you I was at university once?'

'You dropped out after your parents passed away.'

'I did… yes. Well, while I was there, I was studying art and art history.'

'Ah,' she smiled, 'I thought so. A fellow creative. I can always tell.'

'You too?' I turned to her, but I shouldn't have been surprised, judging by the décor in her kitchen. And the way she dressed; although she was braver than I was, and a lot more stylish.

'I'll tell you about my work one day,' she said, 'but I want to know about you right now. Did you have a career in mind if you'd gained your degree?'

That was where it got nebulous. I turned towards the river again, picking my way cautiously through the past. I'd once been so passionate about anything art related, I'd felt myself pulled in countless directions.

A couple of week's work experience in a small local gallery hadn't helped. Certain circles of the art world were too pretentious, too niche. All I knew was, I wanted my art to be inclusive and appeal to the masses. Oh, and I also knew my preferred media wasn't paint and canvas, pencils and paper. Not that I was bad at drawing or painting, because my art teacher at school – the lovely Miss Wells – had always raved about my work. It just didn't grip me enough.

A tutor at uni had suggested fashion as a module, but I hadn't wanted to go down that route at the time either; although it appealed to me more these days, having taught myself to sew a few years back from YouTube tutorials.

I felt myself drifting away, too far and too fast, and reeled myself back to the bench and Perdita.

'I didn't have a particular career in my head,' I admitted. 'I just knew I couldn't do anything that wasn't connected to art in some way. And it had to be perfect and accessible and meaningful. Which was idealistic and silly, because art's subjective. It all *means* something. And "perfect" doesn't exist.' I blew air through my nostrils. 'You wouldn't think any of this, would you? From appearances? I don't look like much of an artist.'

'What does an artist look like? Are we supposed to be missing an ear, sporting a monobrow, smoking cannabis for inspiration every chance we get? We're all different and unique.'

'Yes, but just *look* at me. Properly. I'm… insipid.'

'You're not insipid, Cara! You're intriguing. There are entire galaxies hidden in those big dark eyes of yours. And any man who can see that is worth holding on to. Trust me.'

'Oh, back to men again, are we? That didn't last long. Epic fail on the Bechdel Test.'

'Poor, dear, hapless souls,' Perdita chuckled. 'What would they do without us?'

I nudged her gently. 'Very true. But listen, I'm getting too chilly out here now, even if you're not.' The fact she was all skin and bone surely meant she would feel the cold more than me. Though thankfully it was only mild, compared to other December days. 'Shall we go back inside?'

'Good idea. I'm feeling rather tired, too, if I'm honest.'

'Well.' I helped her up, perturbed again by the feather-light weight of her. 'I'll leave you to have a rest, then. Thank you so much for tea, and for showing me this garden. I won't forget Riverside in a hurry.'

'You won't forget it at all, Cara.' She adjusted her gloves, and her glorious pink beret.

'I suppose not. A view like this, you ought to be able to bottle it – the way it can make you feel.'

'I've been a very fortunate woman, I admit. But I've never stopped being grateful. That's the secret, you see. I've never once taken any of this for granted, or stopped saying thank you.'

A lump in my throat, I rolled up the blanket and tucked it in the crook of my elbow before taking Perdita's arm again. As a substitute for her walking stick, I supported her as we headed along the path, back towards the door in the wall. Somehow, though, it felt as if I was leaning on her as much as she leaned on me.

That evening, I opened my old but trusty laptop and booted it up, making myself a cup of tea in the time it took for the start screen to appear. Finally, cross-legged on the bed, my mug on the bedside table beside me, I opened up the browser and hesitated, my hands hovering over the keyboard for what seemed forever.

I didn't know what I was looking for exactly, I just wanted to see what was out there; do something *pro*active for once, rather than reactive.

An hour later, I logged off, and closed the lid with a frown. Half a mug of tea had gone cold.

There was so much out there. Too much, perhaps. Paid courses, free courses, online, in person, full-time, part-time... I could take my pick, within reason. I had my job at the café to consider, and the hovel, the Pembrokes, my friends here in Pebblestow. Anyway, art had almost limitless forms; I still didn't know what excited me the most.

My gaze wandered to the rail, and the flamboyant clothes I was repurposing with the aim of selling on, compared to the staid grey, black and navy of my own clothes on the other side. Could something related to fashion still be a valid option? Would it get me anywhere? Or would I just be that moth again, flailing against the light?

The end result might never be as important as the journey, though.

Perdita, for example – her life wasn't standing still; it was constantly moving, unspooling, even at her age. The key point was how she'd lived it so far, to the absolute fullest, with every breath and heartbeat and every ounce of spirit.

As I got ready for bed, I lingered in front of the tarnished mirror over the washbasin, looking myself in the eye, searching for those galaxies.

'It might not matter that you're a moth, Cara,' I said to my reflection, though how persuasive

I sounded was debatable. 'Maybe all that truly matters is the fact you've got wings.'

Chapter 13

'I'd like to say I made the pesto from scratch, but I'd be lying.'

'It's fine. All fine. Delicious, in fact. Regardless of how you made it.' Greg dug his fork into the tagliatelle and twirled it around.

'Good.' I tried to offer him a soft smile across the table. As enigmatic as the *Mona Lisa*. He smiled back, matching me for softness, although maybe we both failed at the enigmatic part.

'It's great to see you again, Cara, rather than just messaging or calling.'

'Same. It's good to see you, too.'

I'd stayed on in the café following my shift today, and Sallie had left me to it a while later, with a cheeky wink I'd pretended not to notice as she turned the sign to 'Closed' on the door. Before doing anything, I'd pulled down all the blinds so passers-by wouldn't see what was going on, although I suspected the village grapevine would be red-hot by tonight, regardless. I'd then spent the next couple of hours cooking, tweaking, and attempting to get the ambience right, not that my meal was as gourmet as I'd originally envisaged.

Picking a table against the wall – rather than the one at the back where Perdita liked to sit – I'd spread out a red and white checked tablecloth, lit votive candles and switched on the fairy lights Sallie had strung from the dado rail back in November.

The overhead lights were off, but I'd left on a couple of lamps for a rosy glow. Without them, even with the candles and fairy lights, it had still felt too dark, as if we were having a séance. Although then I'd fretted whether the rosiness made it seem like a brothel.

When Greg had arrived, though, my mood had lifted. And as I let him in and locked the door again, my heart-rate had calmed. Why had I been so panicky? With a sheepish grin, he'd handed over a bottle of wine and told me I looked pretty. After I'd blushed, and told him he looked good, too, he'd immediately asked if there was something he could do to help.

But I'd had it all in hand. And now we were chatting genially, just as we did the last time, at Aqua Vitae. Nothing stilted or stuttery about the evening. Greg obviously didn't get tongue-tied or knotted-up in my presence.

The thought jabbed its way into my head: a painful spiky thing, which I quickly tried to push out again.

'The choice of cuisine's apt,' he went on, twisting tendrils of pasta around his fork again. 'But then I shouldn't be surprised, finding out Italian food is your specialty.'

'Oh? Why's that?'

He paused, his fork mid-way to his mouth. 'You're half Italian, aren't you? Sorry, Laurence mentioned it the other day. I was surprised you hadn't brought it up yourself, especially when we were at Aqua Vitae.'

I shifted on my chair. 'Does it matter? I didn't think it was important.'

'No… I mean, it isn't. It just explains your name, though, and the way you look.'

'The way I look?'

He frowned. 'You've got a Mediterranean air about you… All that dark hair, your olive skin… I'm sorry, Cara. I feel like I'm putting my foot in it, but I don't know why. I intended it as a compliment.'

'Yes, I know. I'm sorry.' My smile was tight now. 'My mother was from Italy. But we never visited. And I never learned the language. There's not much else to say, really.'

'You don't have family over there?'

I thought of my aunt, who'd never replied when I'd written to tell her my mother was dead, and the cousins I knew I had, although no one had ever told me their names.

'No,' I said. 'No, I don't.'

It wasn't fair of me to go all cold on him like

this. But I couldn't face talking about it tonight. I wanted to relax and enjoy myself. My life beyond the café was growing ever more complicated, and I needed whatever this was with Greg to be simple. The easier and more straightforward, the more I could think of it as fate. The more I could believe that I was meant to be here, and nowhere else. With no one else.

'What about you?' I challenged, staring at him over my wine glass. 'You can't have told me everything about yourself yet.'

Greg finished off the last few morsels on his plate before answering. 'No. But a bloke's got to retain some mystery.' He leaned back in his chair with another smile, folding his napkin. 'Seriously, though, I'm an open book. What you see is what you get. Sorry if that disappoints.'

The smile vanished, as if he'd just realised something unpleasant.

I felt a twinge of alarm. 'Why should I be disappointed?'

'My life's not that exciting, really. But I'd prefer to be self-employed. Something to do with marketing and PR, perhaps. It's what I trained in. I still feel like there's loads of time ahead, but if there isn't,' he shrugged, 'I've done okay for myself, relatively speaking.'

There was something about him now that tore at my gut. 'Greg, there's nothing wrong with you. Or your life.'

'Deborah didn't think so.'

Damn. Were we going to do this? Tonight? Go there. The wasteland haunted by our exes.

'Deborah,' I said, 'was she just a girlfriend? Or the woman you lived with, or…?'

He leaned across the table, holding out his hand. 'We lived together. But look, Cara. I am over her. It isn't that I want her back, because I don't. She wasn't good for me. It's just… I can't have someone screwing with my head like that again. I think that's why I put myself down when I know I shouldn't. I still see myself through her eyes.'

I stared at him, paralysed for a second too long before taking his hand. 'Greg, I'm sorry she made you feel that way.' I swallowed. 'Because I think you're lovely. A lovely, kind, decent man.'

He pulled a face. 'Just what a bloke likes to hear.'

'No, Greg, I mean it in a good sense.'

'So, okay, I'm not a jerk like that guy the other day. Will, or whatever his name. The way he barged in, demanding your attention. And I get that you still work for JoJo Pembroke, sort of, but… I regret leaving the way I did. I should have stuck around. Shown you some support.'

'Oh.' A wave of shame lapped against me. 'It's okay. JoJo was in a panic about something and her brother was just worried about her. He didn't mean to act like that. In fact, I was supposed to apologise to you on his behalf.'

A fib, but I felt Greg needed to hear it. And I

didn't want him to think badly of Wilf.

Although… if he knew the truth…

I let go of his hand and pushed back my chair, keen to change the subject. 'Almost forgetting – I made tiramisu. I still don't think the Italian theme was intentional, though.'

After dessert, and coffee with Baileys, Greg offered to help me clear up. He followed me into the kitchen where I washed and he dried.

'I'd love to repay you, Cara. Cook dinner for you sometime soon."

'Right.'

'I'm not a bad cook. I enjoy it. And I promise not to poison you, either.'

'Who says I haven't poisoned you? It might be too soon for symptoms to show.'

He laughed. 'Just so long as I'm not stuck in the loo all day tomorrow.'

'Don't tell me if you are. Too much information.'

The laughter dwindled into contemplative smiles.

'So,' he said, 'our next date. When? Or even… *if*?'

'Not an "if". A definitely. And I've always liked a man who knows his way around a kitchen. Particularly his own.'

He put down the tea-towel, and rested a hand lightly on my back. 'I just need to say, I get why you wanted to have this evening here.'

'You do?'

'It's neutral ground. Not your place or mine.'

'Sallie just offered. My place is small.'

'There's also less expectation.'

'I guess.' I'm not sure Sallie had viewed it that way. I dreaded to think where her imagination had taken her. I turned to face Greg. His hand dropped back to his side. 'But if I come over for dinner at yours…?'

'Also no pressure. Just dinner. I like spending time with you, Cara. And I'm happy for you to set the pace.'

Warmed and lulled by alcohol and his sheer *nice*ness, I blinked up at him and instinctively put a hand to his chest, spreading my fingers across his shirt. I didn't know what I'd done to find myself with someone like this. I needed to sort my head out. Fast.

'Greg, that's very sweet.'

'But…?'

'No buts.' I had to listen to Sallie and Nushrat's advice. I'd be a fool if I didn't try to make this work. 'I'd love to come over to yours. And then… we'll see where it goes from there.'

A slow smile widened his lips, and I stretched up, kissing him gently, leaning into him. After a few moments, his hands pressed into the small of my back, pulling me close as I arched into the hollow of his body. A less urgent clinch than last time, at least to begin with. He was a good kisser, taking his time, and I felt a gradual heat build inside me, his own need evident as we pushed against each other. But something didn't feel right, and it wasn't just the worktop digging into me.

Greg must have sensed my retreat. He leaned back, staring down with darkened eyes, his chest rising and falling in shallow breaths. But he smiled again, and cleared his throat.

'If we're done cleaning up here, Cara, I should phone for a taxi. We'll go via yours and drop you off.'

'That's kind... Are you sure?'

'Of course I'm sure. I'll call now.'

I nodded, as he took out his phone and absently rubbed a hand through his hair.

A good man. A decent man. I could do much worse. *Had* done worse with the likes of Sid, who hadn't stopped when I'd retreated, making me feel I'd already consented to him staying the night by allowing him to sit on my bed and kiss me. And I'd convinced myself I wanted him to stay as I'd trailed my hands over his ripped torso, so conspicuous under his tight T-shirt, and let him push me back against the pillows. Because... who wouldn't want someone who looked like him? I was so out of his league, I ought to be grateful he wanted me. And looking back, I'd felt like that the entire time we were going out. Always retreating, then surrendering, telling myself I ought to be grateful.

Now, I watched Greg make the call and pocket his phone again. 'Ten minutes. Less of a wait than I thought there'd be, this time of year.'

'I'll finish tidying up, make sure everything's turned off and the candles are out. Sallie would never forgive me if I set the place ablaze.'

All the way to mine, in the back of the taxi, Greg held my hand; the warmth of his fingers soothing against mine. And he kissed my cheek and told me not to worry as we pulled into the Pembrokes' drive and I offered to pay a portion of the fare.

'Dinner at my place soon,' he said, 'okay?'

'I'd like that. I'll check my diary and let you know.'

Adults said that, in real life. They had busy schedules, with all sorts going on. I wanted to be just like them, I realised. But living a life I loved; a fulfilling grown-up life, which I'd built for myself. As I watched the tail lights of the taxi fade into the night, though, I wondered why I let myself regress so often lately into a little girl, gazing at a carousel from a broken snow-globe, waiting for the seemingly impossible to happen.

Chapter 14

'What exactly are we doing?' I almost crashed into JoJo as she came to an abrupt halt. Her hand went up; the iceberg on her left hand, next to her wedding ring, flashing as it caught the light.

'Wait.'

'For what?' My voice dropped to a whisper, although I don't know why, considering the level of noise around us. Revellers – probably from some office do – had tumbled out of a Dickensian pub into the cobbled street. It was almost two o'clock. In the afternoon. Doubting they were going back to their workplace in that state, I watched as they swayed raucously up Crooks Lane and disappeared into an almost identical Dickensian pub to the one they'd just exited.

I turned back to JoJo. She hadn't seemed to register any of it. 'What's going on?' I pressed. 'Why are we here?'

It wasn't odd that she'd wanted me to accompany her into town. Des was out, and she'd asked Wilf to pick up the girls from school. She'd found me in the hovel that morning crocheting a new project I'd dreamed up the night before, and peered down at my handiwork with her sharp emerald eyes (make-up impeccable, as always), as I'd explained what it was and who it was for.

'That's a kind thing to do, Cara.' Although 'kind' didn't automatically sound like a compliment when she said it. 'But I've got something fun lined up for us.'

It would have been no use explaining I was having fun already.

So here I was, trailing around town, carrying shopping bags from one boutique to another, and having my suggestions overridden by JoJo and numerous snooty shop assistants. Accompanying her on a shopping expedition wasn't anything new. Usually it was to buy gifts for her daughters, like today, and she always claimed she needed my input, although she rarely took it on board.

In the end, I'd shut my mouth and said nothing, simply nodded on cue. But then curiously we'd found ourselves in a part of town where there were more bars and restaurants than high-end shops, and JoJo had begun to act shiftily, as if she were in a spy thriller, turning up the collar of her sage green coat and donning huge sunglasses, even though there was no hint of sun.

'Try to look less conspicuous, Cara,' she hissed over her shoulder.

I was dressed in my usual blacks and greys, and would have blended in fine if I wasn't carrying a million shopping bags with logos screaming 'Uber-Chic' and 'You Might Need a Mortgage to Afford Me'.

As she crept towards the street corner, and I lumbered grouchily behind, I noticed JoJo take a sharp breath. Every part of her seemed to stiffen. I craned around the sage green coat to see what she was looking at.

It was an upscale bar-restaurant I hadn't come across before. New ones were always popping up in town. An expanse of dark glass frontage with scrawly white writing. Dominico's. Or, at least, I thought that was what it said. It was loopy and squiggly, and looked as if someone had tried to write it with their non-dominant hand. Potted bay trees, perfectly clipped into neat balls, stood either side of the doorway, seasonal red ribbons tied in bows around their slender trunks.

My attention was diverted to the street in front, where a man was greeting a woman enthusiastically as she climbed out of a car. He gestured towards the bar-restaurant, and they both walked in, side by side. I said nothing. I didn't know what I could say, under the circumstances.

JoJo's body seemed to fold, the stiffness collapsing into itself, and she drew back into Crooks Lane and leaned against the nearest wall.

'I didn't want to believe it,' she murmured.

Okay, Cara, think. You need to defuse this. Cut

the right wire, or it'll all blow up.

How had she even known he'd be here?

'JoJo, it might be nothing…'

'Or it might be everything,' she said caustically, so expressionless behind those giant sunglasses. 'It was in his calendar. "Two o'clock. Dominico's." It didn't say who he was meeting.'

'You sneaked a look at his calendar? On his phone?'

'I asked to borrow it for a moment. I said mine was out of charge, and he lent me his. Don't judge me, Cara.'

'I'm not judging. I'm just saying, don't jump to conclusions.'

'I never imagined it would be *her*… She's always been so… loyal.'

I didn't respond to that.

There might be a perfectly logical explanation for why Des was about to have drinks or a late lunch with JoJo's personal assistant Alyson. I couldn't think of one right that second, but I also knew taking things at face value wasn't necessarily the best move. Situations weren't always what they seemed.

'Right.' I had to take charge, before JoJo crumpled into a wretched heap and ruined her make-up and that gorgeous coat. 'Come with me.' The shopping bags hampered me from taking her arm, so I pulled my best Cara-Knows-What-To-Do face and nodded up the lane. 'Please, JoJo… just follow me.'

Slowly, she budged, and swore at the cobbles as she tottered after me in her narrow heeled, knee-high boots. I spotted a small bar on a corner where I'd gone with Sallie and Nushrat a few times. Seedy-looking from the street, it wasn't so bad inside. The servers were friendly without being flirty, and the tables and booths well-spaced out. Thankfully, it wasn't too busy for an afternoon in December. A few people finishing off late lunches, but plenty of space. I led JoJo to a booth at the back and dumped all the bags on the banquette.

'Right.' I flexed my stiff fingers. 'What would you like to drink?'

She slid on to the curved seat, still with her sunglasses on and that blank Terminator stare. 'I don't care. Just get me whatever you're having,' she said dully.

At the bar, I ordered two small glasses of house red. 'Please tell me you take Apple Pay.'

The barman smiled and slid the machine towards me. I held my phone over it, thumb on the home button, eyes closed. I heard the ping as the payment went through, and sighed with relief. And regret.

But when I returned to the booth with the drinks, there was a crisp twenty-pound note on the table. I eyed it cautiously.

'Take it.' JoJo removed her sunglasses. She looked washed-out, even under all that make-up. 'Let me cover this.'

'You don't need to… That's too much, anyway.'

'Consider it a tip. Cara, please, I'm not stupid. Don't act all proud. We wouldn't be here if it wasn't for me. What I mean is,' she swallowed, 'this is my fault. I dragged you out today, and I should have been more honest with you.'

I tucked the note into my purse, and shuffled on to the banquette opposite her. 'Thank you.'

'You're the best out of all of them, and sometimes I treat you like crap.'

'I wouldn't say—'

'I know what I'm like. But I am grateful for everything you do for me. For my family. I may not always show my appreciation, but when I say you're a "star" it's because you are.'

I stared into my wine as Wilf stalked into my head the way he often did. Magnificent. Confusing.

Still off limits, I assumed.

'Have you suspected Des for a while?' I asked, after a long pause, as JoJo attacked her wine. 'I know he's been "out" a lot more than usual. His car's not in the drive as much.'

I wasn't sure I ought to be talking like this, or if JoJo even wanted to confide in me.

'You know I have. Wilfred dragged you into it, that night when Des didn't come home till late and I couldn't get hold of him. It's been going on for a while, I'm sure. Alyson's been acting weird, as well. But I never once thought…' She blinked furiously as if tears were beating behind her eyes. 'Such a stereotype. It's ridiculous.'

'But isn't it... too public? Them meeting like that? In a bar, in the middle of the day?'

Didn't people go to hotels to conduct affairs? Or was that only the sexual aspect of the betrayal? If love was involved, the motive behind it even, being out in public like that might be a desperate cry for recognition. Then again, I'd never crept around, seeing someone I shouldn't be seeing.

'She's supposed to be in the office today,' JoJo responded. 'I bet if I call there, the rest of them will cover for her.'

'The whole office?' I raised my eyebrows. 'That's almost... paranoid. You can't think like that.'

'They're probably all laughing behind my back.'

'I'm sure no one's laughing.'

I didn't even think Des and Alyson would find any of this funny, but maybe I was too trusting, too naïve still. I hadn't grown up enough, even now.

JoJo demolished the last of her wine, and slid off her seat in one graceful, fluid movement. 'Do you want another, Cara?'

I'd barely touched mine; she was asking out of courtesy. 'Maybe we should be going soon?' I said hesitantly instead.

'We've only just got here. And this was your

idea, remember? I don't mind paying for your company. After all, I'd pay you if you were my therapist, right? But don't pretend you brought me to a bar and expected me to drink lemonade.'

Of course I hadn't. Then again, I'd just thought she was in shock and needed a quiet drink and a shoulder to cry on, or someone to tell her everything would be okay. I hadn't expected her to go on a bender in the middle of the afternoon. I should have taken her to Starbucks or Costa. A sugary tea might have been all she needed.

Realising one of us had to drive back, I pushed my own glass away. Personally, I didn't imbibe alcohol before climbing behind the wheel of a car. And lunch had only been a quick, measly salad, between boutiques. 'Actually, could you please get me a soda water. Ice and lemon.'

I think she caught the edge to my voice. JoJo hovered by the table, hesitating, just for a moment, before sashaying to the bar.

Over the next half-hour, she downed a fresh glass of red (a large) along with the small one I'd left. Her features softened again, her eyes glazing a little, but not with tears. If I drank like that when I was sad, I'd have been blubbing after ten minutes.

But she was the inimitable JoJo Pem. She wouldn't go down without a fight.

'I think you need to ask Des about it.' I attempted to counsel her. 'Just ask him for the truth. You'll only think the worst if you don't.'

'Oh, I intend to. Although I'm speaking to my solicitor first.'

'Don't do anything in a hurry. Not without talking to Des—'

'So he can lie to my face?'

'He might not lie.'

'Barely anyone around me is as truthful as you, Cara.' She held my gaze now, sharp-eyed again. 'I've watched you grow up. You were just a girl, effectively, when I first met you. And now you're probably the only true friend I've got left. I'd trust you with my life.'

Damn. She was laying it on thick. Should I be getting emotional? If I'd been drinking, I might have told her she was my friend, too, and that I trusted her back. But I was too much like a marionette, with JoJo pulling the strings. It all felt so one-sided.

Yes, I was living in her annexe, but I knew she'd never intended to let it to a tenant, in an official capacity. She didn't need the income. I was there out of convenience, however much she might state otherwise. She didn't know the minutiae of my life the way Sallie and Nushrat did. And Sallie never treated me like an employee when I was off the clock.

That wasn't to say JoJo had never had to console me when my relationships, if you could even call them that, imploded. But I seldom argued with her over anything she asked me to do, the way a true friend might; someone who felt entirely at ease around her.

From where I sat, I wasn't sure I could ever see JoJo as just a pal to the extent she seemed to see me. And I wondered if that was the real reason she'd had a hard time keeping hold of friends in the past – because they'd all felt that way around her?

Was that how Des felt, too? More beholden to her than perhaps a husband ought to, living in her shadow all these years? Even taking her name when they'd married, so that he wasn't plain old Desmond Jones any more. Not that I knew the full story around that, just the superficial details.

'On the other hand,' JoJo murmured into another empty glass, 'it might be best if I leave it for now.'

'Leave what?' She'd already finished the wine; she couldn't be talking about that.

'Leave the inevitable till later. Postpone talking to Des about it until after Christmas. For the girls' sake.'

It struck me that maybe he was waiting, too. Unless he was going to act like it never happened and carry on as before.

'I suppose,' I said. 'But… could you actually keep up the pretence?'

Her eyes shot fire at me, and a strange defiance, even as her shoulders remained slumped. 'You'd be surprised what I can hide.'

'O-kay.' I sighed inwardly, suddenly drained from the melodrama and trailing around in her wake. 'Do you think it's time to head back...? Belle and Vicki will be home by now.'

And Wilf would be with them. He could take over from me with JoJo. Do a better job, no doubt. All I'd done was get her slightly drunk.

She snapped upright, blinking all around her before she gulped and nodded.

We walked back to the car without speaking, JoJo carrying half the shopping bags.

∞∞∞

'In what universe did you think it was a good idea letting her drink like that during the day?'

The voice – achingly familiar already, and blush-inducing – halted me in my tracks. I held the key inches from my back door. I'd almost made it across the yard in one piece. So near, yet so far.

I turned reluctantly. He was walking towards me, brow knotted in confusion.

'Wilf, I didn't know she'd want more than one glass. You had to have been there—'

'If I had, I wouldn't have let her near a bar in the first place. Now Belle and Vicki have to see their mother like this.'

'She's not that drunk.'

'It's still obvious she's been drinking.'

I'd deposited JoJo in her kitchen a couple of minutes ago, leaving the shopping in the boot of the car, so the girls wouldn't spot their gifts. Wilf had been on the other side of the kitchen island. I'd mumbled some form of hello, and made a dash for it.

'Listen,' I said now, 'you need to talk to JoJo rather than me. Somewhere the girls won't overhear you. It's about Des.'

Wilf's shoulders tensed, noticeable even under the hoodie he was wearing, some Canadian sports team emblazoned on the front. 'Right. I see. You won't enlighten me yourself?'

'Just speak to your sister. Please. I've done what I can for now. It's your turn.'

'You can't pawn her off like that.'

'I'm not pawning her off. I just don't know what to say exactly. If I'm helping, or making things worse. Believe me, Wilf, I don't want to see her in that state.'

'No.' A muscle twitched behind the stubble. 'That makes two of us.'

He was close enough that I could see his face in detail. Close enough that I could have reached out and touched him and told him I understood.

He stepped back. 'Thank you, Cara – for just being with her, I guess. Letting her vent, if that's what she needed.'

'It's fine. But fetch me if you think I can be of any use again, okay? I don't mind. You know where to find me.'

He nodded but didn't speak. And I turned and let myself into the hovel.

Chapter 15

A conveyer belt of alternative scenarios stuttered through my head all evening and overnight, and I caught little sleep in between.

The likeliest (and I wanted so much to believe it) was that Des was simply trying to organise an extra-special Christmas surprise for JoJo, and had enlisted Alyson's help, rather than mine for a change.

And why would he have handed over his phone to JoJo, just like that, if he knew it contained incriminating evidence? Wouldn't she have found more than a vague date in a calendar? Illicit messages, for example? Emails and texts. Maybe the odd photo.

My brain wouldn't shut up. Or shut down.

It was brutal.

Exhausting.

The birds had just started their dawn chorus when I staggered out from under the duvet, shivering as I pulled on a cardie and wriggled into my duck-shaped slippers before heading to make myself a tea. No, not tea. Coffee. I'd need regular caffeine hits to get me through the day. As the kettle boiled, I went to the loo, but as I stepped back into the corridor, I immediately noticed something poking under the back door. A folded sheet of paper from a notepad. It hadn't been there a couple of minutes ago.

With a frown, I picked it up and read it, unlocked the door with another shiver and peered out. Light was only just bleeding into the sky. There was no one there. No light on in the house, although a faint glow emanated from the games room. I wavered, almost setting foot in the frosty yard, but then stepped back and slammed the door shut.

I locked it, and re-read the note. Short, to the point, yet somehow carrying a fateful weight.

> *'JoJo told me everything.*
>
> *I thought you should have my number in case something like that happens again. Text me yours and I'll save you as a contact.*
>
> *Wilf.*
>
> *PS. Thank you again.'*

His number was at the bottom, each digit neatly formed, difficult to misinterpret. As for the message itself – what could I interpret from that?

I made my coffee and took it back to bed.

Sitting nestled under the duvet, mug on the bedside table, I tapped Wilf's number into my phone and saved it. Before I could chicken out, I drafted a reply.

—Thanks for your note, here's my number in return. You're right, it's a good idea, in case of emergencies.

I almost stopped there, but my thumbs took over with a life of their own.

Don't know about you, but I couldn't sleep much last night going over it all. If there might be a logical and non-dodgy reason for Des being so absent lately, or for him to be meeting Alyson on his own. I keep thinking there's more to it than the obvious. Any thoughts yourself…?

I stared at the screen, blood rushing in my ears. I couldn't go through with sending that – could I? It invited a response. Initiated a conversation and made us collaborators, in a way. An alliance. And yet, it was for purely selfless reasons.

I hit send, before I could warn myself there wasn't much that was pure about it.

A minute later, as my heart seemed to be trying to thump its way out of my chest, my phone pinged.

—So you're awake too. Saw your light on but didn't want to assume. Couldn't sleep either. I think you're right. I'd talk to Des myself but JoJo made me promise not to and maybe she's right and it should wait until after Christmas but I

don't like to see her like this.

Didn't Wilf know what a comma was for, considering he was such a language geek? Either way, I didn't care. Allowing my coffee to go cold, I lay back on my pillows and started typing again.

—For the girls' sake, that makes sense. I don't know if JoJo is going to last that long though. Plus the girls are old enough to notice something's wrong. A crappy time of year for this to happen. Again, there might be a good reason, but how are we going to find out?

I didn't have to wait long for an answer.

—How well do you know Alyson?

Damn.

—Not well enough to talk to her about this, if that's what you're getting at? Have you met her yourself yet?

—She's been to see JoJo a couple of times, so yes.

(Hallelujah, a comma.)

He continued:

JoJo's warned me to watch out though. Apparently I'm just her type?! Can't say I noticed her flirting but maybe JoJo's warned her off. Think most women around here have been warned off by my darling sister. Another pro for Bristol??

My eyes widened with a rush of adrenaline. This conversation was veering off topic. But I knew I wanted it to. I could hear his voice in my head, as if he was propped up on his elbow next to me, smiling, smoothing the hair back from my face…

I dropped the phone, which might as well have stung me. It lay on the duvet, looking at me accusingly. Surely I had to answer now, though. I couldn't leave him hanging. But maybe I needed to inject some humour into this, before I told Wilf how much I didn't want him to leave Pebblestow.

—Relieved Alyson hasn't tried it on with you. TBH, you wouldn't have stood a chance. She eats men like you for breakfast. And your sister's got so many followers, I don't rate your chances with any woman, unless she's part of some remote tribe somewhere and hasn't heard of the internet.

His reply was swift. Assured.

—Yikes. I prefer eggs on a breakfast menu. I'd rather not be on the menu myself. Guess I'll become a eunuch or go live in the Amazon then. Talking of breakfast…

—Drastic measures. Both sound painful. Breakfast sounds much better. Cornflakes today, I think. What about you? What's your meal of choice this morning?

—Has to be eggs now they're in my head. I make a mean omelette.

—Wow, really? It talks back? Calls you names? Spits in your face? Seriously, how mean are we talking?

I waited. But no dots appeared, to indicate he was typing. Frowning, I checked over my last message, but there was nothing there that might put him off – was there?

Put him off what, exactly?

I sat up, kicking away the duvet. This was not good. I'd been tired and groggy and indulged in something I shouldn't have indulged in. Let myself get carried away.

Regretting that I hadn't spotted his note until I'd been fully conscious and primed for battle, I padded into the kitchen to heat up my coffee. Now I didn't even feel like cornflakes. I didn't feel like eating anything. My appetite had been replaced by something else, but I didn't know what.

Ten minutes later, as I stood sipping from my mug and shaping the contours of the day in my head, I jumped at a knock on the back door. Hot coffee slopped over my hand. I swore, and reached for a tea-towel, before answering what sounded worryingly like a JoJo knock.

But it was JoJo's brother. All shorts and sweatshirt, bed-hair and stubble. Holding a plate with a rather yummy-looking breakfast, fluffy and golden, steaming hot.

Suddenly, I was hungry again.

Wilf held out the plate to me. 'I thought you might like a mean omelette of your own. If you eat eggs...?'

I pretended to recoil. 'I do, but my imagination's going wild here. Will it bite? Shout at me? Tell me I look hideous?' I leaned over to address the omelette directly. 'Look, I admit I haven't showered or done anything with my hair yet, so you might have a point. But cut a girl some slack, it's still really early.'

Wilf grinned. 'I lied. It's actually very polite. As egg dishes go.'

'All right then, if you're sure.' I took the plate from him with a wide smile of my own. 'It's very kind of you. Do you want to come in? Fetch your own and eat it here...?' I stood back from the door, the blood rushing in my ears again.

Wilf stared past me, ruffling a hand through his hair at the back, working his way forward, caressing the curls I wanted to stroke myself, the compulsion mounting with each passing second.

'Nah... I'd better not. The others will be up soon. JoJo would shoot us both if she saw me coming out of your place first thing in the morning.'

'Ha! Yes.' I laughed weakly. 'Not quite how I planned to spend my day. Target practice for your sister.'

'No,' he agreed. 'Then again... plans can change. Things are worth the trouble sometimes, aren't they?'

'Sometimes... but rarely.' My smile was bleak now. 'Not in my experience.' I indicated the plate, and resorted to common courtesy to smother the lump in my throat. 'Thanks for this.'

Wilf was already turning and walking away. 'No problem. I won't accept anything less than "excellent" on TripAdvisor, though. And, Cara...'

'Yes?'

'You could never look hideous.'

Chapter 16

I hadn't ever thought of a churchyard as a place I would choose to spend time in. Walking around this one with Perdita, though, curiously made me want to come back another day, as I realised I'd been missing out on this jewel in the centre of the village all these years.

I'd walked past Pebblestow's parish church on enough occasions, peering over the stone wall into the cool, leafy shade in summer, admiring the pearly pink blossoms in springtime, or the golden hues of autumn. But I'd never wanted to venture through the lychgate and just wander idly among the listing headstones. What was the point of reminding myself I wouldn't exist one day, either, like these poor souls? My hopes, dreams, memories – just snuffed out forever. Everything that made me, *me*, essentially.

Yet there was something cathartic about all this today, my arm looped through Perdita's as she stopped every so often to read out old names and dates on a headstone. Hard to explain how I found it grounding in a good way. As if it might cast things in a fresh light, if I allowed it to.

'I haven't told you this before, Cara, but my husband and I were married here.' Perdita gestured to the church on our left with its mellow stonework and small stained glass windows. 'Not a huge wedding, like some people dream of. Just close friends, and the little family he had. A few well-wishers from the village, of course, waiting for us when we came out.'

'Really? That must have been lovely. It's a gorgeous building.'

I hadn't stopped to appreciate it fully in the past, and I'd never set foot inside. I'd never had the need. Sallie and Laurence had been married a few years back in the most coveted wedding venue in the area – a plush hotel just outside town, set in acres of landscaped gardens complete with ponds, fountains and a renowned maze.

I'd been a bridesmaid along with Nushrat; pursued by one of the male guests all afternoon until finally, after too much champagne, I'd given in under a rose-scented arbour near the maze and let him kiss me. He'd been twenty-ish years my senior. A silver fox divorcee. Later, though, while everyone was busy sending off the bride and groom, he'd slipped me a key-card to his room, his smile wolfish as his sweaty hand lingered in mine. I'd felt instantly sick. On my way out, to catch a taxi back to Pebblestow with Nushrat and her boyfriend at the time, I'd handed the key-card into reception, and trembled with indignation all the way home.

There was something charming and intimate about this church in the centre of Pebblestow, which that other venue lacked. It was beautifully fitting for a small wedding. I couldn't imagine any of Perdita's bridesmaids – if she'd had any – being propositioned by some random bloke, either.

'Spring blossom was absolutely everywhere,' Perdita reminisced, as she wobbled a little at my side. 'Even down the front of my dress. So much of it fluttering around, we didn't need confetti. My husband had fun picking it out of my lingerie on our wedding night.'

I laughed. "Perdita! I'm shocked. You probably put it there deliberately.'

'Not at all.' She smiled. 'It was a gorgeous, sunny day. The happiest day of my life up until then. Or maybe the second happiest... I'd been with him over a year, after all.' She drifted off into her memories where I couldn't reach her, so I left her to it for a while before resuming the conversation.

'You lived in Pebblestow a long time,' I broached gently. 'Is your husband buried here? Or any other family?' I glanced around the churchyard, wondering if this was why she'd wanted to come here, but hadn't been able to bring herself to tell me. She'd simply taken my arm as we'd left the café and said she could do with a stroll before I dropped her off at home. It was my lunchbreak and I hadn't minded. I'd grab a quick sandwich later, when I returned from driving her back up to Riverside.

'My husband was cremated,' she said, just as gently in return. 'The children helped me scatter his ashes down by the river, off the jetty. One of the saddest days of my life, but not one I've dwelled on. I just pray we'll be together again soon.' She blinked, as if suppressing tears. 'Sooner than anyone knows.'

I stopped walking. 'Are you okay? I mean, you aren't...?'

She looked at me, her eyes dimmer than usual, the dark depths less twinkly. 'No. I'm just old, my darling. Older than I'd like to say. Sometimes I feel I might crumble in the wind and blow away, as if I was never even here.'

'Perdita, no.' I turned to face her, holding her hand. 'You're the most *alive* person I know. You're not crumbling or blowing away anywhere. At least not on my watch. Your children would never forgive me, would they?'

Her lips puckered into a rosebud smile. 'No, they wouldn't. Although I think they couldn't help but love you, Cara, whatever you did.'

'Perdita, do you mind me asking how many children you actually have? You've never said.'

'Haven't I?' She looked past me, as if she had to think about the answer. 'Too many, perhaps;

although each one's etched on my heart.'

'Sorry?'

She patted my face. 'Don't look so worried, I didn't give birth to all of them. Just two or three.' She chuckled. 'You see, when our own weren't so small any more, my husband and I decided to foster. Riverside's so large, and it was such a happy place, it felt a waste not to share it with others. And I cared about them all dearly. Especially the "outcasts", with their dazzling, divergent minds. The ones other people couldn't handle, even though one of my own was like that, too, so I knew how difficult it could be. My husband was just as dazzling and divergent, you see. He had an affinity with children like that. The ones who don't seem to belong anywhere. Instead of shaping them to fit the world, he showed them how to make their world fit them.'

I felt the prickle of tears behind my own eyes. 'Your husband sounds amazing.' My voice was choked and unsteady, clogged with emotion. 'You don't meet people like that every day. You must really miss him.'

'I'm sure you've met folk like that yourself, even if you didn't know it at the time. And yes, I miss him as if a part of myself left, too. But you mustn't worry about that now, my dear.' She touched my face again, stroking it with the pad of her thumb. 'You mustn't be anxious about letting go of your fear and loving someone, just because you might lose them one day.'

'I don't… That isn't…' I frowned.

Perdita stepped back, as if to survey me better, and leaned both hands on her walking stick. 'You told me your parents died, your mother shortly after your father; how she couldn't live without him. You said you were scared to put your happiness in someone else's hands like that.'

'Yes. But…'

'Sometimes we have to, though. Because it's that or nothing. Unless we take the risk, we might never be truly happy. And maybe… maybe that other person will never be happy, either.'

I hadn't thought of it like that. How my parents had taken the gamble to be together, and what their lives might have been like if they'd stayed apart. My dad's life had revolved around my mother and me. I'd never once doubted his love, and I knew the lengths he'd gone to, to give me a rainbow of happy memories to counteract the bad. As for my mother, she might still have carried her sadness around with her all her life. Even more so, if she hadn't married my dad. She might never have lived for nearly two decades alongside the man she adored; a man who adored her back, and tragically died defending the sanctuary he'd created for her.

How many people knew a love that fierce and loyal? I'd got so hung up on the ending, it had shadowed too much of what went before. They'd both adored me, too. Their precious only daughter. A living, breathing expression of their passion, however accidental. They'd never once made me feel that I wasn't meant-to-be, or that I'd held back their lives in any way. No child should be made to feel otherwise. And I understood why Perdita had wanted to foster. Even now, even here, in this peaceful churchyard, she was doing nothing less than being a parent to me.

But then, almost rudely, the tranquillity was shattered. Yipping filled the crisp, December air, and I blinked back a mist of tears and turned to see a familiar ginger furball bounding towards me, trailing his lead.

Perdita laughed with delight as I scooped him up.

'What on earth…? What are you doing here?' I rubbed his tummy, and looked in the direction he'd come from. A rush of heat hit me as a fraught-looking Wilf appeared at the lychgate. The dog had obviously jerked at his lead and run off. Unlike him to do that, but he might have been hissed at by a bolshy cat, or snarled at by a bigger dog. 'Walking around the village for a change, were you, Loki?' He licked my face in response.

'This is JoJo's dog.' I turned to explain to Perdita. She wasn't laughing or smiling now, just leaning on her walking stick and staring towards the lychgate. 'That's Wilf,' I muttered, hoping my blush wasn't too incandescent. 'JoJo's brother.

Will you wait here a minute? Loki must have run away from him.'

'Hey.' Wilf sounded slightly out of breath as I approached. 'Loki just shot off. I've been chasing him half-way down Swallowtail Lane and round the village. It's like he was possessed or something.'

'Odd.' I stroked the dog under his tiny muzzle.

'Damn, I really need to join some gym in the new year. Or start running again.' Wilf shook his head. 'I'm so out of shape.'

He looked in fine shape to me, but I didn't comment. I managed to hold on to my dignity, for once. 'Well, thankfully, Loki's okay. It could have been worse.'

'I had nightmare visions of him running out in front of a car.'

'It's rare that he tugs at his lead like that, he's so small. But if he gets spooked and it catches you by surprise, he's off and running before you know it.'

Wilf took him from me. 'Fast, for something with such little legs.'

'Me, or the dog?' I quipped, before I could stop myself.

'Your legs seem great, Cara, from what I've seen of them. But I think I'd still be able to catch you without any problem.'

My blush grew hotter. Possibly radioactive.

'Compared to Loki.' Wilf pushed a hand

through his mop, and coughed. 'Sorry. That sounded really different in my head. So, what are you doing here?' He nodded past me towards the churchyard.

'I'm on a break, and Perdita wanted to come. Not that she's got family buried here. Or even old friends, by the look of it. Which is strange, now that I've said it. Unless they've all been cremated, too. I think most of the people she must have known once in Pebblestow are gone. That's so sad, isn't it? To be the last one left?'

'I wouldn't be keen on it myself.' Wilf frowned over my shoulder. 'Where is she, though? Perdita?'

I looked round. 'Oh... She was right over there. I wanted you to meet her.'

'Maybe she's gone inside the church?'

'Didn't you see her?' I frowned, too. 'You must have – when you first got here?' Although there were a few trees and headstones in the way, and Perdita was so tiny...

'I can't say I did. Sorry, my attention was... elsewhere.' He held my gaze a moment too long, then shifted away. 'I'd, er, better be getting back. I said to JoJo I'd help her with something, and I should have been back already. She'll be worrying.'

'That's what sisters are for.' I smiled feebly.

'More accurately, they're there to be annoying. Anyway,' he nodded behind me, 'you'd better find this Perdita, before she gets up to mischief.

I'd try inside the church.'

'She can't have got far. She's not a demon on her feet like Loki here.' I gave the dog one last stroke between the ears. 'Don't be naughty and run off for your Uncle Wilf again.'

'He won't. I won't let him.' Wilf lifted the dog's paw as if waving goodbye. 'Say "See you later," to your Aunty Cara.'

I laughed, but it was brittle. 'I've never been Aunty Cara in my life, I'm not about to start now. It makes me sound ancient.'

'Fair enough.' Wilf coughed again and checked his watch, which was lighting up imperiously on his left wrist. 'Ouch, I'm being summoned. I'll catch you later.' He turned at the lychgate, throwing me a brazen look over his shoulder. 'I don't mean literally.'

'Ha-ha.' I threw an impudent grimace back, and spun to face the church. 'Perdita, where are you?' I muttered, taking a deep, steadying breath. There was only so much drama and innocuous flirting I could handle in one lunchbreak. And was the flirting even that innocent and harmless, or as charged as the messages Wilf and I had somehow got into the routine of sending each other, every morning, discussing our breakfast habits?

The studded wood door to the church was slightly ajar. Tentatively, I pushed it open further and stepped inside. The last two times I'd been anywhere like this had been for my parents' funerals, agonisingly close together. But this was nothing like that church, which had just been a chapel really, attached to the crematorium: blazing white and modern, with sharp angles and jarring music.

This place hummed with a million soft breaths, a thousand voices in song; tears of sorrow, too, mixed with candlelight and flowers and prayer. The stone walls were warm as honey, the wood pews and pulpit polished to a glossy walnut brown. So many vows to love and honour, repeated beneath this high, vaulted roof. The echoes of babies, gasping and crying at water poured over their heads.

It all seemed to rush at me at once, out of the archaic stillness. I swayed for a moment, disorientated, before I spotted a splash of pink. The familiar beret.

She was perched on the far edge of a pew to my left, conversing with an angel. I blinked, clearing my vision. It was just a marble statue, Perdita's head dipped towards it as if sharing a confidence. Beads in numerous colours were scattered across the worn stone floor. But that was an illusion, too. Merely the light filtering through the stained glass, the windows so much brighter looking outwards.

The old woman lifted her head as I drew close. 'Ah, you found me.' She glanced past me briefly, as if reassuring herself I was alone.

'You just vanished. I thought I'd lost you. Trying to live up to your name?'

'Not intentionally.' Her smile was rueful. 'I thought I should give you and your young man some privacy.'

'Oh… Wilf and I – we're not – he isn't…'

'Isn't he? The way your face lit up, I'd say that he was *something*. And you make a lovely couple. If you don't mind me saying so.'

I lowered myself on to the end of an adjacent pew. 'But we can't. He's JoJo's brother. And besides… I'm seeing Greg.'

'Ah. Of course.' Perdita blinked at the angel, and nodded. 'Wilf Brooks is only the spanner in the works. The one you're not supposed to like. Except you do like him. It's obvious.'

'Yes, but' – I kept my voice low; after all, we were in a church – 'it's just that I fancy him. You know, *fancy* him. And it's clouding everything else.'

Her faint brows pulled together as she turned to me. 'Well, I "fancied" my husband, Cara. That didn't stop me falling in love with him, too. I don't see what the problem is. It's not uncommon for them to go together in a healthy relationship. But you implied the other day that you also "fancy" this other man, Greg?'

'Yes.' I stared at my feet, and bit my lip, sensing Perdita's watchful gaze on me. 'Not as much, though. I mean – it wasn't instant. Not like with Wilf.' I looked up again. 'But that's the problem. I need to listen to my head in all this. Just because I was blown away by Wilf the first time I met him, I can't get all "whoa, this is destiny, blah, blah," when it isn't.'

'But why couldn't it be? Because you liked him at first sight? Cupid's arrows strike from all angles, none less valid than any other. Anyway, how does Wilf feel? Have you considered his point of view?'

I straightened my back, almost sneering as I said, 'Cupid and his arrows have nothing to do with it. Wilf barely knows me. He just likes me a lot, apparently. He came out and said so. There's a connection, but...' I pulled a face, because I still couldn't quite believe he'd said that. 'If the circumstances were different, maybe we'd do something about it. But they're not. It could get really messy, and it wouldn't be worth it. Wilf understands that, too.'

'Well.' Shrugging her thin shoulders, Perdita turned back to the marble angel again. 'As long as you're both honest with yourselves, and everyone around you... That's what counts. I don't want to be remembered as the meddling old lady.'

I smiled, unable to resist. 'I'd say you're more of a fairy godmother.'

'Oh! I like the idea of that.' But she rapidly grew sober again, as if other thoughts had overtaken her. With her walking stick, she tapped a slab of brass inlaid at the angel's feet. 'Do you see this, Cara? All these names?'

I shifted to get a better look. 'What about them?'

'They're the children and young people who died in the village when the Spanish flu swept through it a century ago. Pebblestow was hit particularly hard. So many young ones lost.'

'Oh…' I blinked down at the list. It was horrifically long. 'I didn't know.'

'But you've seen the war memorial in Market Square? A generation of men – like Wilf and Greg – just wiped out a hundred years ago, too.'

'I laid a poppy wreath there on Remembrance Day, on behalf of everyone at Sallie's. The memorial's for all the fallen from the village, not just from the First World War.'

'You're right. All those tales, never finished.' Perdita sighed. 'But people still come to this place in hope.' She lifted her quivering head and looked around the church. 'I think that's why I like it here. It has nothing to do with religion for me, of any denomination. It's all to do with people, and *why* they want to believe in something bigger.'

'Because life's short,' I said. 'You don't need to tell me. I understand.'

'Do you? I'm just trying to put a different spin on things. To be truly honest with ourselves sometimes, I think we have to imagine a different life. Another scenario.'

'So then, what exactly are you saying?'

'I'm offering an alternative solution to your problem, Cara. Your dilemma, shall we say. If you lived over a century ago, whose name would you be most afraid to see on a telegram?'

'What?'

'Don't be shy, and don't think too hard. And above all, don't feel guilty. It's just a name on a piece of paper. You don't have to tell me. This is just for your benefit right now.'

Damn. I couldn't get away from it. Perdita was too tenacious. She'd hooked me with her charm and devious ingenuity, and I was trapped now. Cornered.

Doomed.

I stared at the marble angel, imagining myself back then, one of countless women waiting for news from the Front, horror gripping my throat when it arrived and told me the very last thing I wanted to hear.

'Point made,' I said raspily.

My hands were so tightly clenched, if I hadn't been wearing gloves, my nails would have left red dents in my palms.

'I'm sorry if it wasn't the answer you were hoping for, my dear.' A familiar wave of sympathy swept towards me as Perdita held my gaze with her dark, unfaltering eyes. 'I said it was a solution. I never said it would be easy.'

Chapter 17

Injecting cheerfulness into my voice and a spring into my step – neither of which I felt – I hurried into Sallie and Laurence's living room. 'The evening's saved! I'm here now. And, yes, as you can probably tell, I remembered the popcorn.'

'We had every faith in you,' said Sallie, unconvincingly.

'No, we didn't,' said Nushrat, swapping me the two buckets of sweet and salty for a glass of White Zinfandel. 'We thought you weren't coming, you were taking so long. And you weren't answering your phone.'

'Sorry, I forgot to set a reminder. And then it was out of charge.'

'You mean you were asleep?' Sallie unfolded herself from the sofa to take my coat, as Nushrat eased the cardboard lids off the popcorn buckets and tucked in.

'No, I wasn't!'

I'd been trawling the internet on my laptop

again, looking at various art courses. Anything to distract myself from other areas of my life. I'd surprised myself by becoming so absorbed that I'd lost track of time. A good sign. It implied my world did *not* revolve around men. Or more specifically, one man. The one whose name I couldn't unsee on a telegram that didn't even exist. So perverse of Perdita to tell me I had to let go of my fear, and then force me to make a spur of the moment decision based on nothing less. The fact my subconscious was desperate to get through to me didn't make it any better.

'Hi, ladies.' Laurence appeared in the doorway, rattling his keys. 'Glad to see you made it, Cara. Sal almost sent me out to look for you.'

'Well,' I shrugged, 'I can't miss Christmas movie night. It's tradition, isn't it? And Sal was only worried about the popcorn.'

'Nope.' Laurence shook his head. 'She's got a stash of her own. She hides it and thinks I don't know where it is.'

'You git.' Sallie threw a cushion at him. He caught it with a laugh. 'Giving away my secrets.'

He tossed the cushion back, and blew her a kiss. 'Enjoy your movie marathon, my sweet.'

'What have you got lined up tonight?' Nushrat asked him as he shrugged on his jacket. 'Anything fun?'

'Just seeing a few of the lads from work.' He threw me a glance over his shoulder. 'Including Greg. Do you want me to give him a message,

Cara?'

I turned towards the giant TV on the living room wall. 'No. It's fine. We were only in touch yesterday.'

'Ooh, setting a date for dinner at his place?' Nushrat prodded me. 'When is it, then? Spill.'

'We haven't.' I sank into an armchair, my eyes still fixed on the TV. 'Set a date yet. It was only small-talk. You know.'

'Okay. Well.' Laurence's tone had changed. 'I'll just tell him you said "Hi."'

'If you like.'

Even though I anticipated the sound of the front door closing, the slam still made me jump. A few drops of wine splashed over the edge of my glass. Sallie handed me a tissue.

'You sure you're all right, hun?'

'Why shouldn't I be?'

'I don't know.' She flopped back on to the sofa. 'But you're being all strange again. You're not feeling under any pressure, are you?'

I screwed up my brow. 'Pressure with work? Pressure in general? Pressure—'

'To take things to the next level with Greg already.'

'Oh.' I sniffed. '*That*.'

'Look,' said Sallie, 'we might tease you. And we might all think Greg could be the best thing for you since... well, since anything ever. But none of us want you to rush that side of things if you're not ready.'

'It's not a race.' Nushrat perched on the arm of my chair, and wrapped her arm around my shoulder.

'In fact, Laurence and I were discussing it only last night,' said Sallie.

'You were discussing my sex life with your husband?' My eyes widened. 'Well, thanks.'

'It wasn't like that. I was worried Greg might have got too pushy and that's why you were backing off. I get a sense that you are. But Laurence says Greg's being quite open with him. He really likes you, and he wants you to set the pace. Is that the truth? Because if he's lying to Laurence —'

'He's not lying, Sal. But is *everyone* talking about me behind my back? I thought men didn't discuss stuff like that. No wonder my ears have been aflame. Yes, Greg's said that to me, too. So, here you go: this is me, okay? Setting the pace.' I almost spilled wine again as I flung out my hand. 'Taking things really slow, so no one gets hurt.'

Oh, but pain's inevitable all round, Cara. Isn't it? You're hurting now, just sitting here telling porky-pies.

'Can we just watch one of these movies?' I frowned, shushing the voice in my head. 'What have you got lined up this year?'

Sallie hesitated, and exchanged a look with Nushrat. 'I thought we could kick off with *Miracle in Massachusetts.* It's a new one. Penniless waitress inherits a crumbling old mansion after a random act of kindness, and falls for the guy who helps her restore the place in time for the Christmas Eve extravaganza. And yes, at some point I think he wears a lumberjack shirt.'

'Oh, yay,' I declared darkly. 'I'm a penniless waitress. I wouldn't mind inheriting a mansion, crumbling or otherwise.'

Wordlessly, Nushrat scooped a bowl into one of the buckets of popcorn and passed it to me. Sallie reached for the remote.

The air crackled with a rare unease, even as the multicoloured lights, oblivious to the mood, made the tinsel on Sallie's Christmas tree shimmer with a myriad colours.

I always looked forward to this annual tradition. Sitting around in comfy clothes and comfy chairs with my best friends, watching festive movies. The TV would flicker until the small hours, when Laurence would creep in and cover us all with blankets while we slept. Sallie had landed on her feet with him. Maybe there were more good people around than I gave the world credit for.

But this year, I could barely follow any of the film plots. Women seemed to be slipping around on icy pavements a lot, and handsome men were conveniently catching them; men who seemed beastly at first but turned out to be charitable and kind. Friends were falling out and making up two scenes later, and cute kids were asking for the latest toy in their Christmas stocking, or for their mum and potential stepdad to kiss under the mistletoe.

I probably ought to watch a classic, I realised. Lose myself in an old-fashioned miracle, less centred around the paraphernalia of the season or a man in a checked flannel shirt. Yes, by the time the final credits rolled, either the protagonist or their romantic interest had ended up choosing family, friendship and love, over some stultifying corporate career or similar, but not one character in any of these movies tonight seemed to openly want the same thing I'd wished for, on a night not all that long ago, while riding a carousel I hadn't seen in town since. And yet... as I sat curled up in my cosiest leggings and jumper, in a tight tense ball, I couldn't stop thinking that what I'd wished for might be the most vital thing anyone could want or need.

Chapter 18

I'd downloaded a stack of prospectuses and spent an entire evening sifting through them. At least, it would have been a stack, if they were hard copies. I'm not sure what I hoped to achieve by looking. It was all aspirational... wasn't it? Going to college or university again in my thirties. Applying for finance. Potentially moving away, if I couldn't find anything suitable online or locally. I felt a tug of homesickness for Pebblestow just considering it. But I'd still researched as far afield as Bath Spa, which looked charming and impressive, from the website, and therefore wouldn't be for the likes of me. A couple of courses had a certain allure, though. And it wasn't a million miles from Bristol...

I snapped shut the lid on my laptop, and leaned back against my pillows and the headboard. I was turning into *that* person.

My teenage self would have been doodling his name with a heart around it, or practising signing his surname instead of mine. I ought to know better at my age now, but here I was imagining a life where he sat at his desk, doing… whatever important work he did at his desk, and I flitted about in my studio at the end of the garden, doing something equally important, and arty, though I had no clear vision of what that entailed. We'd come together late afternoon on the patio or in our cosy, country-style kitchen, to drink wine and share our day, and entertain friends and colleagues at the weekends. And a year or two down the line, maybe we'd be decorating the nursery—

Cara! What the hell?

Not this again. Why was I getting so carried away?

I felt my forehead. Was I hot? Feverish? Delirious? Would I even be able to tell when I was using my own hand to check?

If the object of my adolescent-style infatuation could see inside my head right now, he'd cringe in horror and flee south, leaving nothing but a trail of dust. My fantasies were mortifying.

I looked at my phone as it let out a 'choo-choo' on the bed beside me. I wasn't surprised he was messaging, although usually it was in the mornings. I'd quickly grown used to the new alert tone I'd assigned to him, hearing it with increasing frequency.

—I know it's late but your light's still on. If you're awake I'm having an early breakfast. Really fancied Eggs Benedict. Ever tried it?

I shook my head as if to dislodge the basest of my thoughts. My thumbs hovered over the phone while I worked out how to respond.

—Yes, I'm awake. And no, I haven't tried Eggs Benedict.

—Which begs the question Cara Mia: would you like to?

Did he realise he'd effectively just called me his darling in Italian? Of course not, I snapped at myself, because then he wouldn't have done it. I needed to get a grip.

— Breakfast right NOW? Wouldn't it be more like a late supper?

Where was he leading with this?

—Too early for you? I could meet you in the games room in twenty? You eat bacon don't you?

The whole thing was bizarre. Still, as my stomach gave a grumble, I accepted it wasn't the worst proposal I'd heard. It had been ages since dinner.

—Yes. OK, I'll see you there. You bring the food. I'll bring…?

—Yourself preferably. Unless you've got decent decaf coffee? I live in hope.

I squirmed, typing my reply.

—I have normal and decaf. Both Fairtrade, if that's what you mean by decent (and they taste good too). Not filter or cafetiere stuff, or anything like that though, sorry. I only have a kettle, spoon, mug and jar. (Well I have more than one spoon and mug, but you get the idea.)

—Naturally. How could you entertain guests otherwise?

—I hardly entertain guests ever. I just don't wash up every five minutes.

—Well I know what I'm getting you for Christmas. That's one gift sorted.

Oh! Would it be coffee or washing-up related? My thoughts skittered from sophisticated, expensive cafetiere all the way to Marigold rubber gloves. I'd only bought him a wallet, which came with a matching keyring in a gift box, and even that had been Nushrat's idea.

I puffed out my cheeks and exhaled, ruffling the wispy curls around my face. What was I doing? Where was this going? This thing inside me, snowballing out of control for someone I knew so little about.

But I answered him, nevertheless.

—I'll see you soon. 20-ish minutes. I'll bring myself and the decaf, as requested.

I rolled off the bed, and immediately swapped my stained pyjama top for a grey vest, with a black jumper over the top that I'd knitted myself, soft and tactile, and casually flattering. It had batwing sleeves, and a slashed neckline that shifted around to reveal a glimpse of shoulder now and again, although the vest straps underneath stopped it being overly provocative. The tartan PJ bottoms ought to stay; I couldn't look as if I'd made too much effort. Which also meant no make-up. I teased out the tangles from my hair with a large-tooth comb, though, and fluffed up the curls before weighing up whether to go with a messy bun or leave it loose. I tried both ways and went with loose. Dabbing the shine from my nose with a tissue, I suddenly remembered I still had to make the coffee.

I deliberated over the mugs. I owned six, and none of them matched, but they all had a story behind them. In the end, I chose my favourite for myself with the floral print I loved, a clever cross between a William Morris design and an Orla Kiely pattern; reserved for special occasions. For Wilf, I chose the largest mug I owned, plain white, with 'Flirty & 30' in fancy writing around it, given to me by Belle and Vicki for my milestone birthday. I only tended to use it for hot chocolate, particularly if I was adding whipped cream and marshmallows.

Waiting for the kettle to boil, I faced my reflection in the slit of a window above the sink. I looked like a ghost in the inky glass, but also wild-eyed and determined. I knew why I was doing this. I knew why I had to. It was his name on that telegram. And I could either lie to myself until it was too late to do anything about it – or face it head on and see where it took me.

Chapter 19

Guilt skewered me the instant Wilf opened the games room door.

'Hey.' His voice low, he glanced towards the house, all in darkness. The security light had flashed on automatically in the yard, but there wasn't much we could do about that. It would go off again after a few seconds.

'I apologise straight off about the mug,' I said. 'You can blame your nieces; they gave it to me.' I followed the glow of the fairy lights twisted around twigs in vases, to the sofa that faced the TV. The hang-out area where the girls often slumped around with their friends. Two plates were waiting on the low table, and I put down the mugs before smoothing out my jumper. Tea-lights burned in little glass holders, and the image on the TV was a flickering log fire. My heart seemed suddenly too large for my chest. Wilf cleared his throat.

'Look, um, all this,' he began, 'I know it doesn't look entirely platonic—'

'It's okay,' I cut in. 'You don't want to draw too much attention, from the house. If you put all the lights on...'

'Yeah.' He nodded. 'Exactly. You, er, look nice.'

'Oh... Thanks. So do you.' His dark green sweatshirt accentuated the emerald flecks in his eyes, and his jeans hugged his lower half and made him look even taller.

I pushed remorse over Greg out of my head, though it lingered at the edges, glowering at me. The timing was rubbish, and I knew what I had to do as soon as it was reasonably possible, but I could hardly ring him at this time of night and tell him we had to talk. Besides, I couldn't have a conversation like that over the phone; I needed to do it face to face. I had experience of being ghosted by boyfriends, or dumped by text. Though at least Sid had been gracious enough to tell me in person, albeit over Sunday lunch at a pub after staying over at the hovel the night before.

I could count the number of times I'd been out with Greg on one hand, but the way he talked, he had every intention of trying to make it work. And maybe, in a different situation, it would have been enough for me. But right now...

'Oh my gosh.' I looked up from my plate, after devouring the first mouthful of Eggs Benedict. 'Wilf, this is amazing. Is there anything you can't do with an egg?'

'Probably not. Although to the best of my

knowledge I haven't fertilised one yet.'

I almost choked on the second mouthful, lifting my hand in a stop sign when it looked as if he was about to thump me on the back. 'I'm okay,' I rasped.

'I've never laid one, either,' he added, then laughed, though there was an edge to it. 'Sorry, Cara. Your face. I wish you could see it. But it's an *old* joke.'

'I meant food-wise. You know I did.'

'And you should have known I'd be facetious, given the opportunity.'

'I don't know you that well, Wilf Brooks.'

'You know me well enough, Cara Shaw. Ever since I met you, I've twisted nearly anything you've said to me into a joke or an argument. I ought to apologise, but I think you've enjoyed it.'

'I wouldn't say "*enjoyed.*"'

'Then I'm sorry.' He faltered. 'Moving on swiftly... this coffee's good, by the way.' Wilf held up his mug.

'Thanks,' I muttered, remembering the meal at Aqua Vitae with Greg, and my invitation to him afterwards. It wasn't all that long ago. I was a horrible, horrible person. No better than Sid Atkinson. The fires of hell raged on the TV screen behind Wilf's head.

'I probably know more about you, than you know about me,' he continued, growing serious, 'and that's not fair. Or balanced.'

'Oh? And what do you think you know about

me?'

'Stuff I've picked up from JoJo. And Belle and Vicki are even easier to interrogate. My sister thinks a lot of you, but she's also convinced you're a car crash when it comes to relationships.'

'Wow.' I shook my head. 'JoJo said that?'

Wilf stared into his coffee. 'It's obvious she's issuing a warning. But I also think she's exaggerating.' He lifted his gaze. 'Belle and Vicki can't sing your praises highly enough. They both think the men you've dated have been wrong for you.'

I swallowed. 'Greg isn't like the others. Then again... the girls haven't met him.'

A pause. 'So you're still seeing him?'

Another pause. 'Technically I haven't stopped seeing him. It's only been a few dates, and we've never...' My cheeks flared with heat.

'There's a "but" there.'

'I'm going to have to break it off. My friends won't be happy. They set us up.'

'So why...?'

'It doesn't feel right. And Greg deserves more than that.'

Wilf ate a few mouthfuls of the muffin with bacon, eggs, and the hollandaise sauce on top, and made no further comment.

'Anyway.' I sat upright. 'Belle and Vicki were praising me, were they?'

'Why are you surprised? You've always been

in their lives, as far as they're concerned. They can't really remember a time when you weren't. And even when you stopped being their nanny, you've still been there for them in other ways. I know teenagers don't necessarily show it, but they both think the world of you. I'm paraphrasing, of course. But you get the idea, don't you? Because I think you need to hear it – how much you mean to that family. I'm not satisfied they show it enough.'

I blinked at the first sting of tears. Wilf looked away.

'Well, you're wrong,' I said after a moment, 'they do mention it, because JoJo's always calling me a "star."'

He grunted. 'I can just hear her saying it, straight after she's asked you to do her a massive favour. Am I right? I know JoJo better than anyone, Cara. Even better than Des knows her, I think, when it comes to certain things. She means well, *some* of the time. But how could she not turn into a diva, when she has thousands of devotees on the socials blowing smoke up her arse every day?'

I let out a cross between a snort and a laugh. 'You're probably the only person who can get away with saying that.'

He put down his fork. 'There's not much I could do that she wouldn't forgive.'

'And that's the difference between us. You only have to hear the way she talks about your ex.'

'Zoe?'

'She despises her. It's obvious she can't forgive anyone who hurts you.'

Wilf abandoned his plate on the low table, half the food untouched, before slumping back on the sofa. He dragged his hands over his face. 'Damn. I know. I *know*. She's always been too protective. But she has her reasons. And anyone who threatens us – they're instantly in the firing line. Like Des, and Zoe. I know it sounds dramatic…'

'It's a strong bond, Wilf. You shouldn't mock it.'

'I wasn't.'

'But you have in the past.' I couldn't help sounding deflated as I put my own plate on the table. 'I often imagine what it would have been like, if I'd had a brother or sister to share stuff with, especially when…'

'When what?' There was a cloudiness to his gaze now. I think it was sadness. And I think it mirrored my own.

I burned to tell him. To get the words out. And something assured me Wilf would understand.

'I was away at uni when it happened. The break-in. My parents were asleep upstairs. Dad woke up though, told my mum to call the police. She begged him not to go down, not to confront them.'

'Cara.' Wilf leaned forwards again, pressing

his hands together. 'JoJo told me. I wasn't prying, I just…'

'Can I tell you myself, though – the full version? In my own words? She might not have told you everything.'

He nodded. 'Go on.'

'It was an accident, effectively. Mum witnessed it. She followed my dad down; she couldn't let him go alone. But if Dad had only left it… Not played the hero. If he'd let them take what they wanted… There was a scuffle and he slipped. Cracked his head on the hearth. The men – boys really, they were younger than me, Mum thought – panicked and got away long before the police or the paramedics arrived.'

'Shit,' hissed Wilf, 'I'm sorry. JoJo said they were never caught?'

'No. And Dad was gone so fast, apparently. He'd hit his head too hard. The wrong angle…'

'And your mum?'

I took a deep breath, swallowed. 'The thing with Mum was, she was already clinically depressed. She should have had more help after Dad went, rather than being forced to go over what happened, again and again. And maybe I should have seen the signs, or someone – a professional – should have flagged something sooner…'

Wilf's hand was on my arm. 'You don't have to say it.'

'I want to. I need to. I really believe she was

trying, for my sake, to fight it. Fight through her pain. And maybe that's what everyone else saw. But it was too much for her. The note said she couldn't go on without him. She basically took anything she could lay her hands on. I found her in bed; tried to wake her up… I should have done more before that, though. I should have realised what she might attempt. Got rid of—'

'Cara.' Wilf's grip tightened on my arm as he moved closer. '*Don't.* Don't go there. People who are that desperate – they find a way. Look, I know it's not the same, but I spent weeks after my mum died blaming myself for not noticing something was wrong sooner; for not spotting some sign and pushing her to go to her doctor. And all the while, Zoe was sleeping with some guy from her firm, making plans to leave me, once I was over the worst. And she might have waited and not told me when she did, except she'd just found out that morning she was pregnant with his baby.'

'My God…' I blinked at him. 'JoJo never told me that.'

'She had a boy, before you ask. Premature, I heard, but all fine now.'

'That's – good. For her. Not for you. I mean—'

'I never wished harm on the kid, whatever I felt about Zoe. And I meant it, Cara, when I said I was over her.'

That was never entirely true, though, was it? People who'd been so much a part of our lives…

they lived permanently in our heads if not our hearts.

'The worst of it was,' said Wilf, 'all the time we were together, she claimed she never wanted kids. She'd almost convinced me it was a bad idea for *me* to want them, to even contemplate having any of my own because of...'

I felt his sharp intake of breath. The retreat. I'd done it enough times myself not to recognise it in someone else. Instinctively I wanted to ask, 'Because of what?' But if he was reluctant to tell me without a prompt, I didn't want to push it. His hand had slipped from my arm, and he'd shifted away to the other end of the sofa.

We'd both opened up, but now we were closing down again, withdrawing into our shells even as fake firelight flickered off the walls, and candles and fairy lights glimmered. My pain was a raw, exposed nerve, and yet... it was *out there*, accepted by another human being, who'd let me have a glimpse of his own agony in return.

This hadn't been Wilf's intention by asking me here surely, and it hadn't been mine by accepting. What I didn't understand, was how it had all gone wrong. Or maybe, conversely, it was all going right. I knew him slightly better now, and I was aware how much he knew about me; how badly he'd *wanted* to know, and how he wasn't put off by anything the Pembrokes had told him. The notion coiled around my stomach and tightened into a need I almost couldn't bear, it was so intense.

I stood up, sniffed, brushed imaginary crumbs from my PJ bottoms. 'Do you play "foos-ball"?'

'What?' Wilf looked up distractedly.

I went over to the table football in the corner, flicking on the small spotlight overhead. 'Fancy a game?'

He lifted an eyebrow. 'Tell me you're not a pro.'

'I used to play sometimes with my dad. He loved it.' I had to stop running from the fact I'd loved it, too.

'Ah.' Wilf unfolded himself. 'This is where you thrash me, right?'

'Oh, I have every intention of doing so. I may look sweet and innocent, but I'm ferociously competitive.'

'I can see that. But never underestimate a tall man. I have more of an aerial view. First to get to five? And no three-sixty-degree spins.'

I laughed. And promptly scored five goals, only conceding one.

'Damn you, Cara.' Brow knotted, Wilf swore worse than that and rounded the table. I circled it to get away, laughing again.

'I told you I was competitive.'

He let out a stream of words then, in a language I recognised, although I had no idea what he was saying.

My face fell. 'I didn't know you spoke Italian.

I mean… no clue what you just said, but I recognise the language.'

'I don't.' He hesitated. 'Not fluently. I spent a month or two in Rome about ten years ago. My accent's terrible. I speak French, too.'

'Right. Of course you do.'

''You don't know Italian yourself, though?'

'No. Languages aren't my thing.'

'JoJo said you didn't. I was surprised but…'

'She told you I was half Italian.' I leant against the pool table, too worn down to stay terse for long. 'My mum never taught me, and I never once heard her speak it. The story of how my parents met… how Mum fell out with her family… Not even JoJo knows it in full.'

'And I don't need to know yet, either. I'd like you to tell me, when you're ready, but I think you've put yourself through enough for one night.'

I felt him closing in then, until the tips of his shoes were almost touching mine in the ballerina flats I'd slipped on to come to the games room. He loomed over me, the solid mass of him, broad shoulders, narrow hips. I could have moved to the side, stepped away, he wasn't pinning me in. He was just there. I lifted my chin and blinked up at him. For a moment we didn't move, and then I spread my hands over his chest and upwards, to the soft hair at the nape of his neck. I felt an intake of breath again, but he wasn't in retreat. And neither was I. His eyes never left mine.

And then we were kissing. More than kissing. It was ridiculous. As if we couldn't get to each other fast enough. Yet it seemed to go on forever. I'd never known anything like it. He lifted me off my feet, carried me back to the sofa.

'Did you lock the door?' I said croakily, combusting in his arms.

'I locked it when you came in. You saw me.'

'Did I?' His lips were on my neck, my hands under his sweatshirt. 'Wait, Wilf – have you got a… Because I've got a box in one of my drawers. Not drawers as in old-fashioned knickers—'

'Cara,' he stared at me, smoothed back my hair, 'I wasn't planning this… I didn't…'

I grappled urgently with my jumper. Too hot to leave it on, even if we were about to migrate to the hovel. 'I want to, though. I wanted you the first time I saw you. I felt the connection, too. I just fought it. But it's more than I thought it was. Much more.' I was gabbling, my chest rising and falling, the jumper somehow tangled around me. 'I've never felt like this before.'

The third intake of breath. A retreat this time. I stopped fighting with my top and looked up at him again. His face seemed to be caving in, but he didn't let go of me or stop smoothing back my hair.

'You have no idea what I said to you in Italian, Cara Mia?'

I shook my head, like ice inside when a second ago I'd been on fire.

'I can't do this now…' his own chest rose and fell steeply '…I'm sorry, I—'

'Can't?' I looked down. Pressed against me, everything felt in working order.

'Not like this. Not here.'

I frowned. 'We're going over to mine, aren't we…?'

'It's killing me, but that isn't it. And it's not you… This is on me. I need to be sure. For your sake.'

I'd heard words to that effect before, although never at this point in the proceedings. *It's not you, it's me*. Such a tired cliché.

The air vibrated between us. Wilf's eyes looked haunted as a flood of emotions crashed through me.

And then I was batting his hands away. 'Well, at least you're telling me this now, not afterwards. Thank you for that.'

'Cara—'

'It's fine. I get it. But please have the courtesy to move back while you're friend-zoning me, or whatever this is.'

'I'm not rejecting you, Cara. I'm doing this for you.'

'Doing what? You're not making sense. One second you want me, the next you don't. You chase me for days and then you back off.'

'Exactly.' Wilf moved away from me, across the sofa, stabbing his fingers through his hair. 'This is what I'm like. And it's not that I don't want you – I do. But for how long? How do I know I won't hurt you? I'm not scared of you. I believe you, when you say you feel different this time. I'm worried what *I* might do.'

'What might you do? I don't understand. Zoe left you. You didn't cheat on her.' I hesitated. 'Did you?'

He scrunched up his face. 'No! Never. But maybe she wouldn't have done it if I'd been different.'

'Or maybe she just wasn't right for you. Maybe that whole life you had over there wasn't right. I don't know. Or… do you think I'm going to do what she did?' Straightening my jumper, I shrank against the back of the sofa, all my bubbles bursting. 'You think I'm capable of it, because of what I'm doing to Greg? I don't want anyone to get hurt, but I don't know what I'm supposed to do. I never asked to feel like this.'

Wilf winced. He visibly winced, and my blood ran even colder. 'I told you: if you feel different with me, then I believe you. We can't help the timing. But the fact you feel this way… I can't let you get more involved. You don't know what I'm like, and you ought to be more than just my next dopamine hit.'

'Your next *what*…?' Had he said that? Had those words actually left his mouth?

'I want to commit, Cara. To my work, to a relationship. To a single course of action. And I try my hardest to. But then it all goes wrong. So what if I can't? What if I'll always be chasing that next high, never totally satisfied with what I've got at any given point?'

I screwed up my brow, even more confused. What was he trying to tell me? That he was some kind of addict?

'Wilf, are you saying you're on drugs? Or you've been on drugs, or…?' I felt so naïve all of a sudden. Helpless.

'Not drugs the way you think.' He turned away, pressed his palms to his forehead, his elbows on his knees. I ached to stretch out and touch his back, tell him everything would work out; but the ache didn't transfer into deed. 'You're so lovely and funny and sweet,' he went on, 'and this is the last thing I expected to happen when I decided to come back here, to the UK. But it's the absolute worst time for me. I have no real clue what I'm doing next, or where I'm going. I'm torn in so many directions, you have no idea.'

'Actually, I do.' My voice was small. It filled the silence his admission had carved. 'I'm torn about stuff, too. I want to go back to art school, in some capacity. I need to do something more with my life than I'm doing now. But I don't know where that's going to take me.'

Slowly, he turned his head to the side, and put out his hand. A peace offering. 'I'm not rejecting you. Trust me when I say that. If I didn't care, we could just do this, whatever it is.' He gestured to the sofa and I felt my cheeks redden. 'For however long it might last. If you only wanted something casual. But you don't. Not really. And I don't, either. But I need time to work out exactly what I *do* want, and you need to figure out your next move, too.'

I sighed, bit my lip, let my hand slide across to link with his. 'So, this is an impasse?'

'In a way, I guess. I think it has to be. For now.' His fingers stroked mine, and he lifted my hand and pressed it to his lips for a brief moment. 'I'm sorry.'

I blinked back the mist forming in my eyes.

Maybe we were both feeling more than we ought to at this stage, and we'd felt it too fast for us to know how to process it. I'd never gone for his type, personality-wise, yet here I was, snatching at any spare minutes in his company. But he was right, the timing couldn't be worse. And the fact that no one would be on our side, except an old woman who'd read too many romance novels and had evidently been one of the lucky ones when it came to love.

'I'll clear up here,' he said, switching to pragmatic mode after an endless, harrowing silence.

'And I'll take the mugs back to mine,' I added, proving I could be practical, too. I rocked to my feet. 'Wilf… Look… Just don't be a stranger, okay? Don't go all moody and act like I don't exist. If you need help with JoJo…'

'I'll never pretend you don't exist, Cara Mia.'

Swallowing the prickly, hot lump in my

throat, I nodded. My hands shook as I reached for the mugs. As I walked towards the door without daring to glance back, I realised that if Wilf spoke Italian to some extent, it was more than likely he knew what *cara mia* meant.

Chapter 20

I'd never broken up with anyone at a garden centre before. Not that I'd ever been the one to actually speak the words and admit that something wasn't working. But I was determined to do it with more compassion and respect than any of my past mistakes had ever shown me. I wasn't counting Wilf in that list. He wasn't in my past; and he wasn't a mistake, as far as I was concerned. I just didn't know yet if he was my future.

Greg had wanted me here to help him pick a Christmas tree, and in my nervousness over the phone when he'd asked, I'd heard myself agreeing before I could say anything else. The last thing I wanted was to lead him on. To Sallie's delight, though, I'd asked him to pick me up from the café; merely so no one would spot him at the hovel. Just before he'd arrived, my best friend had adjusted my beanie hat and pinched my cheeks.

'Ow!' I'd scowled. 'What was that for?'

'You looked pale. And it's what they used to do in the old days, when they didn't have blusher.'

'I'm only going to the garden centre with him. Not taking a turn around the ballroom.'

'You should ask Perdita, she'd know what I mean. I haven't seen her in the café for a few days. Is she okay?'

'I haven't seen her, either. But she phoned while I was in the bath and left a message. She wants me to go up to Riverside again, and she'd like to order a box of your mince pies.'

'Ooh, good. That can be arranged. Just let me know when you're going and I'll get them sorted for you.'

Greg had arrived then, and Sallie had waved us off as if she was my doting mother and he was the nice, smart boy with prospects that every girl in the village dreamed of stepping out with.

'I don't want a *massive*, massive tree,' Greg was saying now, as we wove through the giddying selection at the garden centre.

I turned over a tag and read the price. My eyes watered. 'Are you sure you want a tree from here at all?'

'They last. I've got one from here the past couple of years. Just small ones, to make an effort. I thought I'd push the boat out this year. Perhaps you could come over and help me decorate it?' He smiled.

I smiled back; a mirror reflex. Inside I was

wailing and cursing. No idea how to start.

'Listen.' Greg pulled me behind a row of trees, out of view of the other customers. 'I understand why you want to take it slow, and I'm fine with that. But a kiss can't hurt, can it?' And his lips were on mine before I could react. Soft and gentle. This time I felt nothing, though, except mild shock. He straightened. 'I've missed you, Cara. You seem too busy to say much when I message you. Is everything all right? What have you been up to?'

I raised my eyebrows, felt my ribcage constrict. What had I been up to?

'Greg, I'm sorry,' I whispered.

His eyes narrowed with confusion. 'What about? Why are you sorry?'

I pulled off my hat, running a hand through my hair until it hit a tangle. And then I tugged through the knot, because, unlike my remorse, it was a pain I could handle. 'You don't deserve someone like me.'

Was I really doing this? Hitting him with a formulaic bullet from the off? The way I was reacting, I might as well have been his wife, not just someone he'd been on a handful of dates with. Was I going overboard? Taking on someone else's guilt? Was this how Zoe had approached Wilf on Valentine's Day, except she might have had her hand over her still-flat belly, unconsciously defending a tiny life that had nothing to do with him?

'I've been seeing someone else,' I said.

Another cliché. This entire situation was a bloody cliché.

'Someone else?' Greg echoed, still perplexed. 'Who? What are you talking about?'

'It just sneaked up on me.' I shook my head. 'No, that's not quite right. It came out of nowhere, at the start. *He* came out of nowhere. On a plane from Canada. And the thing is, we both felt it. It wasn't just me.'

'Whoa.' Greg grabbed me by the shoulders. Not hard or threatening, simply to slow me down. 'Are you talking about JoJo's brother...? Will, or...?'

'Wilfred. He prefers being called Wilf. And I know you said he was acting like a jerk when you first met, which was childish—'

'But it was only because he likes you?' Greg dipped his head, trying to get me to meet his eye.

'I've been fighting it, because it complicates everything, but a couple of nights ago...'

'You slept with him.' It was a statement, not a question. His hands slid from my shoulders.

I shook my head vigorously. 'No. No, I didn't. Well, nearly. And I wasn't the one who stopped it, so I might as well have, I suppose. I'm *so* sorry, Greg. I should have told you sooner that I was having doubts about us, but I wasn't sure if I was reading everything wrong. I didn't know how strongly I felt about him. And it wasn't really till Perdita asked me to imagine the telegram, that I stopped resisting it.'

'Telegram?' His handsome face was a mass of lines and creases.

But I couldn't tell Greg the whole story. I truly wanted him to have a long, healthy, happy life with someone who appreciated him and wouldn't do something this contemptible in the middle of a garden centre.

'The telegram part doesn't matter.' I flapped my hand, casting it aside. 'What matters is, I can't keep misleading myself, or you. I honestly don't want to hurt you, Greg…'

'It's okay.' The creases were ironing out, the jaw stiffening; as if someone had injected him with Botox. 'Cara, it's fine. We've only been on a few dates. We never discussed the topic of seeing other people or not. I haven't even referred to you as my girlfriend in conversation with anyone.'

The last sentence didn't ring true. His voice was too flat.

'But exclusivity was implied, Greg. Sal told me it was. And neither of us are the sort who could have romantic dinner dates with one person and then jump into bed with someone else.'

He just looked at me and hooked an eyebrow, and I realised what I'd said.

'It wasn't like that,' I muttered.

Except it was. Minus the jumping and the bed and the actually going through with it. Heat billowed at the memory, and pooled in my stomach.

'So – you're with him now? With Wilf?' Greg

shoved his hands into the pocket of his coat.

'Not officially. And not unofficially, either. It's still complicated.'

'You said you weren't the one who stopped it?'

'The almost…?' I slipped my beanie hat back on, and frowned at the price tag on the nearest tree, registering that it wasn't as high as some of the others. 'He wants to play it cautiously, too. We're both in a difficult spot, with JoJo especially. And we need to figure some things out individually first.'

'He must really care about you, if you'd already given your consent.'

'You think so?'

'I know so. Unless he couldn't…'

'He could,' I mumbled.

'Then you mean more to him than just a quick shag. I'm sorry if that's too blunt. I'm just letting you know how it looks, from my perspective.'

There it was. The bitterness. Inevitable, I suppose. Greg was as human as the rest of us.

I turned away, nauseous now.

'How about this one?' I held out the label. 'It's more reasonable. You don't need to take out a loan to afford it.'

I felt his eyes boring into me. 'I'm not really in the mood.'

'Greg… please. Let's just find you a tree and get out of here.'

He hesitated, but then: 'No… No. Look at me, Cara – I don't want a tree any more. I can't be bothered. I don't want to take it home and decorate it on my own again this year. I wanted to do it with you. Because he isn't the only one who cares, okay? And I can keep playing it down, or I can just tell you. Unlike him, it seems, I *can* picture you clearly in my life. Or, at least, I could.'

'Greg, I'm—'

'No. *Listen*. I've got a steady enough income right now, my own home; I would have looked after you, supported you. You wouldn't have had to work that dead-end job in the café any more. Or any job. If things had carried on as well as they were with us, at some point next year you could have moved in with me. I haven't been in your place, but Laurence told me about it. You're suffocating in there, he says, it's so small. I would have shared all I've got, gladly, because I think we might have stood a chance, we could have been happy—'

He stopped, as a middle-aged couple rounded the row of trees, arguing over which one they liked best.

'But what about what *I* might have wanted?' I said, as Greg brushed past me to get to an open space again. I'd never asked for a knight in shining armour.

I trailed after him, through an archway, out into the car park, stunned by his admission. Another man who'd managed to floor me.

'Greg.' I finally caught up with him and pawed at his sleeve. 'That wasn't my vision. You didn't have to do that for me. Slot me into your life like that.'

He blipped open his car before swinging round. 'Then what was your vision? What do you want with *him*?'

For a moment, I thought Greg was going to abandon me there at Leafley's Garden Centre, as an icy gust of wind blew out of nowhere and snatched my breath and my guilt away.

He was above that sort of petulant behaviour, though. Greg opened the passenger door and held it for me, as the wind buffeted it and tugged at my hat and my hair. But I couldn't move until I'd answered him.

'I want to be his equal,' I said simply, meeting the disappointment and the challenge in Greg's eyes. 'I want us to rescue each other.'

That night, I had trouble sleeping again. So much so, I switched on my lamp in the end and picked up a book, in a vain attempt to distract myself. There were too many things drilling into my brain at once. I dreaded my friends' reaction over Greg, and I didn't want to fall out with them. They meant too much to me. Sallie and Nushrat saw him as a solid, stabilising influence, and at one time in my life I might have needed someone like that.

But Greg had been mapping everything out for us – without me. Making plans to play the hero, perhaps to boost his own self-esteem. I felt awful that I'd caused him pain, yet the more I thought about it, the more indignant I became and the less apologetic. I wasn't little Cara, stuck in a perpetual rut, any more. Most of my todays recently hadn't been the same as my yesterdays, and my tomorrows were even more uncertain. Yet there was a curious excitement to that, sizzling around my anxiety. A frisson of anything-might-be-possible.

I put aside the book and grabbed a pillow instead, hugging it tightly, attempting to contain the thrill tangled up with the fear. My friends might not understand my motives one bit. It was more than likely they wouldn't, in fact.

Wrongly or rightly, I hadn't told them I was re-evaluating my career prospects, or researching ways I could return to my studies. The whole concept was still so hazy, I hadn't felt ready to share, except with Perdita – or the other day with Wilf. In Sallie and Nushrat's shoes, I might have looked a gift horse in the mouth by ditching Greg. He was trying to be noble and dependable. But the entire notion of presuming I *needed* a man to take care of me, to make me whole… it felt like a tiny crack that might have deepened into a fissure.

On the face of it, though, I'd given up the chance of a relatively worry-free future. The way spirited heroines in historical novels sometimes did, even though their real-life counterparts wouldn't have had the safety net of a fictional happy ever after. Once upon a time, after all, even in this village, it might have been a straight choice between starvation or matrimony.

A hundred years ago, for instance, if Wilf had been killed in battle and Greg had come back and asked for my hand in marriage, I probably would have accepted, if I was destitute and alone. And given time, I might have been content and satisfied enough, because I wouldn't have known any better. I would have filled my days – and nights – being a dutiful wife, a loving mother, an asset to the village, even if a hidden fragment of my heart remained broken, and faithful to a dead man until my own dying breath...

Cara, stop it! I snapped upright in bed. *Stop killing Wilf off, even hypothetically.* It had to end now. There were women who'd lost their lovers for real. I was so ungrateful.

I lived in a different age, and there was nothing to say I couldn't have followed my dreams to study art again with Greg's backing, once he knew what it meant to me. So what had I sacrificed all that for? A man who wasn't offering me anything right now, not even an informal romp in the proverbial hay. A man I seemed to understand less and less, the more I learned about him.

Wilf wasn't reliable or steady, or giving any firm assurance he might be able to behave that way. It didn't matter how much he told me he was putting space between us because he cared too much not to; my friends were never going to see it like he did. Part of me didn't blame them, because I couldn't quite see it, either.

In a burst of despair, I threw aside the pillow and duvet, and dived out of bed into the cold air long enough to pick up the broken snow-globe from the coffee table. I wriggled back under the duvet, and held the miniature carousel out in front of me, studying it closely, the way I did so often lately, as if it held all the answers.

Did I believe in magic, and men with stars in their earlobes? Meeting Angelo at the Christmas market felt oddly like a dream now, and of course I didn't believe any of it. I just *wanted* to.

It was purely a coincidence that before that night my life hadn't been in such a spin. After all, I'd already been introduced to Greg a couple of hours before; and three-thousand-odd miles away, Wilf had already made plans to come to Pebblestow. Even Perdita, with her wisdom and her inspiring past, hadn't turned up in the village in a puff of smoke. Their lives didn't revolve around a wish I'd made.

The carousel had only had the power to stir up a wildness within me. A stronger desire for change, perhaps. But right now, as I lay alone –

and, yes, I admit, *lonely* – in my double bed, fizzing from all the choices I could make, frustrated over Wilf, vindicated yet still upset when it came to Greg, scared of how my dearest, closest friends might judge me... I couldn't see how that heartfelt wish had much chance of ever coming true.

Chapter 21

Perdita was an angel and consoled me with a pot of tea. We also somehow demolished six mince pies between us. It was clear she felt partly responsible for my predicament. I slumped at her kitchen table, head in my hands, slightly queasy. The pies had something to do with my churning stomach, along with Sallie's mood when I'd picked them up from the café.

I didn't have a shift today, but I'd just popped in, cheeks stinging from my brisk walk down into the village. The café had been busy, which might have contributed to Sallie's sourness, and I'd offered to stay and help her and Polly, but she'd refused. The box with the mince pies had been ready and waiting; I'd already texted Sallie my request that morning. I'd offered to pay on Perdita's behalf, too, but my best friend had said curtly that she'd take it out of my tips, and I could settle it with Perdita any way I liked. And that was that. I'd left the café with my cheeks stinging even more – a combination of embarrassment, discomfort and exasperation – and trudged up the north road to Riverside.

'So your friends know now, that it wasn't working out with your young man Greg?' Perdita had asked, over our pot of tea.

'Sort of. I messaged them after I saw Greg – just quickly, to say something didn't feel right and I'd ended it. Sallie would have probably heard it from Laurence, otherwise. I don't know, I should have told them face to face – shouldn't I? I suppose that's partly why their replies were so… crisp.' Although that was putting it nicely. 'I just didn't want to leave it. They needed to hear it from me, not second hand.'

'It's hard, I know. They want the best for you. But even your closest friends might not be aware what that is. I don't doubt their past advice came from a good place, and they've probably taken offence that you didn't follow it. Which leaves you in a pickle, unfortunately.'

'I haven't just *not* followed their advice,' I pointed out glumly, dusting icing sugar from my hands, 'I've done virtually everything they told me not to.'

'I'm sure they'll come around eventually.'

'The thing is, I understand where they're coming from. I do. And they're invested in it more than normal, I suppose, because they set me up with Greg in the first place. They're convinced he's right for me. He represents stability. Wilf – not so much.'

Perdita sighed. 'If it helps at all, Cara, my husband was a little… scattered, I suppose you could say, when I first met him. And he was allowing it to limit him. He had so many wonderful ideas, but every time he had a fresh craze or urge, he used to panic and think: what if it fades? What if I can't see it through? He needed help to focus on just one, and with my encouragement and the mentors he met along the way, he turned it into a success.'

I let my ears prick up even more. Perdita's words were always so relevant. 'That sounds a lot like Wilf's problem. What did your husband end up doing?'

'He ran an independent publishing company. Small, but lucrative enough. He was very selective about the books he brought out, both fiction and non-fiction. I wouldn't say the novels were literary, or ever up for the Booker. There was never anything pretentious about them, but they were relevant for the times. He captured the zeitgeist, as they say. And his merry band of authors did win other awards.'

'Would I know any? The books and the authors, I mean.'

'Possibly. But I'm afraid my memory's not what it used to be.' She pushed herself back shakily from the table. 'Would you be kind enough to help me clear up, dear? I need to unload the dishwasher, too, before I can load it again.'

'Of course.' As she handed me a tea-towel, I realised that she wasn't going to expand on her husband's business, and I didn't want to be pushy. Certain memories might be harder and more painful to dredge up, so I changed the subject. 'This tea-towel's gorgeous, Perdita. The pattern…' I looked towards the window-seat. 'It matches your upholstery.'

'I should hope so.' Her etched face twinkled again. 'I designed it.'

I scrutinised the rectangle of cloth in my hand; a good weight and quality. The floral pattern was somehow modern yet retro, with a faint nod to Scandi design. And the colours… I didn't know how to start describing them. The palette was inspired. 'You had them made for you, bespoke, you mean?'

'That's not what I mean at all, Cara. Don't you remember, I said I was a creative soul, too? I suppose you've never heard of Perdita Rivers. It was my brand name. Oh, I was never up there with the likes of Laura Ashley or Cath Kidston, but I was popular enough. I earned a living.'

'Perdita Rivers.' I couldn't say it rang a bell. I was polite enough not to say so, though.

'And my husband's company was Riverside House Press. You see, we borrowed flagrantly from this place. But Perdita Riverside didn't sound right, so I just went with Rivers. It had a certain glamour.'

'It's a fabulous name. And a stunning fabric;

I've always thought so.'

'Look closely, Cara. There's more than one pattern, but I designed them to coordinate seamlessly, to work in combination.'

I looked again, and this time picked out noticeable differences. 'You have animal silhouettes in some, not just flowers.'

'And a fairy-tale theme, too. Of course, these are just a selection of my favourite prints. There were many more.'

I stooped to empty the dishwasher. Most of the crockery was already bone dry; she probably didn't put a wash on daily, with just herself here. 'So, is that what you studied – textile design?'

She nodded. 'My husband supported me to begin with, and in return I helped with his business. A joint effort. And it wasn't all that long before the children arrived. Very much a joint effort, too. As procreating often is.' She twinkled impishly again. 'We somehow fitted it all in. Beautifully chaotic. I wouldn't have missed being with him for the world. I'd make the same choice, over and over, if I had to.'

Her smile was genuine and so full of gratitude, sadness deluged me over my own situation. I just wanted what Perdita had had. The confidence to grasp a dream. The courage to push through with it. Someone at my side who was cheering for me as much as I was cheering for him. But in that moment, comparing it to Perdita's success story, it all felt hopeless.

The old woman seemed to read my thoughts, and turned to face me. 'Things will work out, Cara. Not without effort on your part; nothing that worthwhile is ever as easy as it sounds. But I have faith in you.'

'At least someone does.'

She let out a small raspy laugh. 'Perhaps that's enough for now. My believing in you. Until you start to believe it yourself.'

I smiled back wanly. 'Maybe.'

Once the dishwasher was empty, and re-loaded, and Perdita was safely back in her chair, I retrieved my backpack from the pegs by the door. 'I have a gift for you, by the way.'

'A gift?' Her face lit up again.

'Think of it as an early Christmas present. I know you won't be here in Pebblestow much longer… But… I wanted to give you something to remember me by.'

'Oh, I'm not going to forget you, Cara. You've brightened up my stay so much, I can never thank you enough.'

'I think you're the one who's done the brightening up…' I looked to the row of pegs, where my coat also hung, and for the first time I allowed myself to touch Perdita's vivid pink beret and the scarf that almost matched it. Up close, I could tell that the beret was vintage and screamed quality. The scarf, on the other hand, looked as if it had been made from ordinary acrylic yarn; bobbly and slightly faded.

'You like those,' Perdita noted, a smile in her voice. 'The beret's older, as you can probably tell. You have an innate eye for that sort of thing, I suspect. The scarf was made by one of my foster daughters, many years later. I taught her how to knit.'

I fingered the scarf tenderly, imagining the love and patience looped into each stitch. 'I had to teach myself. It wasn't my mum's sort of thing.' With even more caution, I touched the beret again. 'What about this? It's not home-made.'

'Ah, no. My husband gave me that. His first ever gift to me. We were only just starting out as sweethearts...' She wore that familiar distant look for a moment. 'It's precious to me, as you can imagine. I used to wear it a lot in the early days, and then I worried it was too fragile. But he made me promise that I'd bring it out of hibernation. So here it is, and here I am. As I think I already told you, my dear, I haven't broken a promise to him yet.'

'You did tell me.' I smiled, encircled by her warmth; by the love that still burned so fiercely for a man who was no longer at her side. 'I think it's lovely. The beret *and* the promise.'

'So – my gift then?' She rubbed her knobbly hands together, and I laughed.

It was in my backpack. The cushion I'd made for her. Freeform crochet flowers splashed all over it. I felt bashful as Perdita opened the brown paper package tied with string (like the song, it was one of my favourite things, too), and held up the cushion in obvious delight.

'Oh, it's stunning, Cara!'

'Do you really like it?'

'I love it! I'd be silly not to.'

'I thought you could put it on the window-seat. Or take it back home with you. Your other home.'

She creaked out of the chair and shuffled over to the window-seat. 'The colours match so well with my prints. You were spot on, picking those out. A keen eye for colour and texture yourself.'

Even I had to admit I'd done a good job, but my phone let out a 'choo-choo' just then, and I gave a small start.

Perdita eyed me astutely. 'Is that him? Your Wilf? You've gone pink. Any brighter and you'd match my beret.'

'It's him.' I fished the phone out of the back-pack.

He was still sending me messages. Just checking in, mainly; asking if I was okay. I wasn't sure if we'd both deliberately stayed out of each other's way, or whether I was avoiding him and he was letting me. The messages had lost their sparkle and humour, and I didn't know what he was trying to imply by sending them. Perhaps that he was still interested. That he wasn't going anywhere – *yet.* I don't know. My own responses were equally non-committal and vague.

This message from him now was more direct, though. It caught me unawares.

—I'm walking Loki down by the river. If you're free do you want to meet me? Don't worry if you can't. Just let me know so I don't freeze to death waiting. Actually I won't wait that long. You might not see this till later. Sorry if I'm rambling. I'll either see you or I won't.

'He wants to meet me,' I said. 'Right now. He's out walking JoJo's dog.'

'Are you going?' said Perdita.

'You think I should?'

'If I still had legs that worked as well as yours, my dear, I'd be running down there.'

I smiled nervously, and messaged back.

—I can be by the old stone bridge in fifteen minutes. Would that be OK? Do you know the one I mean? Not the new one.

—Only one old stone bridge that I've found. I'll see you there.

Perdita was living vicariously again, her excitement palpable. 'Off with you then, Cara. Hurry, hurry. Find out what he wants, what he has to say.'

'I think it's just a walk. Nothing exciting.'

But I ached to see him again, however futile. Which was exhilarating enough. And Perdita could sense that. It seemed she could understand me right now better than anyone.

Chapter 22

I didn't run down the hill, I was too afraid of tripping over. But I walked quickly enough so that I was out of puff by the time I reached the eastern edge of the village, where the old narrow bridge curved over the River Pebble. I saw him down on the path that ran along the bank, and instantly I felt it, the sharp tug. I wanted to be beside him, even at his worst, at my worst.

And my mother's words resonated in my head again. How sometimes it came at you out of nowhere, loud and brash and glorious, and other times it simply crept up and overtook you. And then those rare occasions when, somehow, it managed both. That last one was how this felt. As if something loud had come at me out of nowhere, and then something much quieter, yet just as powerful, had overtaken it.

Loki spun with joy when he saw me. By the look on Wilf's face, I thought he was about to do the same.

'I got here as fast as I could,' I said breathlessly. 'I hope you haven't got chilblains while you waited. Don't they make your hands all purple?'

'Just as well I've got thermal gloves on.'

I bent to stroke Loki. 'So – a walk then?'

'I wasn't sure you'd be free. I saw you go out earlier, but I didn't know if you were working. I went past the café but I couldn't see you. There was a woman behind the counter who just glared at me through the glass.'

'Tall? Blonde?' When he nodded, I sighed. 'That's Sallie. She probably recognised Loki and guessed who you were.'

'Great,' he said grimly, and beckoned left. 'Shall we go this way? If you're fine being out in public with me…?'

'I don't know, are you fine being seen with *me*? My mates already know that I called it a day with Greg. I won't repeat their opinions, but I haven't had much opportunity to talk to them about it properly. Polly asked for extra shifts at the café, and Sallie said she didn't need me, so…'

Wilf frowned. 'Aren't you desperate for the money yourself, though? I'm sorry,' he added instantly, 'that came out wrong.'

'Aside from spending more time with Perdita, it's given me a chance to work on some stuff I wanted to upload to Depop and Etsy, anyway.'

I took out my phone as we ambled along the path. There was no one around. In the warmer months, there were villagers fishing sometimes, or kids splashing around where the riverbank sloped to a shallow, pebbly spot. I showed Wilf what I was currently selling, and the items I'd sold in the past.

'People really pay that much?'

'Some do,' I said. 'For unique finds. Quality was often better before fast fashion became a thing. I mend and tweak, too. Make things wearable again. It's nowhere near enough to call it a living, but it helps a bit. And I also make my own designs from scratch. Some of my crocheted cardies have sold well, but they're time-consuming, and I have to re-invest in the yarn, as well as buying new stuff to revamp.'

'Amazing.' He sighed and shook his head. 'I guess I'm always surprised by how much people pay for JoJo's concoctions. I admire her, and everything she's achieved, but lately... I'm not sure of the cost she's paid, on a personal level.'

'This thing with Des? Do you know more?' I picked uncomfortably at the edge of my beanie hat. 'I feel horrible keeping out of her way. But I haven't been avoiding her because of the Des and Alyson business. It's not that.'

'You've been avoiding her because of us,' Wilf said softly.

Us. Was there an Us? 'Does she suspect something, do you think?'

It was possible she was too concerned over Des to pay much attention to her brother right now.

'She knows me well enough,' said Wilf. 'She's tried eliciting information, but I'm not telling her what she wants. I'm neither denying, nor confirming.'

'Same with Sallie and Nushrat. Maybe that's part of the problem. I haven't been completely honest with them, and they hate that.'

But might it damage our friendship irreparably? I couldn't bear to think it would get worse.

'I'm sorry.' His gloved hand fumbled for mine. 'I've missed you, though.'

You can't miss something you never truly had.

But I didn't say that, because I knew what he meant. I'd missed him, too.

It was all so absurd, I wanted to scream. I wanted to share how I felt. Overtaken. Overwhelmed. Upside down. I even wanted to tell him about the mysterious carousel and my earnest wish – and I hadn't felt safe enough to tell anyone about that. Not even Perdita.

But the words piled up in my throat and nothing came out.

'How did Greg take it?' Wilf asked sombrely, after a while, as we approached the edge of the woods, still holding hands. The footpath veered away from the river here and twisted back through the trees, eventually coming out again in the park near the duck pond, where the ice cream van liked to park in the summer. I knew we wouldn't go all the way around today; it would get dark soon, and the temperature was dropping.

'Better than the matchmakers who paired us.' I frowned. 'To be fair to Greg, he could have reacted worse. But you'd have thought we'd been seeing each other much longer, the stuff he'd planned already…'

It was one thing to daydream one-sidedly and indulge in flights of fantasy, another to be deadly serious about it.

'Like what?' said Wilf.

'Like me moving in with him next year.'

'O-*kay*. And had he factored your own views into this?'

'No. But there I was, thinking dating was supposed to be fun. More relaxed, these days.'

'If you're using dating apps, maybe. I've never seen the attraction of those, though. You'd have thought they'd be perfect for me. The novelty aspect. But… Have you used them yourself?'

'Sallie signed me up for one once. I lasted about a week. It brought me out in hives.'

'Maybe dating *can* be casual and fun, if you're not emotionally invested.'

I stopped as Loki shot across the path to sniff a harmless-looking bush and I almost tripped over the lead Wilf was holding. 'Emotions.' I tutted. 'Those pesky things.'

Wilf turned to face me. 'They suck out all the pleasure.' His fingers left mine and his gloved hand lightly touched my cheek. We stood there for a moment, before he murmured, 'You're flushed from the cold.'

'I don't think it's purely from the cold.'

Loki prodded my calf hard with his nose, catching me by surprise. I stepped forwards. It was all the invitation Wilf needed. He slipped his free arm around me, below my backpack, and pulled me against him. My legs turned to putty alarmingly fast. I grabbed his coat to orientate myself. And then we were kissing again. But languorously, without the rabid impatience of the other night. Pressed close to him like this, I was helpless. Undone. I couldn't fight it, and I didn't want to. The music was there. Coming from inside me. I couldn't *un*hear it.

The dog was barking. A frenzied yapping. Wilf straightened up, and I looked round, dazed and detached from the world.

'Nooo,' I whispered.

In full running gear, complete with reflective stripes, Nushrat's boyfriend stood stock-still, staring at us. He'd evidently run out from the woods. And we were blocking his path.

'Hiya, Tod,' I whimpered, aware I was still clinging to Wilf, who wasn't letting go of me, either.

'Hiya, Cara.' Tod pulled an AirPod from his ear. 'How, um, are you?'

'Fine.' I swallowed. 'This is, er, Wilf... JoJo's brother.'

'Yeah.' Tod nodded at him stiffly. 'I heard

about you from Nushrat.'

Wilf tensed. 'Well, I'm public enemy number one around here.' He seemed to realise I was still locked in his embrace, and his arm slid away. 'Good to meet you, Tod.'

'Likewise.'

Under the circumstances, neither of them meant it. I wanted the soil to swallow me up as I stepped aside to let Tod pass.

'I'll tell Nushrat you said "Hi" then, Cara.'

'Lovely. Yes. Tell her I'll call.'

But I wouldn't call first. I wouldn't have the guts. Tod would tell her what had happened. Nushrat would tell Sallie, and then I'd get an earful from both of them. Tod jogged off, glancing over his shoulder. Loki sniffed, as if to say, 'I tried to warn you.'

Wilf closed his eyes briefly. 'I'm sorry. Again.'

'It's fine,' I lied. 'It'll be fine.' I dug my hands in my pockets and frowned.

'Cara…'

I couldn't cope with the apology in his eyes. I couldn't bear what he was apologising for. And so I talked over it.

'Don't worry. They'll just say I'm self-sabotaging. Apparently it's what I always do. But what they don't get is, those men weren't a good match for me. Not even Greg, however compatible we seemed. They weren't the right ones for me to open up to. And they'll think I'm doing this now because I just can't control myself around you, but I'm so tired of them thinking that. It isn't only like that with you, not any more. I'll stand up to them alone, though, because I know you're not ready to stand with me. But I need to do it, anyway. So don't feel bad about anything. Don't say you're sorry.'

I started walking back along the path, Tod already far ahead. Loki barked again, and probably strained at his lead to follow me, because Wilf was suddenly right behind, catching up with his long strides.

'You're not alone, Cara. I'm still here.'

I jolted to a stop. 'But you're not here, as in *here*. Are you? Nothing's changed since the other night... has it?'

Our breath plumed in front of us, merging in the cold air. It could be as easy as that, I thought. To be together. Why was everyone making it so complicated? And if Wilf was hearing the music, too, he wouldn't be acting like this. He wouldn't be able to *un*hear it, either.

'I wanted to see you,' was all he said at first; and then, after an excruciating pause: 'I was a fool. And selfish. I shouldn't have asked you to meet me.'

'No. You shouldn't.' Squidging my boots in the sludgy, shingled path, I turned and trudged off again. This time, no one caught up with me. 'But I was a bigger fool for agreeing,' I muttered.

Chapter 23

I called in sick. Well, first I called Polly, to see how she felt about taking on even more extra shifts. She leapt at the chance. Christmas was an expensive time of year, she emphasised.

I'd already bought all my gifts, so I had no more expenses than the usual; and I wasn't planning any wild nights out, or wild nights in, or whatever Polly did when she was with her twenty-something friends.

It seemed an age since I'd been twenty-something, and as I slumped in bed, sniffling as if I had a cold (it made me feel less guilty about taking time off), either reading my library books, or bingeing on Netflix on my phone on the Pembrokes' account, I felt like a has-been. As if the best parts of my life were over.

I'd dug myself into a hole with Sallie and Nushrat, and Laurence wasn't happy with me, either. Their initial response: I should have waited until after Christmas to break it off with Greg. It was a bad time of year to be alone; as if I didn't know that.

But leading him on had seemed worse to me. Wouldn't he have realised something was wrong if I kept fending off his amorous advances after welcoming them only days before? That was the problem with upside down and inside out. This feeling I couldn't shake off, didn't want to shake off, because it made me alive, and giddy with anticipation, and full of despair, all at once. I couldn't go back to Greg's arms now that I knew how it felt to be in Wilf's.

Basically, I was being penalised for not wanting to lie. And I bristled with resentment at the same time as accepting my friends only wanted the best for me. Tod wouldn't have kept his mouth shut about stumbling across Wilf and me by the river, so Nushrat and Sallie now had their worst suspicions confirmed.

After the first flurry of *what the hells*, following my trip to the garden centre with Greg, they hadn't gone on to bombard me with moral support, which would have been the usual procedure, and I agonised that this time I'd pushed them too far. The radio silence after the incident with Tod was thunderous. Then again, on this occasion, I wasn't the one who'd been cheated on. Why should they offer me sympathy when I'd done the very thing they'd told me not to?

So here I was, hiding from everyone, including the Pembrokes; a pile of laundry festering in the corner because I didn't dare venture across the yard to the outbuilding. But however hard I tried, I couldn't hide from my own thoughts. They crowded around me, clamouring for my attention, stumbling over themselves to get to me. I tried my best to swat them away, although some were more obstinate than others.

I also attempted to downplay the odd 'choo-choo' from my phone, because the messages pierced my heart too much. They weren't telling me anything I wanted to hear. He was just checking up on me, asking if I was all right. Eventually I replied that I had a cold and was taking things easy.

It was much harder to ignore the barrage of knocks on the back door, which came one afternoon when I was on the final episode of some tricksy psychological thriller. I was only watching it with one eye, but it sounded as if someone was trying to break my door down; both eyes flew open in alarm.

My first thought was Wilf, checking that I wasn't unravelling like my mother, which had crossed my mind too often the last few days, as well. A secret fear that all this would trigger something in me; unlock some genetic code which would certify that I was just like her, and make it impossible for me to feel the light again. But when I forced myself to sweep aside the duvet and stumble to the door, I discovered it was just Belle Pembroke, grinning away at me with a large, flat parcel in her arms; her teeth an immaculate beam of white, and hazel eyes that now reminded me too much of Wilf's.

The grin wavered when she looked me up and down. 'Cara, are you okay?'

I peered around her into the yard, but she was alone.

'Don't worry.' I shivered. 'I'm just a bit under the weather.'

Belle didn't wait for me to invite her in, and I was too far back from the threshold to block her path. I had to step aside completely, or she would have bashed me with the parcel. She strode right in through the kitchen, and I closed the back door with a resigned sigh.

'So,' she said animatedly, as I dragged an outsized cardie over my manky PJs, 'this just got delivered for you, and Mum asked me to bring it over.'

'For me?' I stared at the package. 'How? I mean...'

'By special courier. But he didn't know what it meant by "The Hovel, 5 Swallowtail Lane," so he knocked on our door. It's addressed to you, though. "Miss C. M. Shaw."'

My eyes popped wider, even as a sheepish blush warmed my face. I'd never referred to the annexe as 'the hovel' in front of the Pembrokes. The only people who knew about the nickname were Sallie and Nushrat, and I dare say their other halves. But even if they were still cross with me, which was highly likely, they wouldn't have risked shaming me like this.

Belle put the parcel on the bed before flopping on to my sofa, all arms and legs and poker-straight, Rumpelstiltskin-spun hair. 'Why would anyone call this place a hovel? When I go to uni, I want to decorate my room in halls just like this. It'll probably be even smaller, and I won't have my own kitchen, unless I get one of those studio flats.'

'I suppose.'

I didn't know what I supposed, really. I was too distracted by the brown paper parcel, tied with string. Very like the one I'd given Perdita, only bigger. The handwriting looked vaguely familiar, but it was in block capitals, and had a spidery quality, as if the hand that had written it was trembling at the time.

'Are you going to open it?' Belle said, without masking her curiosity. 'I'm trying to guess what it might be. And why "The Hovel"? Your official address is "The Annexe".'

'I don't know,' I mumbled, reluctant to open it with an onlooker present. But JoJo's eldest daughter was like an excitable filly. And she evidently wasn't budging from my sofa until her curiosity was satisfied.

Belle curled her legs underneath her, making herself comfortable. She looked at me expectantly. '*Well*? I need to know what it is.'

I frowned, reminding myself who was the

adult around here, even though she'd overtaken me in height when she was twelve. 'It won't be anything exciting, so you don't need to stick around.'

'Ooh.' Now it was her turn to widen her eyes. 'Have you been ordering stuff? You know, *stuff*. They send it out in discreet packaging.'

I felt old and stale, like the bread I'd tried to toast that morning. She could have meant all sorts by that, and she was only fifteen, so I wasn't going to go there. 'No, I haven't ordered "stuff". But I'd still appreciate a little privacy.'

'Oh.' Her face dropped, and I felt a twinge of guilt. 'I thought I might hang out here a bit. Vicki's got Jade and Savannah in the games room, and I can't be in the same space as Jade ever since she told Harrison Kirk I fancied him. But I don't. He's got serious hygiene issues. And even if he didn't, his whole attitude's douchey. So anyway, I hate Jade. Not hate, like I want her dead. I just don't want to see her smug face right now. So I'm not talking to Vicki because she knows how I feel.'

'Right... I'm sorry—'

'And Mum, Dad and Uncle Wilf are at each other's throats, too. Mum practically threw the parcel at me to bring over to you. I think she's stressed about the party. Usually, you'd be helping her, but she said to me she couldn't ask you this year. Uncle Wilf had told her to stop taking the piss; I overheard him. He said you had your own life, and you weren't at her beck and call, even if you did live here rent-free.'

I blinked down at Belle, trying to take it all in, but the only thing that held my attention was the last part, about Wilf. 'He… he said that? To your Mum's face?'

'Well, he really likes you, doesn't he?' Belle threw me a knowing look. 'He thought he was being all casual when he grilled me and Vicki about you, but OMG, he's so into you he can't hide it, even though he tries. I think that's why Mum's so annoyed; or one of the reasons, at least… Because it's not just Uncle Wilf. She's livid with Dad, too.'

A bleakness crossed Belle's face for a moment, and I wanted to wrap my arm around her the way I used to when she was little, foolhardily reassuring her I'd fix everything. Except I couldn't blow away the storm that lurked on the horizon for her parents. I could only put aside my own concerns, and lend a listening ear, if she needed it.

'Mum thinks you're going to hurt Uncle Wilf, the way Zoe hurt him, because you're such a loser when it comes to relationships.' Belle tipped her head back to look at me, an earnest gleam in her eyes now. 'I heard her say it. But Uncle Wilf said he's more afraid of hurting you than the other way round, and it didn't mean you'd failed with those other men if they weren't right for you. Dad says Mum's over-reacting. And *I* just think it would be really cool if you and Uncle Wilf got together. You'd make such a cute couple. *Wilara.* Or *Carilf.*' She creased her brow. 'Which sounds better?'

Neither! I twisted a chunk of my hair aggressively around my fingers. It was a cop-out – and a damn irony – for Wilf to keep saying he didn't want to cause me pain, when in actual fact he was inflicting it by his very ambivalence, by blowing hot and cold.

'You do like him back, don't you, Cara?'

I realised Belle was still talking. She'd asked me a question.

I could lie. Pretend to be blithe about it. But I was done with lying about this.

It took all my energy, and all that remained of my dignity, to answer her.

'Yes. Yes, I like him.'

'I guessed you did.' Belle lit up with the broadest smile she'd bestowed on me in ages. 'He's sweet, really. Like a big shaggy bear. Though he said he's seen a bear up close, and it wasn't as sweet as it looked. Now, are you going to open that? *Please.*' She made puppy-dog eyes at me as she gestured to the parcel. 'I'm dying here.'

'Er... okay.' I blinked, dazed, as if I wasn't wholly in my own body, and pulled at the string tied in a neat bow. The wrapping fell away to reveal a classy cardboard box. With care, I lifted the lid to find a mass of tissue paper. Putting the lid aside, I parted the flimsy, rustling layers to reveal a glimpse of wine-red lace.

As Belle leaned forwards, I winced, but when I gingerly revealed more I could tell the lace wasn't sheer but lined with matching satin, and there was just too much of it to be lingerie. Slowly, with mounting confusion, I lifted the dress out of the box.

'Whoa,' said Belle. 'That's so *gorge*!'

I couldn't argue. It was the most beautiful item of clothing I'd ever handled. The lace was intricate and soft under my fingertips; the quality and workmanship exquisite. From the fifties, I guessed, or modelled on that era. Cap sleeves, pinched waist, layers of underskirt flaring outwards. Tiny, lace-covered buttons ran down to the waist from a sweetheart neckline. There was no label, though. As if the dress had been handmade. A one-off.

'What the…?' I didn't understand, and then I spotted a pale pink sheet of A4 paper at the bottom of the box, folded in half. I draped the dress on the bed as Belle reverently fussed over it.

Again, the handwriting was oddly familiar, but still shaky.

'Dearest Cara,

I hope you'll accept this early Christmas present, in return for yours. This dress should fit you perfectly, I think. It brought me passion and joy when I was your age and needed more colour in my life. Wear it bravely, and with that lovely smile of yours.

With love from your fairy godmother.

(Perdita x)'

I gulped.

I could never wear this. I'd draw far more attention to myself than I'd be comfortable with. And it probably wouldn't suit me, anyway. I couldn't carry it off. Yes, it was a dark red, but still brighter than anything I usually wore. I just wouldn't feel like me.

But the sentiment behind it…

I didn't notice Belle was on her feet reading over my shoulder until I heard her ask, 'Who's Perdita?'

'Oh.' I hesitated, wondering how best to describe her. Fairy godmother seemed apt, but would take too long to explain. 'A friend of mine. An old lady who used to live in the village.'

'A generous friend.' Belle stroked the dress. 'Although I guess, if she already owned it…'

What about her own children and grandchildren, though? Daughters? Daughters-in-law? She should have passed the dress on to family. Unless it wouldn't have fitted any of them, and she felt it was going to waste. I held it up again. It didn't even smell musty. And it was clearly made for a petite person. But still… Not me. Not *this* petite person.

'Try it on,' urged Belle. 'I want to see how it

looks on you.'

I chewed my bottom lip. 'No... No, I couldn't. It wouldn't look right. I can't accept this gift.'

'"Wear it bravely,"' Belle quoted. 'Come on. You're only trying it on.' She pushed it towards me.

'I'm not sure...'

'Well, I am. Go change in the bathroom. I'll wait here. Come out like they do on that TV show – what's it called? – *Say Yes to the Dress* or something.'

'When did you get to be so bossy?'

'When I was about six. Don't you remember? Vicki and I used to order you about.'

'I've conveniently erased it from memory.'

'Try on the dress, *please*, Cara. Pretend I'm your favourite niece and I'm asking you really nicely.'

I frowned. 'How did you suddenly become my pretend niece? Let alone my favourite one?'

'When you "pretend" hooked-up with my only uncle.' Belle giggled, and shoved me towards the bathroom. 'But it's okay. I gave you both permission. I don't think it's cringe, even at your age.'

Belle was definitely more outspoken than ever. At the same time, the way she'd blown through my misery had flipped a switch in me. She'd got me up out of bed and conversing with another human being again. Someone who also seemed to be on my side. I couldn't help but feel grateful.

But what was Perdita thinking by giving me this dress? I was just someone she'd met a few weeks ago. I didn't understand why she had such a vested interest, besides living through me vicariously. And had I let slip in front of her that I called this place the hovel? It was so odd.

In the bathroom, as I shed the PJs and carefully stepped into the dress, the speculation stole over me that maybe the old woman was trying to recreate her *own* youth, through mine. Those heady early days with the man she would later marry. The tumultuous thrill of a new romance. All the more evocative and poignant because he was no longer with her. This would be her first Christmas without her husband in over half a century.

'Damn.' I sat on the edge of the bath for a couple of minutes, the sense of loss strangely visceral. And then I took a deep breath, fastened the buttons at the front, the bodice perfectly sculpted and fitted, and wiped the dampness from my eyes.

Right, Cara. I stood up again, the material swishing around me, and walked back out, relishing the alien satisfaction of seeing Belle's jaw drop.

'Cara, you look…'

'Is it all right?'

'See for yourself.' She excitedly turned me towards my full-length mirror, hanging on the wall beside my clothes rail. 'This was *made* for you.'

The woman who stared back at me oozed confidence, even an understated glamour and panache, as if she always wore this sort of thing and felt at ease in it. The dress fitted every contour like a comfortable glove to the waistline, before the skirt flared out crisply to my knees. The colour didn't overwhelm me, either. Against my dark hair, the red looked deeper; somehow there was even a delicate bloom in my cheeks. I didn't look as if I'd been eating rubbish, or hadn't washed my hair in days. I seemed civilised. Maybe even pretty.

'You look amazing!' Belle enthused. 'Cinderella gets to go to the ball, yet again. I loved all those stories you used to tell us, you know, when Vicki and I were kids. And the films we'd watch with you. *Beauty and the Beast... Tangled...*'

'You loved Disney, you mean.'

Belle wouldn't have taken kindly to me adding that she was still technically a child. 'So what ball am I going to?' I said instead.

'Mum's Christmas party on Saturday, duh.'

'This?' I blinked. 'You think I should wear *this*? I'm not even sure I'm going to go. I've been feeling so bleurgh...'

'You seem fine to me. And you've got to be there. Uncle Wilf won't know what to do with himself when he sees you in that dress. I'll come over before and do your hair and make-up. Don't look at me like that. I know you prefer it subtle. I'm not like Mum. But you're not the best at doing it yourself, admit it.'

I stared into the mirror, and a calm, assured woman blinked back at me. I couldn't possibly... Could I? I wasn't in the right frame of mind for a party, let alone Christmas. Let alone facing JoJo. Or seeing Wilf, knowing how pointless it probably all was, whatever Belle claimed. But maybe this was more than just a dress, and Perdita understood that better than anyone. Maybe this was armour.

'Be here at six?' I swung round to the teenager, the dress swinging with me. 'Does that give you enough time?'

Belle let out a squeal, and for the first time in years I glimpsed that cherubic little girl who'd twirled around the old house, waving a wand that shed glitter, and half-convincing me to believe in magic, too, as I hoovered up behind her.

And I think what I felt in that moment was just as strong a love as any aunt might feel.

'More than enough.' She grinned.

Chapter 24

'Cara…' JoJo straightened up, staring at me. 'You look… different.'

I decided to take that as a compliment, even though it hadn't sounded like one.

She'd been stooping to get a stash of napkins from a cupboard. 'Caterers didn't supply any,' she went on. 'Can you believe it? This whole thing's cost me enough.'

'Or maybe it's that I wasn't here to help organise it?' I shrugged. 'If you had the same firm as usual, then it's always been an optional extra.'

I'd let myself in through the back, slightly earlier than the time stated on the invitation. In the past, when JoJo had thrown a party, I would have spent all afternoon helping her set up. Even though she always hired caterers to supply the buffet, she never paid anyone to serve. Her parties were too informal for that, she claimed. She didn't want strangers hovering around, detracting from her hostess skills, though it was entirely acceptable for me to devote my night to serving and detracting.

She tossed back yards of hair, so like Belle's, and slapped the napkins on the granite island. Her dress was an ankle-length sheath of bronze silk, with barely-there straps. As always, JoJo was stunning. The focal point of any room. Like a feature wall.

'You're busy enough, Cara. I can't keep imposing on you the way I do. Besides, I heard you haven't been well. Feeling any better? I wasn't sure you'd be up for this tonight.'

'I'm much better, thank you.'

She eyed my dress, her green eyes narrowing. 'Is that new?'

'No. It's old.'

'New for *you*. It's not the kind of thing you normally wear.'

'It isn't, but it feels right. Like I've worn it before.'

JoJo curled her lip. 'In another life, you mean?'

'Not exactly. I don't know what I mean, to be honest.'

'Cara?' Des came down the hall from his study, carrying Loki. 'You look—'

'Different, I know,' JoJo snapped. 'I've already said that.'

Des didn't look at her. 'I was going to say "lovely", if that's appropriate?'

'I can't stop you complimenting other women.' JoJo flashed him a saccharine smile.

'Even if you have known them since they were children.'

'Cara was nineteen when she joined us, as I recall,' Des said smoothly. 'Not strictly a child. But did I ever say anything I shouldn't have?' He frowned at me. 'Or behave in any way that made you uncomfortable?'

'Sorry?' This had taken a strange turn, rather fast. 'No. Never.' I looked from husband to wife, about to speak again when Belle and Vicki squawked and sniggered through the hall. Arm in arm, in platform sandals, they tottered under the archway into the kitchen.

Belle seemed to have forgiven her sister, from what she'd said while doing my hair and make-up earlier. Apparently Harrison Kirk had asked Savannah out, of all people, and Jade wasn't speaking to Savannah now, because it turned out Jade actually fancied him, although neither of the Pembroke sisters could fathom why. He still hadn't heard of personal hygiene, and he was always shitty to the unpopular girls, even though they couldn't help being unpopular. It didn't mean boys like Harrison could treat them like dirt. Did it?

'No,' I'd agreed with Belle, remembering my own school days. I'd always seemed to hover somewhere in the middle. Neither popular, nor unpopular. A bit nerdy, overly fond of books, but exotic enough in other ways and too quick with my tongue to let anyone put me down. I could remember those days easily, but that girl I'd been… Only bits of her still existed. She wasn't whole, like she used to be. She'd been patched together into something else.

Belle let go of her sister, and ran over to me; if you could call it running in those heels. She threaded her arm through mine. 'Doesn't Cara look amazing? I did her make-up. But she never needs much, she's pretty enough without it.'

'That's the charm of big dark eyes and high cheekbones,' said JoJo. 'Our little Cara has blossomed over the years. Inevitable, I suppose.'

'Gorgeous dress.' Vicki smiled at me, genuinely, and I smiled back, trying to ignore the barbed edge to JoJo's voice.

Her two daughters, so tall and slim, had wriggled into the Lycra mini dresses their generation seemed to favour. Belle's was gold, Vicki's silver. For an instant, I felt like a stale old lump of bread again.

The doorbell chimed, and Loki squirmed in Des's arms, yipping agitatedly.

Des frowned. 'Shall I shut him in my study?'

'I can take him to the annexe, if you like?' It wouldn't have been the first time I'd left Loki on my sofa with one of his favourite teddies while a party raged next door. He seemed to settle fine like that, by some miracle.

'I'll do it.'

I turned at the sound of that familiar, husky voice. Wilf filled the archway. Our eyes locked, as

I knew they would, they seemed unable not to fuse even when I knew they shouldn't. And then slowly his gaze slid over me as a whole. My make-up, as subtle as Belle had promised. My hair, most of it a tumble of curls down my back, with just a section, like the swag of a curtain, caught up in a large clip Belle had lent me, with a butterfly design. But when I'd examined it closely, I'd realised it was a moth. A shimmering, silver moth. A sign – to remind me I had wings.

It had been too short notice to hunt for new shoes in the pre-Christmas sales, so I'd had to make do with a pair of silver kitten heels, with multicoloured jewels, which had been my mum's. Bought for her by my dad when she'd turned thirty-five. She'd seemed to love them, though they'd rarely been worn. I'd kept them, to feel close to her, and worn them once or twice. But they'd never felt right on me – too ostentatious, too bright – and I'd just put them away under my bed. My other going-out shoes, wedged and black, wouldn't have matched this outfit.

'You don't want to get dog hair on that dress,' Wilf said, with unearthly calmness, even as his Adam's apple bobbed above the open collar of his charcoal shirt.

'But you don't want to get hairs on that shirt, either,' I said, my eyes still glued to him.

Des sighed. 'Let me do it – seeing as I'm holding Loki already. I'll just use the lint roller when I get back.'

I turned to Des again; dazed, as if I'd already been drinking, when I hadn't been near a drop. 'All right. Thank you. My key…' I pulled it out of a beaded vintage purse, shaped like a daffodil bulb and looped around my wrist, large enough for a tissue and a tin of lip balm, too. Another charity shop bargain I hadn't wanted to sell on, though I wasn't sure who would buy it if it couldn't accommodate a phone.

'Here.' Vicki plucked a teddy from a basket by the back door. 'Take this, Dad. It's Loki's favourite at the moment. He likes to snuggle with it.'

'Don't forget to put some water down. Grab a bowl from here,' said Belle. 'Actually – I'll help. You're running out of hands…'

'And I need more hairspray.' Vicki frowned as she examined a strand of her immaculate-looking hair, and toddled past her uncle towards the stairs.

The doorbell chimed again, and JoJo snapped at Wilf.

'Are you going to answer it, then? Or just stand there salivating over Cara? This whole night's in your honour, the least you could do is pay attention to the other guests.'

A blush that might have matched my dress blazed over my cheeks. 'JoJo…'

'It's fine.' She frowned, hands on hips. 'Wilfred's old enough to make his own mistakes, I'm not stopping him. He's as much a sap as his mum was. So, do your worst, Cara. It's what you're best at.'

A dark gash across his brow, Wilf stabbed a finger towards his sister. '*Uncalled for*, Jo. And I never asked for this bloody party. Don't take it out on Cara, just because you can't control me the way you want to control everything else around here.'

After a deep breath in and out, he pivoted and headed for the front door. Flinging it open, he greeted the first guests as if he hadn't been slamming this party only seconds before.

The next couple of hours passed in a half-dream, half-nightmare. I didn't talk to JoJo, and she didn't talk to me. Old habits died hard, though, and I found myself circling on auto-pilot, offering to top up guests' drinks, or wafting around with plates of caramelised pork belly skewers, and fig and goat's cheese puffs, and other things I couldn't identify without checking the description from the caterers.

Wilf mingled, wearing a megawatt smile, while men pumped his hand, and women – unavailable or not – flirted shamelessly. Sometimes the occasional man flirted and a woman pumped Wilf's hand, but on the whole, the pattern remained stable. Yet ridiculously often, he would catch my eye across a crowded space full of scintillating, influential people, and we might as well have been alone. Eyes holding a private conversation that no one else was privy to.

Except maybe JoJo. That was the nightmarish

part. I could feel her own gaze following me, but when I looked at her, she would turn away and follow Des or Wilf. I wanted to corner her, demand to talk. This dress gave me courage, not the other way around, if that made sense. I wasn't wearing it bravely, it felt more as if it was wearing me. And the champagne helped, because I wouldn't be able to confront JoJo without either; the dress and the alcohol combined created a reckless alchemy.

What was going on in JoJo's head? Was it jealousy? Possessiveness? I thought I knew her better than this, but now I wondered if I'd ever known her at all.

Alyson, her PA, was conspicuous by her absence.

'Oh, she's in Swansea,' Belle said, when I nonchalantly mentioned it as we passed in the kitchen. 'Gone to stay with family for the holidays already.'

'Right. Shame she's missing this, though.'

Belle shrugged. 'I don't know. Haven't seen much of her lately, to be honest.' And she drifted off, while I drank a glass of water to hydrate.

Realising I was desperate for the loo, I decided I might as well kill two birds with one stone, and check on Loki. Minutes later, I was about to step out into the yard again when I saw it. The anomaly. The shadow that shouldn't have been there, at the edge of my vision, leaning against the annexe. And then, abruptly, the shadow was flesh and blood, blocking my path, foul whisky-breath and cigar smoke, his paunch straining the belt buckle of his trousers.

'Hello, there.' He leered, swaying worryingly close.

'Hi,' I muttered, trying to pull the door shut behind me. There was no way I was going to step back.

'I don't think we've been introduced,' he said. 'I'm Quentin Fortescue.'

More like Fiftescue. 'Good for you.'

'And I know who *you* are, Cara. I asked who the pretty little thing was in the red dress. I also asked if your significant other was here. Apparently you're unattached at the moment, according to JoJo... Maybe I can help with that?'

Any more forward, and I'd be his trophy wife already. Anger took root. 'I'm sorry, Quentin, but you've been misinformed. There is someone, and he's fairly significant.'

'Oh. But not here this minute... is he? Don't worry, I won't tell. We could have a drink or whatever? Except it's rather crowded in the house...' He looked past me into the hovel. I felt a thump of disgust. A lurch of nausea, too, as he leaned closer.

But then I heard a rumble, a growl, and looked down. The Pom was at my ankles, his tiny teeth bared as he stared up at Quentin.

'This is Loki.' I smiled. 'He doesn't like strangers much.'

'Well, hello, little fellow. You're not that fearsome, though, really?'

'How about the big fellow?' I pointed over Quentin's shoulder. 'Behind you. Is he fearsome enough?'

'What?' Quentin looked at me, perplexed, then turned round.

The big fellow was younger, taller, his shoulders broader. I knew who my money was on. By the homicidal glint in Wilf's eyes, I also knew I had to intervene. I stepped in front of Quentin, who'd ducked back into the shadows.

'It's fine.' I put my hand to Wilf's chest. 'Please. It's not worth it.' I looked round at Quentin again. 'Maybe you should call a taxi. I wouldn't hang around, I think this party might be over – at least for you. There's a path round there that leads to the front.'

He didn't need to be told twice. I was awesomely powerful in this dress, especially with Wilf and Loki as back-up. The security lights chased Quentin away, down the side of the annexe, and the Pomeranian stopped growling and licked my ankle. I let my hand drop from Wilf's chest, although I wanted to leave it there indefinitely.

'Come on, Loki, let's get you inside again.' I ushered the little dog back into the hovel, where I settled him on the sofa and stroked his head, telepathically conveying my thanks.

I knew Wilf was right behind me. His presence dominated the small space. 'Are you okay?'

'I'm fine,' I said. 'I could have handled Quentin, you know.'

'I wasn't going to take that risk. I saw him watching you, in the house.'

'Well, he's gone now. And we should go back.'

But Wilf didn't move. 'I'm sorry about JoJo. The way she's acting… I'm sorry about everything. The other day, by the river…' he tailed off.

We could keep going round and round, or one of us could do something definitive. Resolve the tension. Words alone weren't going to cut it.

'On second thoughts,' I glanced around, as if I didn't recognise the place, 'we don't have to go back. We could stay right here? There's no rush. I've got wine in the fridge.'

'I'm guest of honour, though,' he pointed out ruefully. 'I think they'd notice if I wasn't there. But I'd hide away with you all evening, if I could.'

As he moved away, I swallowed. 'How about all night, Wilf? Would you hide with me here all night?'

He stopped, looked back. 'What?'

'After the party. After everyone's gone home, whatever time that is… We'll go back to the house now, play our part. But later…'

'Cara—'

'It doesn't have to mean anything. I just don't want to be on my own. I know what I'm saying, what I'm asking. It's a two-way thing, this dopamine hit business. Maybe I need the distraction, too? A few hours where I don't have to worry about anything else.'

'Look, we have to go.' He frowned. 'Come on. I'm not letting you lock up without me. That prick Quentin might still be around.'

'Fine.' I brushed past Wilf, heading for the door, humiliation clogging my throat. 'Forget I said anything, then. I know when—'

But he caught me round the waist, turning me to face him; my raspy, jarring words evaporating at the heat in his eyes. 'I can't forget, though,' he admitted, his voice delectably low and gravelly, even more so than usual. 'I don't know who you are in that dress... I can't stop looking at you. You're *luminous* tonight.'

'Am I?' I stepped closer, insinuating myself into his embrace. 'Right now I feel tired, Wilf. Not sleepy... just exhausted by all this. Everyone knows about us now, even though there isn't actually an "us" the way they all assume. So we're just getting all the aggro without reaping any of the benefits. Even the short-term ones.'

'That's a powerful argument.' His gaze, stained with unmistakeable yearning, glided across my face, from my eyes to my lips. 'You're very persuasive, Cara Mia...' And then his mouth on mine filled in all the blanks, his hands and arms left me in no doubt. '*Later*, though.' He peeled himself away with a groan.

I leaned against the wall, my knees weak, my heart galloping hard. I could have locked the door right then and blocked everything else out, except Loki let out a grumble as if we were disturbing him, and I remembered the little dog was there, eyeing us from the sofa.

So instead, I straightened my dress and my hair and my composure, and laughed at Wilf as he pretended he couldn't walk, although I'm not sure he was entirely pretending. And we went back to the party, drunk on anticipation.

Chapter 25

It was gone two by the time JoJo shut the door on the last of her guests. I was already clearing up, and even Belle and Vicki were helping; sort of. There was a lot of yawning going on, and flopping of limbs as they padded around, barefoot now, having abandoned their sandals around midnight.

'Girls,' said Des, carrying a tray with empty glasses into the kitchen and depositing it by the sink, 'get to bed, both of you. You look shattered. Thanks for all your help, though. The cleaners will be here on Monday, as usual; they'll finish off the job.'

JoJo tippety-tapped into the kitchen, still in her heels, swaying precariously. 'Yes,' she gushed, 'thank you, my darlings. You're the absolute best daughters ever.' She leaned against the island for support. 'I hope you enjoyed yourselves. Sorry we couldn't have had more of your own friends here. You know how it is, though. The adults have to play, too.'

'It's fine, Mum.' Belle smiled thinly. 'We've got our New Year thing going on.'

'And anyway,' said Vicki, 'we *love* chatting to all your friends. Quentin, especially.'

I stiffened at this, and frowned as the sisters exchanged glances.

'What about Quentin?' JoJo picked up a half-drunk glass of champagne from the counter, and was about to knock it back when Des swiped it from her hand. She scowled. 'He's *your* friend, Des, so what happened? He disappeared suddenly. And what's so great about him?' She eyed the girls warily.

'Nothing, Mum,' sighed Vicki. 'I was being sarcastic.'

'He was vile.' Belle scrunched up her face. 'So gross, the way he kept licking his lips all the time.' She shuddered as Vicki pretended to retch.

'I didn't think he was that bad,' said their mother. 'He seemed interested enough in whether Cara was spoken for.'

In the past, I would have shrugged it off; not that I'd ever been in such a tight spot with a man because of her. But I wouldn't have risked an argument. Tonight, though, I wasn't one of JoJo Pem's official employees, or the friend JoJo badly claimed to want, or one of the many sycophants who'd spent the evening under her roof, quaffing Moët and guzzling maple-glazed sausage blinis. I was that in-between thing, who'd finally seemed to have found a voice I'd lost a long time ago.

'Yes, thanks for that, by the way, JoJo. It was kind of you to think of me.'

'Telling him you were unattached, you mean?' She met my eye with a flicker of apprehension. 'Well, he's loaded... Isn't he, Des?' She swung round to her husband for confirmation, but Des was looking at her as if an alien might have taken over her body. JoJo swivelled to face me again, pulling up one of her spaghetti straps as it slid off her shoulder. 'I thought I was doing you a favour, Cara.'

'Jo – you put that creep up to it?' Wilf reappeared from clearing up in the garden, an ashtray in each hand, but he'd obviously caught what his sister had said.

'Put him up to what?'

'Harassing Cara. Following her to the annexe.'

Des tipped the dregs of a champagne bottle down the sink as JoJo made a lunge for it. 'He did *what*?' Des glared at his wife, then looked over his shoulder at me. 'Cara, are you all right?'

'It was nothing. I'm fine.' But I didn't know how far Quentin might have pushed it, if he hadn't been interrupted. 'Wilf got rid of him,' I said, keeping it simple, not wanting to think of all the ways it might have gone down if I'd been alone.

'Ooh, you hero!' Vicki lavished her uncle with a sassy grin. 'I'd have paid for tickets to that.'

'Right.' Des turned to his daughters. 'You girls

get upstairs now. I think it's way past your bedtime.'

'We're not *kids*, Dad.' Belle pulled a face, but still locked arms with her sister. 'Come on, Vicks. We're not staying where we're not wanted.'

Vicki protested theatrically, even as she let Belle drag her away. I frowned into the fish tank, lit up in calming blue, as Thor and Odin circled an aquarium decoration I hadn't noticed before, shaped like a Christmas tree. Trust JoJo to have bought that. Or the girls.

Des waited until the giggling and chatter faded up the stairs, then turned to his wife again. 'That was low,' he said hoarsely. 'Even for you these days. Quentin Fortescue is a twat. I don't care if his brother-in-law's in the House of Lords, or his sister's a bloody hedge fund manager, or how many acres of Shropshire or Cheshire he owns – he's not setting foot back in this house. You should have *warned* Cara about him when you heard how he was talking.' Des shook his head, his skin tinged with grey. 'Do you have any idea what could have happened...? Men like that don't like hearing "no". What would you do or say, if someone ever put Belle or Vicki in that position?'

'You invited him here tonight,' snapped JoJo, after a cringeworthy pause. 'You always blame me, Des, but this one is on you. I don't know the man from Adam.'

Des closed his eyes briefly. 'I take full responsibility for that. But if I'd been aware of what he said to you... or that he actually followed Cara to the annexe... *Hell*, JoJo. Sometimes you haven't got a clue, have you? I've cushioned you too much. Everyone has, so you can live in your ivory tower and focus on what you do best. We're all to blame here. All of us.' He looked from me to Wilf, his gaze heavy with sympathy though, not recrimination, before turning back to his wife. 'But we can only do so much, my love, when the thing we have to protect you from most is yourself.'

I stood transfixed. I'd never seen Des assert himself like this in all the years I'd known him. He was still grey-faced, though, and the way he'd called her 'my love'... The manner in which he was looking at her now, as she withered in front of us like a scorched flower... It wasn't the look of a man who was about to leave her for someone else.

But what did I know? Except... I'd seen my dad look at my mum that way, after she'd spent hours alone in the bedroom with the curtains closed, before she finally managed to venture downstairs, to join us at the dining table.

'Des.' JoJo reached out, clutching his shirt-sleeve. 'I'm sorry...'

'It's okay.' His voice was low, almost crooning, as he ushered her into his arms. She nuzzled her head into his chest. 'We'll get through this,' he said. 'We always do.' He looked at Wilf and me, over JoJo's shoulder, and indicated with his head for us to leave, a weak smile on his lips momentarily and what might have been gratitude in his eyes. It was hard to tell, they looked red and watery.

Wilf walked me wordlessly back to the annexe, scooped up Loki and disappeared. I sat on the edge of my bed, slipped off my shoes and swore, clueless as to whether he'd be back. Any bolstering effects of the alcohol had worn off and my adrenaline levels had plummeted. Stress and nerves, and the simple fact I was occupying the same space as Wilf, had carried me through the last few hours, along with the magic of this red dress. Now, though, I shuddered from the cold, realising the boiler had switched off automatically at midnight. The minutes ticked by, and I lay down and pulled the duvet over me.

He wasn't coming back, was he?

I closed my eyes, reliving how we'd followed each other around the crowded space but never quite found ourselves in the same group. We'd smiled furtively as we dipped in and out of conversations, enjoying the suspense, the game, like two lovers who'd made an illicit pact. The Romeo and Juliet of Pebblestow. We had our assigned rendezvous, our secret language. We both knew where it was heading, and the drama of it all was delicious. The expensive fizz, and the dress worn so boldly once by Perdita, had suppressed my doubts and fears, but now the negativity was pressing its way towards the surface again.

'Why is it so cold in here?' The voice stirred me from semi-consciousness, and I blinked and focussed, as Wilf leaned over the bed and swept a spiral of my hair back from my face. I sat up, and he immediately straightened, and perched across from me on the sofa. 'Sorry I took so long. Des was still trying to get JoJo upstairs, and I had to settle Loki.'

'The heating goes off overnight,' I said, answering his question and adding, 'I wasn't sure you were coming back.'

'You said you didn't want to be alone. And you hadn't locked the door. But listen, I'll leave if you want. Or I'll crash on the couch. Either way… I think you need to change into something warm and get some sleep. You haven't been well.'

'I wasn't sick.' I frowned. 'I was skiving. Well, actually I was hiding. But then Perdita sent me this dress, and Belle was so persuasive, and I thought *screw it*, just go to the damn party and face up to it all. Face JoJo, and *you*. And…' I ran out of steam.

Wilf held out his hand, and I rocked to my feet and went and sat beside him, welcoming the warmth of his large, solid body next to mine. 'I don't want you to have to hide.' He put his arm around me, and my head dropped against his shoulder. I closed my eyes again. 'Look,' he went on, after a drawn out, dreamy moment, 'we need to have a long talk. There's stuff I have to tell you, about myself. It's just… sometimes it's hard to know where to start. All this happened so fast with you. But now the conversation's overdue. And I don't want to hide any more, either.'

I squeezed his fingers. 'You can tell me anything. I need you to know that.'

He squeezed back. 'But not now.' His lips brushed the top of my head. 'You're drained. I'm not sure how much you'll understand.'

'Okay,' I snapped upright on the sofa, 'I'll get to bed. We'll talk tomorrow, or whenever. But there's no way you're going to fit on this and get any sleep.'

He let out a wry grunt, and helped me untangle the clip with the moth motif from my curls. I put it to one side, as he fanned out my hair, sparks shooting the length of my spine at the gentleness of his touch, until I shivered, needing more. Standing up, I turned to face him.

'I'd better just go then,' he said.

'But you promised you'd stay the whole night.'

'Technically, I never promised anything.'

'Don't try to inveigle your way out of a formal agreement.' My fingers, clumsy with tiredness and impatience, fumbled with the top button of my dress, then the second.

'What are you doing?' he muttered.

'What does it look like? Are you going to help me, or just sit there?'

He put his hands over mine, and stilled them. 'I'm not sure you're sure enough.'

'What?' My brow wrinkled. 'Do you need me to consent to consenting? I don't know what you mean. What do you need me to say? A few hours ago, you were more than up for it.'

'I'm more than up for it now, Cara, but I don't want you to regret this.'

He was so different from Sid. Maybe not so different from Greg, in some ways. But I didn't want to think about other men. My concentration was on Wilf. Every part of me wanted to belong to him and for him to belong to me, for as long as we had. Tonight. Weeks. A lifetime.

'I could never regret you,' I said. 'Or this, or us. And, for the record, that *is* a promise. I didn't even wish for you, but then there you were.'

'Wish for me?'

'Don't ask. You were straight out of a storybook, though.'

'Ah.' He nodded, though a brow curved sceptically. 'Prince Charming?'

'You've a high opinion of yourself, Wilf. I was going to say more like some bad-tempered, jet-lagged giant.'

His laugh, soft with happiness at the memory, caressed my face. 'It was an act. The ladies love it.'

'Do they now?' I laughed, too, but then my lips found his again and the laughter was quickly smothered. Desire screamed out of my exhaustion as his mouth responded with more emotion than ever. The kiss tipped from sweet to feverish, and at last, when I thought I couldn't bear it any more, his hands took over from mine, fumbling with the lace-covered buttons.

Chapter 26

It wasn't yet dawn when I lifted an eyelid, but I could see a glow coming from somewhere. I tilted my head a fraction, and saw it originated from the sofa. Wilf was slumped across it awkwardly, the crocheted blanket around his shoulders, reading one of my books by the torch on his phone.

The man was just too perfect.

I bit my lip, suppressing a smile, though why I was suppressing it I didn't know. Unless I felt I might jinx all this by revelling in my joy. I couldn't believe he wasn't as drained as I was by the long day, the drama of the evening, everything we'd done after I'd insisted the dress needed to be hung up neatly, because it deserved more respect than Wilf's hasty dumping of his attire on the floor...

I wriggled my toes at the more recent recollections and burrowed into the pillow, the duvet snug around me. Sated, and still heavy with sleep, I drifted off again, woken by daylight filtering through the curtains the next time I opened my eyes, although the gentle hand rubbing my shoulder might also have been implicated.

'Hey… Sleepy-head, I made you a coffee.'

'Hmm?' I blinked at Wilf as he knelt beside me. The hovel felt roasting hot now; the heating had clearly come on hours ago.

'I also made a tea. In case you preferred that, first thing.'

'What time is it?' I groped for my phone between the two steaming mugs by the bedside lamp. 'Wow – really? That late?'

'There didn't seem to be any alarms set, but I thought I ought to wake you. You might have plans.'

I heaved myself into a sitting position, the nightshirt I'd pulled on to go to the loo last night plastered to my back; my hair clinging to my neck. Attractive.

'I'm supposed to be going to Perdita's. It's her last day; her family are picking her up tomorrow.' I fanned myself with my hand. 'Did you turn up the radiator in here?'

'Sorry. Around eight. It still felt cold.'

'You can turn it down now a bit, please. Don't you ever sleep? I saw you, you know, reading in the night. I woke up for about five minutes.'

'Did you? You seemed flat out. And no,' he sighed. 'I'm not a good sleeper. Sorry if it disturbed you. I'm used to it now myself, after all these years, but…'

In sympathy, I pushed back the hair from his brow. On the verge of asking how Zoe had coped, I realised she didn't belong in this conversation. None of our exes did.

'It was sweet,' I said, 'seeing you like that. You like reading fiction too, then, not just the non-fiction you borrowed from the library?'

'I'll read pretty much anything you put in front of me. In bursts.' He made himself comfortable on the floor, leaning against the bed, his long, sinewy legs stretched out across the rug. In his boxer shorts, with his shirt flapping open, he was the best sight I could ever recall waking up to.

I tilted my head contemplatively. 'You're a good listener, aren't you? I was watching you at the party. You listen more than you talk. Even with total strangers, you seem genuinely interested in what they've got to say.'

'It doesn't come naturally; I've had to train myself not to butt in all the time. But there's value in other experiences. It's what bonds us, as people. The tales we live for real and the ones we make up. All the way back to the campfire, thousands of years ago, and the storyteller holding everyone around it in their thrall.' Wilf shifted on the rug.

I sat up straighter. 'That's very lyrical. Have you ever thought of being a writer?'

'Me?' He grunted and shook his head. 'Nah. Like you said, I'm a better listener. I'd rather curate other people's stories than bleed to get my own down on paper.'

'Like an anthology?'

Wilf shrugged. 'All I know is, I haven't got the imagination to invent characters from scratch or come up with an ingenious plot. I could just about scrape out a thousand words in exams. You can love languages, without being any good at using them in a creative sense. I'm happier admiring other people's craft.'

Something stirred in my subconscious; a memory, a seed. 'How about publishing?'

'What?'

'Perdita. Her husband had his own publishing company. A small independent press. Maybe you could do something like that, rather than tutoring?'

Wilf folded his arms over his chest, and glanced up at me. 'I can't say I've never thought about it. But I wouldn't know where to start. I've never worked in that field. I've always taught, in some form or other.'

'So maybe it's time to reverse that. You could become the student again?'

He didn't respond, just nodded towards the mugs on the bedside table. I picked up the tea. 'Do you want the coffee?'

He shook his head. 'It's not decaf. I thought you might need the caffeine.'

'The tea, then?'

'Hate the stuff. Don't worry, I had some of

your orange juice. And some toast, but your bread was…'

'Inedible? You don't have to be kind about it.' I blew into the mug, and took a couple of tentative sips. 'May I make another observation? You were barely drinking alcohol last night, I noticed.'

'Well… it's a long time since I've been wasted.' He picked lint off his sleeve. 'I don't like the sensation. Among other things.'

My stomach let out an almighty grumble just then, and I writhed with embarrassment. Wilf laughed. 'You need to eat some breakfast, Cara Mia.' He animated himself into a standing position – did the man ever keep still for long? – tilting over just enough to kiss my head. 'You need your sustenance, and there are three eggs left in your kitchen; I checked. How about an omelette?'

'A mean one? Yes, please. And it's more like brunch now.' I grew serious. 'Won't they be missing you next door?'

He stretched, curving his back, filling the room as much as ever. 'Probably. But Des and the girls aren't going to care. They're not against us. The opposite, in fact.'

'JoJo, though…'

Padding into the kitchen, he threw me a dry look over his shoulder. 'My sister needs to understand, I've got my own life and so do you. We're both adults.'

I stared at him from the bed, drinking my tea

as he clattered around. 'What's changed, Wilf?' I asked, when he brought me his masterpiece, on a shabby old tray I kept down the side of a cupboard.

'Changed?'

'To make you risk this? Unless...' I remembered what I'd said to him the evening before, part way through the party. About it being a one-off. I'd got so caught up in everything, somewhere along the line I'd let myself believe it could be more. The beginning. Not the start and the end, rolled into one. 'I'm not implying last night meant anything. I know I let you off the hook before we even—'

'I didn't let *you* off the hook, though.' He knelt beside the bed again. 'And I didn't let myself off, either. I think it's too late, for both of us.'

'Translate that into English for me... Please?' I waited breathlessly.

He leaned closer, over the tray. 'I'm saying I see constellations of stars in your eyes, Cara Mia Shaw. And as certain as I can be of anything right now, it's going to take me a very long time to map them all.'

I stared at his beautiful, rugged face as I absorbed his words, and a strange feeling tingled through me.

'Oh,' I whispered, then louder: 'So, you're not torn any more?'

He threaded his hand through mine, examining them together, intertwined. 'I wouldn't have let anything happen last night, if I was. I'm torn about a lot of things still, Cara. But you're definitely not one of them. And I'm ready to see where *this* goes. If you want that, too.'

'I'd like that.' I nodded. 'I'd like that more than anything... except perhaps this omelette.' My eyes flicked to the plate.

Wilf snorted. 'There's no romance in your soul. You just want me for my cooking.'

'If you let me replenish my strength, I might be able to remind you what else I want you for.'

He set my hand swiftly back on the tray, and raised his eyebrows. 'How long do you need?'

'Long enough for you to make a start on the washing-up.' I looked towards the kitchen, and the small pile of dirty dishes that had built up over the last few days.

'You're a hard taskmaster.' He scrambled to his feet. 'But you've got a deal.'

It was time for me to say goodbye to Perdita. I didn't want to, though, as if she was close family and I knew I might never see her again. But I wouldn't admit my fear aloud. I merely insisted she had to come back to the village soon. To Riverside.

'You won't forget me, Cara.' Perdita patted my hand. 'I've a feeling you'll forget some of the things I *said*. Although possibly not the essence.'

'I won't forget anything.' I sniffed, a mix of emotions ballooning in my chest. 'Honestly. But this started out as the best day, and now it feels like the worst.'

She smiled; something bittersweet and ominous about it, though. 'I'm glad that things seem to be working out with your Wilf. I knew the dress would do the trick.'

Heat suffused my face. 'You could put it like that, but I won't go into details.'

I'd already thanked her for the gift, by phone the day I'd received it and finally in person this afternoon, when I'd turned up at Riverside.

Perdita pursed her lips before crumpling into laughter. 'I don't need to know. But it's refreshing to see you so happy.'

'It would have been nice if he could have come here to meet you. But it's the last day of the Christmas market. He'd already arranged to take Belle and Vicki. They're meeting friends. And apparently Des is whisking JoJo off somewhere special…' I tailed off.

Wilf had finally left the hovel around half-one. He'd wanted me to join him and the girls, but appreciated how much I wanted to see Perdita before she left. Besides, I didn't want to rub it quite so explicitly in JoJo's face.

Here you go. I finally did the deed with your precious brother. More than once. And now we're inseparable.

It was disconcerting to admit that I understood how she felt. There seemed to be some unspoken societal rule that I should have secured her permission, and it was JoJo's right to turn against me now because she'd once claimed to trust me above all the females in her inner circle.

Wilf couldn't see this, though. He was quite vocal about it; sick of playing adolescent games, at his age. His sister needed to accept he could make his own decisions, his own mistakes. Except, according to him, I was so far from being a mistake I was the only right thing he'd ever done. (I asked him to rephrase that if he felt the need to repeat it to anyone, because, with his interest in language, surely he could see the problem.)

'Families.' Perdita sighed, as if she'd worked out what I'd been trying to say. 'It's all too easy to fall out. To let things fester. And sometimes, rifts can widen until there's no bridging them, however much you want to.'

I thought of my grandmother, buried in some family vault in Verona. Or, at least, that was how I imagined it. A clan I would never be a part of. 'People can be stubborn, though. You might want to reconcile with them, but they won't let you forgive them, and they won't forgive you back.'

'No.' Perdita spread her fingers on the table, staring at her stubby nails varnished in a festive red. She'd asked me to paint them for her. Her hands shook too much, she couldn't do it herself. 'But sometimes, the most obstinate of people turn out to be the ones you least expect.' Her eyes were suddenly pinned to mine. 'Don't let that happen, Cara. Don't let your parents' history repeat itself.'

I stared at her, confused. 'Sorry?'

'I've a feeling… a suspicion… that you might find yourself facing a decision soon, where the easier option might be to run away. To turn your back on everything here, and start again. But I think – from my perspective, my humble viewpoint – running would be a mistake.' She twirled a finger around a wispy lock of white hair that had come loose from her chignon. 'I had to make a decision like that once. And I'm thankful every day that I didn't flee. That I stayed to fight it out.'

I knew it was no good to ask for specifics. Perdita liked her riddles. They weren't disguised as conventional riddles, I'd realised, but when I tried to unravel them afterwards on my own, there was always another strand of mystery that I couldn't get to.

'My mother had to run, though,' I reminded her softly. 'She was too involved. Too in love with my dad, not to.'

'And she had to live with her regrets, and die with them, too.' Perdita reached across the table and clasped my arm. 'I'm sorry, my dear. I didn't mean it to sound so harsh. In her case, it was probably a losing battle. It sounds to me as if your grandmother was far too inflexible, turning her back on you and your mother when your poor mum was fragile enough already. But who knows the battles your grandmother was waging inside her own head. Sometimes, we have to give people the benefit of the doubt.'

'What if it's toxic, though? The relationship? What if it was never equal from the start?'

'Ah. Well. If the other person won't admit their faults, if they keep inflicting pain… it's well within your rights to step away. They have to be genuine, too, if they ask for help. You can't keep giving it, only for them to cast it aside as if it's nothing.'

'But it's hard to know the difference.'

'It can be.'

There was a curious melancholy creeping over me, and although at first I'd put it down to Perdita leaving and having to say goodbye to her, it seemed to be coming from somewhere else, too. I couldn't get JoJo out of my head now. The way she'd been acting lately troubled me, and my happiness over Wilf was becoming less shiny and defensible the more I thought about it.

'We go through life too complacently,' said Perdita. 'Convinced we know so much. But there's always so much more to learn, about ourselves, as well as others. My children, for instance – the ones I gave birth to, and the ones I fostered – they opened up my world beyond measure. I learned things I hadn't ever considered before. Even when everything was difficult, I never found it limiting. It was all about expanding my mindset. Never shoehorn someone into your life, Cara, and get angry with them if they don't fit properly. Just make your own life bigger, to accommodate them.' Perdita pushed a box of tissues across the table. 'And that's all I have left to say, my dear.'

Wiping my snotty nose, I nodded. 'I'm going to miss this. Chatting with you. And your pearls of wisdom… whether I asked for them or not.'

I couldn't resist glancing round the cosy kitchen, drinking it in, inhaling the atmosphere. The laughter infused in the gently fading paintwork. The trace of cinnamon in the air, from the biscuits Perdita had baked. The love, the joy, even the pain and chaos of her life, scratched into the old table.

Her family were coming tomorrow to pick her up; take her to… *wherever* for Christmas. She'd never said exactly. I'd put that down to her age, as well as her love of riddles, but now I wondered if it was simply that she didn't want to tell me. No names, no concrete facts, as if it was too private to share. After all, I was still just an outsider. This house, her family, her world… it had nothing to do with me. I'd been given a glimpse – and a vintage dress – and I would have to content myself with that.

As we said our final goodbyes, though, she gave me back the library books I'd borrowed on her behalf, and I bundled myself in my outdoor gear for the long trudge through the village, sensing the old woman's sadness irrefutably echoing mine. Perdita was feeling this parting as intensely as I was.

She clutched me with a strength and a fierceness I wouldn't have expected from someone so frail, as she hugged me for the last time. 'Believe in yourself from now on, Cara, my dearest. And fly.'

'I'll try,' I said, tears swelling behind my eyes again. 'But only because you told me to.'

Chapter 27

I hadn't expected JoJo's car to be parked outside the house when I got back. Wilf had borrowed it to drive the girls into town, and it seemed early for them to be back. As I was about to unlock the front door to the annexe, the main door to the house flew open and Wilf stepped out, but the smile on my face instantly dissolved at the expression on his.

'Cara – I've been on the look-out. I would have called, but I knew you were with your friend.'

'What's wrong? Has something happened with the girls?'

'Don't worry, Belle and Vicki are fine. It's JoJo.'

'Wasn't she with Des?'

'That didn't go so well. She's here now, and the girls are with their friends. Des will bring them home. Listen, I think I'm going to need your help.' He moved back into the house, making way for me.

But I didn't budge. 'I must be persona non grata right now, though…'

'No more than I am.' Wilf tipped his head, staring at the lintel. 'She's as much afraid of losing you over all this, as me.' He met my gaze again, almost accusing, blaming. 'You're her crutch, Cara. You've propped her up for years. And maybe that's ableist language, and I'm sorry, but it's all I've got right this minute.'

I forced myself to move, brushing past him as I strode into the house, catching his warm citrussy scent, which was now on my pillows, my duvet. The memory of his hands on my skin swirled through me, heating me up in an instant. But we didn't even greet each other with a kiss. As I unwound my scarf and pulled off my hat and gloves, Wilf gave me a hurried, acerbic rundown of what had happened.

It seemed Des wasn't having an affair. It was a mid-life crisis of a different variety. Or maybe that was unfair and derogatory, Wilf shrugged. His brother-in-law had just had enough of living in JoJo's shadow. 'I'm over-simplifying,' he said, 'but you need to have some basic idea of what's going on. That restaurant or bar or whatever, the one you saw him going into when you were with JoJo? He wants to buy into the business. And Alyson's new boyfriend just happens to own it. Des took JoJo there this afternoon, to meet this guy, to explain… Let's just say it didn't go well. They had a bust-up, and JoJo ended up ringing me.'

'So you brought her home, and Des stayed in town?'

'That's the gist of it.'

'Where is she?' I looked around, as Loki came bounding from the depths of the house, spinning with his usual fervour before flipping on to his back, a puddle of cream and ginger fur at my feet. I rubbed his tummy, then straightened. The dog flipped back round again and wagged his tail.

'Upstairs,' said Wilf. 'I can't get her to calm down. The drive back here was hell.'

'I'm sorry.' I dumped my coat and backpack on a chair. 'Is this our fault? Is she taking it out on Des because she's angry with *us*?'

Wilf flexed and unflexed his hands rhythmically, staring off to the side, more agitated than I'd ever seen him. But then again, I'd only known him for a tiny portion of his life so far. How was it I felt such a claim over him?

'She's pissed off with the entire population of the planet right now,' he said. 'I don't know how to get through to her.'

I slid off my boots. 'Come on, then. We're not achieving anything just standing here.'

Wilf went first, and I shut the stairgate behind me. Loki's gaze followed us, his tail dropping disappointedly. I sympathised, my own spirits plummeting with every step.

JoJo was in her room, a vast expanse of cream and rose gold. Leaning against the chenille-upholstered headboard, her knees pulled up to her chest, tapping into her phone, she was still in the outfit she'd probably worn to go out:

a long, sable-coloured skirt and metallic silk top, bangles jangling on both wrists. Tears had cut grooves in her make-up. Piteous and beautiful at the same time, she barely acknowledged us as Wilf approached the bed.

'What are you doing, Jo?' He spoke soothingly, eyeing her phone. 'I switched that off for a reason. You don't need it right now. We're going to sit and talk.'

'But my followers need to hear this. They have to know the truth. It's about time everyone knew. Isn't that what you think, Wilfred – that I should stop lying by omission? Let them see everything. Warts and all.'

'Damn, Jo...' He lunged for the phone, and managed to snatch it away. 'What are you trying to post?' His face turned ashen. 'Did you...? No. You haven't shared yet.'

'Let me do it.' She made a grab for it, but Wilf stepped back.

'Not like *this*. I think you could do good, Jo, if you're honest and open about it. But not this way. Not with this photo, this status. It's uncontrolled. Irresponsible.'

JoJo seemed to notice me then, hovering between the bed and the doorway, and narrowed her eyes as she addressed me. 'Here to gloat, are you? Tell me how you feel differently about him, too, compared to everyone else you've dated? Rub my face in how deliriously happy you both are and how, this time, against the odds, it's going to work out. You're not going to rip each other to shreds and ruin all our lives in the process.'

The colour was leaching from Wilf's face unnervingly fast now. 'Jo, don't do this. You said you wouldn't.'

'I said I wouldn't, what? You shouldn't lie to her, Wilfred.'

'I'm not. But you've made my life, my story, so much a part of yours – I can't extricate myself. Give me a chance to do this right.'

'Poor little Cara…' JoJo turned to me again, her eyes flashing absinthe fire.

'Please, Jo,' said Wilf, a hoarse, begging note in his voice. 'Don't.'

I had no idea what they were talking about. I felt as if I were inside a bell jar, looking out: JoJo's bedroom muffled and distorted. As if I were nothing but an experiment, and couldn't breathe because they were sucking out all the air between them.

JoJo swung back to him. 'She deserves the truth.'

'From *me*, Jo. Yes. And if you'd gone public about it before, it wouldn't even be a thing. You've made this so much more than it had to be.'

'You told Zoe, though. You trusted her enough to tell her when you first met. Like I trusted Des.'

'And I trust Cara.' Wilf twisted JoJo's phone around in his palm, his voice thready. 'But you claim she's your *friend*, Jo. You made her indispensable to you. And you should have been the one to trust her a long time ago, so don't put this on me.'

I summoned my own voice at last. It felt as if I were trying to speak from inside the bell jar, though. As if they might not hear me.

'What are you both talking about? I don't understand. Wilf, please…?' I stared at him, imploring him to look me in the eye. But he wouldn't.

'Our ADHD, Cara,' snapped JoJo, as if her patience had worn so thin she couldn't control it.

'What?' I looked from one to the other, shaking my head.

'Attention deficit hyperactivity disorder,' JoJo ploughed on, over-articulating each syllable. 'Courtesy of our wonderful dad, although it was never official with him, just retrospective. I guess he tried to make up for it by leaving us each a shed-load of cash. Which was nice of him, I suppose. Dear Daddy. Such a screw-up, he couldn't decide between the two women in his life, so he just kept both, and forced them to get on so Wilfred and I could grow up together. One big happy family.'

'Shit.' Wilf was rubbing his brow, his head hanging so low I couldn't see his face.

'I still don't…' I turned back to JoJo; helpless and confused.

'Oh, you must have heard of it, Cara? You

know what it is?'

'ADHD? Of course I've heard of it.'

I'd known a couple of kids in my secondary school diagnosed with it; boys who couldn't keep still, who were always answering back. Fidgets and loudmouths. And yes, I knew there was more to it than that, but I'd never had the need to delve deeper. A few characters on TV; the odd celebrity; some social media 'awareness' posts… the extent of my knowledge as a casual observer. I felt a paroxysm of shame that I was so clueless, so… judgey. And then shame was replaced by something close to anger. And hurt. I felt hurt.

'Wilf,' I said quietly, 'why didn't you tell me?'

He didn't answer. JoJo was doing all the talking now. And loving it.

Oozing smugness, she flicked back her hair. 'My darling brother takes meds for his. Has since the early days. School was a total nightmare for him, until he got diagnosed. And then, when everyone finally woke up and realised I was similar, in a lot of other ways, Dad had me diagnosed, too. Do you know how hard it was, though, for anyone to take us seriously. A *girl*, with *ADHD*? Doing fine at school by comparison: intellectually, socially – as far as appearances went, at least. All the research, the criteria, was so skewed towards boys. Still is, to a degree. But I've managed without medication—'

'You call this managing?' Wilf jerked his head up, his eyes dark, bruised by her words.

'I've made a success of my life, sweetie, unlike you. I've fed off it. Not the reverse. I wouldn't have the business, this house, *anything*. That was always the difference between us. Even with the meds, you let it rule your life. Why d'you think Zoe didn't want kids with you? Why she went and got knocked up by someone else? You're not the best poster boy for how to control it. You're capable of *so* much, my darling, but you just take the easy route, every single time. Anything to get by without having to try.'

Wilf swore again, and tossed JoJo's phone on the bed. 'You know what, Jo – just post that. Post what you damn well like. But if you handled this right, maybe through one of the better charities, you could be one of the major advocates out there. I've always said it. But you've been so scared of rejection. Your mum couldn't handle it, so you think everyone's going to react the same way. And you're ashamed of it, of *us*; so I've hidden it in my own life as much as possible, too. Even from my own nieces. Just for you. And now – now you throw it back in my face…' His voice cracked.

I wanted to reach out, hold him, but my legs wouldn't move.

Why wouldn't they move?

Because I felt stung. Lied to. And yet Wilf hadn't lied. He just hadn't told me – *yet*. But he'd wanted to… hadn't he? He'd wanted to talk. About this? Or was there more to come?

JoJo snorted. 'Between your mum, Cara, and Wilfred's genes, your kids wouldn't stand a chance… Poor little sods. At least Belle and Vicki were spared. They get to fit in. They don't have to pretend they're normal or as good as their friends. Because this is another reason I don't get to have any. *Friends.*'

She smiled at me, so tautly, it looked as if her lips might snap. 'Not only am I just too successful no one wants to be around me just for *me*, I'm also the most destructive person you're likely to meet. Aren't I? Just look at me. Can't keep my mouth shut. My brain's going at a hundred miles an hour one-hundred percent of the time, and yet it's still like a sieve. And it knows when it's doing wrong, but it just can't unstick itself.'

'Jo—' Wilf tried to interrupt, but she cut in again.

'The simple truth is, I love you both. Because *yes*, you're family in my eyes, Cara, even if this is the first time I've said it properly. Yet here I am pushing you away, and tearing you and my brother apart, because I can't help myself. You need to face it, though. You both do, sooner rather than later. Whatever this thing is between you, it doesn't come without a price, and maybe it isn't worth it.'

She stopped talking at last, and slumped against the headboard as if she were an inflatable toy and someone had let out all the air. A deathly silence took over.

Wilf shook his head. 'I can't do this, Jo. I can't do this any more.' His voice, his entire manner, broken.

As he headed for the door without looking at me, I wanted to step into his path. Block his exit. But my socks were glued to the plush carpet. At the end of the day, I didn't know what I was supposed to say. My feet were stuck for a reason. Time stood still. I heard a door slam.

JoJo and I blinked at each other, and then she picked up her phone. 'I'm deleting, not posting. Don't worry,' she said, almost slurring now. 'Wilfred's right. I should do this properly. Be a force for good.'

'I don't know enough about it,' I admitted dully, after she put the phone down again. 'The medication he's on… How it affects him…'

'It's a complex condition. But if you're serious about this, Cara, you need to find out all you can about it. How best to support him. Anything less won't be enough. So – now you see why I'm so protective? The two people I care about most, after Des and the girls, and you might just end up destroying each other. How am I meant to be happy about that?'

'I… I'm not going to destroy him.' I spoke softly, shaking my head. 'You're being dramatic.'

She smiled again as if her lips might snap. 'Then why haven't you gone after him?'

I closed my eyes for a second.

'Exactly, Cara. This is how it starts. He should

have told you. It shouldn't have had to come from me.'

'He wanted to tell me, I think.'

'But he didn't. And you might convince yourself it's no big deal, but this is his whole wiring we're talking about. His neurological make-up. It doesn't define him, whatever that means, but it's too much a part of him to hide from you. He still tried, though.'

My temples were starting to throb, a headache not far behind.

'If you leave us now, Cara... this family... there'll be a void larger than you realise. Why do you think I wanted you to stay when you were thinking of going back to Manchester? We still needed you. And you needed *us*, even if you didn't know it. You had friends here in Pebblestow. And Des, the girls, and me – possibly the nearest thing to a family that you were going to know again. So when you got upset about moving away, I took the opportunity. I gave you the annexe. It wasn't much, but it kept you in the village. It kept you close to us. After everything you'd been through... it was the least we could do.'

My legs were starting to shake. I sank on to the end of the bed. 'I was more than "upset" back then...' I'd crumbled under the pressure of pushing everything down inside me, the good and the ugly, and denying it for so long. 'You paid for my therapy. I still owe you for that.'

She let out a shrill, terrible laugh. It might have been a cackle worthy of any Disney villain, but she wasn't a wicked stepmother or an evil queen. JoJo was a million things, at once. But she wasn't wicked or evil.

'You don't owe me anything, Cara. We all owe *you*. And, yes, I'm furious with my brother. Because I didn't think you were his type at all, and he had to go and prove me wrong. And I'm angry with you, for letting him get so close. And most of all, I'm probably angry with myself, for dissing on everyone. Including Des.'

She pulled her knees up to her ample chest again. Exhaustion slurred her words a little more. 'He just wants his own "thing". I know that. I get it. He's been there for me all these years, by my side, and now I can't be there for him. And I don't know how to change that. I love Des; but, Cara… how do I show it?'

'I don't know,' I said after a while, a darkness, like a mist, spreading through me. Pride or vanity or fear. Whatever it was, I let it condense and solidify. 'Maybe you just let Des do what he needs to right now. If it's harmless, why hold him back?'

I took a breath, and kept it in for a couple of beats before releasing it. My head spun, then settled.

'Are you going to hear Wilfred out?' JoJo pushed hair out of her eyes.

'When he wants to talk, I'll listen. Of course I

will.'

'But not just yet. If he's shut himself in his room, or gone out again – that means he's not ready. Trust me, Cara.'

Trust me.

In that moment, I wasn't sure I trusted anyone. Not even myself. Still, I stood up again, checking my legs were steady, and stared down at the woman on the bed. Employer? Sister? Friend? Some kind of mother figure, even though she was only about to turn forty?

I might never know how to think of her.

'I'll make you a camomile tea, Jo.' I sighed. 'And then you probably ought to get some rest.'

Chapter 28

The café was quiet, empty of customers at this hour. As I approached the door, Polly was on her way out, flipping the sign to 'Closed'. Her smile, when she saw me, was the equivalent of a hug.

I wasn't part of her gang – too old and boring to fit in – yet she always made me feel closer than just a colleague. A gift, I realised, appreciating it for the first time. A warmth, infecting everyone around her. Like someone else I knew…

My heart pinched. I wanted so much for Perdita to still be here. I badly needed to talk to her. I'd even tried her on her mobile, reluctantly. She had to be busy with her own family now, and I hated the idea of intruding on their time together. But it went straight to a recorded voice, anyway, asking me to leave a message, and at that point I ended the call. I didn't know how much to say in a voicemail, or just as vitally, how much to leave out.

'Are you feeling better, Cara?' Polly might be

an exuberant personality, and forever gadding about (compared to me), but she put her all into every interaction, however brief.

I nodded. Even swaddled by a thousand layers of clothing, though, I was still frozen. I hadn't warmed up since yesterday when I'd returned to the annexe on my own and with no appetite for food, collapsed on the bed, utterly depleted. I'd grabbed a pillow, hugged it, but his scent had faded.

Now I was here at Sallie's because I didn't know where else to go. I hadn't spoken with Wilf or any of the Pembrokes today. All I'd had was a text, which Wilf seemed to have sent in the middle of the night.

—I can only guess how you're feeling. And I'm sorry. I wanted to tell you myself. You shouldn't have found out the way you did. Let me know if/when you want to talk.

I hadn't been able to respond yet, because he sounded almost business-like, and I still didn't know where to start. Besides, peeking through a crack in the curtains first thing, at the sound of an engine starting up, I'd seen him drive off in Des's car rather than JoJo's. And by the time I left the hovel that afternoon, it was almost dusk and he still wasn't back.

Polly peered at me now, her smile wavering. 'You sure you're okay?'

'I'll be fine,' I said unconvincingly, and spotted Sallie coming out from the kitchen, to clear up the counter. 'If I don't see you before Christmas, Polly, have a good one.'

She nodded, her brow crinkling. 'You too, Cara. Take care, okay?' She trudged off, and I pushed the door open to the café, nearly buckling with emotion at the tinkle of the bell overhead.

Sallie looked up, surprise and maybe cynicism arching her dark blonde eyebrows. Nevertheless, I had to throw myself on her mercy. When all was said and done, she'd been right. Even if she hadn't been spot-on about Greg, she'd accurately predicted the perils of my attraction to Wilf and where it might lead.

'Cara… hey.' She put down her tray, and dithered for an instant, before fishing in her apron and pulling out her phone. She swiped and tapped, held it to her ear. 'Nushrat – she's here… at the café. Are you free? Right… okay… see you soon.' Sallie slid the phone into the pocket of her apron again.

And then abruptly, she crossed over to me with three long strides, and gathered me into her arms.

'Oh, my lovely, I'm so sorry,' she babbled. 'We're all so, so sorry. Nushrat and me. And Laurence. I spoke to him at lunchtime. We were going to come and see you this evening, but you've beaten us to it.'

I extricated myself, momentarily lost for words. The ones I'd had, all lined up in a well-rehearsed speech, felt redundant now.

'Come and sit down, Cara, hun. I'll clear up later. Do you want a coffee or a tea? Some cake? You look a bit peaky. How about a hot chocolate, extra cream?'

I pulled off my hat and shook out my hair, staring around the café as if I hadn't been here in years. I felt as if I'd aged a lifetime. Sallie was leading me towards a table by the wall, but I resisted, and instead, went over to the one at the back. The table Perdita had liked to occupy. And as if attempting to channel some of the old woman's strength and unflappability, I sat in the chair she'd always used, with a view of the entire café.

'Oh, you want to sit over here?' Sallie continued. 'That's fine. Whatever. Are you sure I can't get you—'

'May I have a mocha, please?'

Sallie screwed up her nose, unsure. 'Do you like mocha?'

'I like coffee and I like hot chocolate. And I fancy trying something new. I've served enough of them to customers.'

'Daring.' She winked.

'It's just a beverage. Hardly life-changing. Maybe I've been stuck in my ways too long.'

Sallie nodded, the cheekiness evaporating. She fussed around getting my drink ready, while I traced the squares on the gingham tablecloth with a short red fingernail. I'd painted mine the same day as Perdita's, to match hers. Festive and bright. A different shade from my favourite. The rest of me had reverted to my usual greys and blacks, though. After the red dress, I seemed to want to preserve the person I'd been that night, not mock her by trying to be something I couldn't sustain. And yet, sitting here in Perdita's spot, I felt oddly empowered again.

Sallie eventually came over with a large mug, but hesitated before putting it in front of me.

'What's wrong?' I said.

'Nothing. I don't know. Just this weird sense of déjà vu. Seeing you sitting there… like she did. Perdita.'

'Oh,' I murmured, basking in the thought, the way I'd basked in the old woman's smile. 'That's nice. Aren't you having anything yourself?'

'No, I'm fine.' Sallie pulled out the chair opposite. 'Nushrat's on her way; she was only doing a half day today, so she was at home. She won't be long. The library's shutting for the holidays now.'

I nodded. 'Sallie—'

'Cara—'

We both spoke at the same time, and dissolved into awkward laughter.

'I'm sorry,' I said, at last.

'You? What are *you* sorry for?'

Before I could answer, Nushrat burst in. The bell above the door tinkled wildly as she rushed over.

'Cara… did Sal tell you we were going to come see you tonight? I was on the phone with her for ages.'

'Yes, she—' But I was crushed in another hug.

Nushrat released me, took off her coat and pulled up a chair. 'I'm sorry, Cara. For everything. I've been such a cow.'

'I've been the bigger cow,' contested Sallie.

'Oh, I don't know.' Nushrat shook her head. 'You should have heard the stuff I came out with, when Tod saw Cara groping Wilf down by the river.'

'I bet it wasn't as bad as the stuff I said to Laurence, when we were discussing Cara dumping Greg.'

'Hello.' I waggled my hand between them. 'I'm right here. I can hear you both. Every word. And I wasn't "groping" Wilf. It was just a very passionate kiss, that's all.' I tugged at my scarf, not so frozen any more.

'I spoke to Laurence after you rang earlier,' Sallie said to Nushrat, although she cupped her hand over mine on the table, as if reassuring me she knew I was there. 'And he's starting to wonder if Greg liked Cara so much for the simple fact their dates weren't a total disaster. Not that Cara's not lovely, but Laurence is speculating that Greg was clinging to her because he knew he could do much worse.'

'Sal' – I coughed for attention – 'you do realise what you just said?'

'Yes, but listen to this… apparently someone spotted him – Greg – at some pub in town yesterday, with the new girl from accounts. They seemed very cosy; if you know what I mean.'

'Well, that's nice.' I gritted my teeth.

Sallie rubbed her thumb soothingly across my knuckles. 'Don't take it personally. You said yourself he wasn't the man for you.'

'Yes. But...' I shrugged. 'I don't understand them. *Men*.'

'What I don't understand, Cara, is why you didn't tell us how you felt.' Nushrat took my other hand, and I looked wistfully at my mocha, in the mug I could no longer hold.

'Tell you how I felt about what?'

'About JoJo's brother.' Sallie squeezed my knuckles, too hard. 'About Wilf.'

'Ow.'

'Sorry! But why didn't you tell us you were actually in love with him, Cara?'

I fell still. All I could hear was the ticking clock, behind us on the wall. I stared at the steam curling out of my mug. Maybe it would burn my lips. Best to wait a while.

'I'm not in love with him,' I said, knitting my brows. 'I like Wilf a lot, more than anyone I've ever been with. But if anything, over the last twenty-four hours, I've come to realise how much I have to learn about him. And...' I stopped. 'How do you know I'm in love? I mean, why would you even think—'

'Perdita,' said Sallie gently. 'She dropped by this morning. Wanted to say goodbye to me before she left, and take a box of my "famous" mince pies back to her family. And then she told me everything.'

'Everything?' I swallowed.

'We know how close you and Wilf have got.' Nushrat's long, dark lashes fluttered sympathetically. 'We thought he was leading you astray, and you were mucking up your best chance of happiness, with Greg. But now we know. Wilf's *The One*. Not Greg. Not Sid. Not any of the others. Wilf's the one you're meant to be with.'

'Whoa.' I extracted my hands forcefully, and drew the mug towards me, spilling a few drops. 'I'm not sure I'm meant to be with anyone. Whatever Perdita might have told you, she's an utter romantic. She had such a long, happy, successful marriage, she's projecting all that destiny and soulmate stuff on to me and Wilf. But she never even got to meet him. She has no idea what he's like.'

'Well, he's a sweetheart, isn't he?' Nushrat's lashes fluttered a little faster.

'There's no disputing he's hot,' I said, squirming in my chair and batting away recollections of Wilf's hotness that I definitely wasn't prepared to share with anyone.

'I'm not talking about the way he looks; though I admit, it's distracting,' said Nushrat. 'I mean he's so… squishy, isn't he? I just wanted to give him a hug this morning, he looked so miserable.'

'This morning?' I snapped my head round to her. 'You saw Wilf this morning? *Where*?'

'In the library, of course. He was handing in the books he'd borrowed. And then he asked if I was due a break, because he really wanted a word, and so I got Agatha to cover and Wilf bought me a coffee next door. An eggnog latte.' She sighed. I wasn't sure if she was sighing over her favourite drink or the fact Wilf had bought it for her. 'And then he told me how he thought he'd "f"-ed things up with you. I'm not repeating his exact words, because you know I don't swear like that.'

'Pure of mouth, pure of heart,' said Sallie.

'Don't take the mick. But he was so upset, Cara. I mean, *really* upset. Like you'd stamped on his dreams, and set fire to them for good measure.'

My grip tightened on the mug. 'I… I haven't done that.'

'No, I know. I'm just trying to explain how he looked. He said it was his fault, anyway, not yours. Okay, so he didn't go into exact details; but it wasn't another woman, or anything along those lines, unless you counted his sister. He didn't seem too happy with JoJo, I've got to be honest.'

'For a man who looks like he does,' said Sallie, 'it sounds as if he's got serious self-worth issues.'

It sounded to *me* as if he was just going on the offensive. Putting his own case forward first.

Which was sneaky. Underhand—

'He said we shouldn't be taking it out on you, or blaming you for any of what happened,' Nushrat went on. 'Said how bad he felt, watching you try to hide how upset you were over the fact we weren't talking to you. But he'd pursued you, he said. Made it really difficult for you to say no, and he feels really guilty for putting you in that position.'

'But… He gave me every opportunity to say no. And in the end, we were as bad as each other. In fact, the night we actually…' My face was aflame now. 'I was the instigator. So why would he go to you, and humiliate himself like that?' I looked at Nushrat again. 'I don't get it.'

'Because he didn't want to have it on his conscience, that we'd fallen out with you.'

'But mainly because he can't stand to see you hurting, Cara.' Sallie pressed her hand over my arm this time, where she could probably inflict less damage. (My knuckles still ached, though not as severely as my heart.) 'Because it's totally obvious he has strong feelings for you, too.'

My friends insisted on walking me back up Swallowtail Lane, depositing me at the hovel with one last conciliatory hug. Des's car still wasn't back in the drive, and there'd been no further texts from Wilf. Panic and anxiety coiled around my stomach, but I let my friends walk off and didn't mention it. They'd helped enough.

I'd talked with Sallie and Nushrat for almost an hour, finally sharing my provisional plans to return to my art studies. I'd drawn the line at telling them the whole truth about Wilf and JoJo, though. It wasn't in the public domain yet, and I wasn't sure if JoJo would go through with coming out about it, either. Their secret wasn't mine to share.

In an unforeseen way, as a consequence of all this, I grasped with more clarity how my mother might have felt, too. Perhaps her depression was another reason she'd walked out on her family in Italy, and not the outcome of her regret. Was it possible she'd lived with it for years – to her own mother's shame – long before she'd even met my dad? I'd never had the chance to talk about it with Mum, adult to adult. And that was *my* regret: the fact I never would.

I could talk to Wilf, though. I wouldn't let myself regret that, years down the line. In spite of my frustration with him, I hadn't spent a good chunk of the day glued to my laptop researching his condition, just to turn my back on him now. But the impulsive nature of it... what if he'd done something silly or rash?

Closing the door on Sallie and Nushrat, I dug out my phone from my pocket and sent Wilf an overdue message.

—I'm sorry I didn't reply sooner. There was a lot to think about. Where are you? Are you OK?? I'm worried about you! And I'm ready to talk as soon as you get back.

I waited, holding my breath as if he'd send me an instant response. But when he didn't, I breathed with some semblance of normality, hung up all my outer gear and went to the fridge to pour myself a glass of rosé. Probably a bad idea, but I couldn't talk myself out of it. Food still didn't appeal. I'd never lost my appetite over a man before; not even Sid. It was something other people did, when romance threw lemons at them and they were too diminished to make lemonade.

After a while of fidgeting restlessly with the edge of my crocheted blanket, I put down the glass on the coffee table and picked up my laptop again.

There was something else I'd tried researching, the other day, although I hadn't got very far. I followed every tenuous link on Google again now, but I still couldn't find any trace of Perdita Rivers the textile designer. Or Riverside House Press. My search threw up other results, but nothing that seemed to be connected to Perdita or her husband. Though I didn't even know his first name. Or their surname. After all, she'd said 'Rivers' had been derived from the house.

I reached for a tissue.

Damn it, Cara, why are you blubbering again?

Because an old woman wanted her privacy?

Or because you feel excluded?

As far as I knew, everything Perdita had told me was true, and I couldn't imagine she would have been left on her own by her children in that large house if they'd felt she wasn't in her right mind.

What if it was all a flight of fancy, though? Her whole life. The picture she'd painted in my mind. The beautiful chaos. What if none of it was true?

Why was I getting so carried away, imagining the worst? After Christmas, I would ask around the village, prod people's memories. I'd had no reason to doubt Perdita before, and I didn't now – except for my own paranoia – but there had to be some tangible proof somewhere to substantiate what she'd told me. Church records of her marriage, for one; although without an exact date, or their full names, where would I begin?

Even if Perdita and her husband had lived like hermits, not that this seemed likely, some of the older villagers ought to have known about them. And yet... Perdita had always sat in the café alone, when I wasn't with her, and there'd been plenty of elderly customers coming and going who'd been residents of Pebblestow for years...

I shook my head, wiped my eyes, sipped my wine. She'd said her friends were gone. It wasn't impossible for her to have sat there, unrecognised. I didn't know how long she and her family had been renting Riverside out as a holiday home, for a start. All she'd implied was that looking after such a large property had become unworkable for her and her husband as they'd grown older. But someone, somewhere around here, would surely know the family's name…?

Perdita's tales had spun so evocatively in my head – despite a lack of explicit detail – now that she wasn't here to spin them any longer all I had was an increasing list of questions. And I dearly wanted to talk to her about Wilf. There was something she'd said, about her husband, his dazzling mind… I felt she might appreciate where I was coming from. Might have something to offer, to help me approach the subject the right way. I knew I would put my foot in it, it was inevitable; but I needed Wilf to understand that I didn't want to be tactless or insensitive. I'd only been able to research the tip of a huge iceberg today, but it was a first step.

When I went to bed that night, he still wasn't home, although by then I knew why. The wine had dulled the panic, yet my stomach was still a tense, hard knot of worry. A couple of hours ago, I'd gone across to the games room and put a wash on, knowing I'd likely run out of underwear if I didn't. Belle had been hanging out with a friend, scoffing pizza in front of the TV. I'd thought she wouldn't say much in front of the other girl, but…

'He'll be back Christmas Eve,' she'd announced, as I clicked the door shut on the washing machine.

I'd looked over. Belle had regarded me with large, doleful eyes over the arm of the sofa.

'Back…?' I'd said. 'From where?'

'Bristol. He drove this time. Took Dad's car.'

'Oh.'

'Are you over at ours Christmas Day, Cara? Like usual?'

I'd sighed grittily, sick inside. But she was old enough to warrant an honest answer. 'I don't know, Belle. We'll have to see.' And I'd sloped back to the annexe.

Finally, gone midnight, I heard from Wilf. I wasn't asleep, so the 'choo-choo' didn't wake me. My hand scrabbled for my phone on the bed as I dragged myself upright.

—Cara I'm so sorry. Your message only just came through or I would have answered sooner. I know I just left without telling you but I couldn't face JoJo. I needed space to breathe. I didn't know what to say to you either and you needed time to weigh up everything too. I'll be round as soon as I get back. I'm in Bristol BTW.

Before I could even draft my reply, another message arrived.

—I need you to know I can't stop thinking about you. About us. Whatever happens, as far as I'm concerned there was always an us.

'Exquisite use of a comma, Mr Brooks,' I whispered into the empty room, before flopping back against my pillows, the phone clutched to my chest.

Chapter 29

Upside down, inside out, back to front. The music I couldn't unhear. Was that really the real thing? I hadn't been able to admit it out loud to Sallie or Nushrat. It still felt too much of a whirlwind. Examining it rationally, Wilf and I were simply two small people (*literally*, on my part), swept up in some big feelings at a crossroads in both our lives when big feelings could only be a hindrance.

But was that one of the reasons we'd latched on to each other this way? To distract ourselves from making critical decisions about the future, because deep down we were both scared of getting it wrong? Of choosing the wrong path. Even if making love had actually felt like making love, for once – at least for me. Even if I now understood the emotional connection of the act, rather than just the physical… It didn't mean this thing with Wilf was going to survive beyond the first flash of brilliance.

I couldn't deny that in years to come, I might

always look back on this December and remember it as nothing less than miraculous and life-changing. But was it just an interlude? A stop-over on a journey where, sooner rather than later, Wilf and I would be going our separate ways?

What if we were never meant to be the destination?

Without Perdita around to fill my head with possibilities and wonders, stark reality was taking her place. By the time Wilf turned up at my door on Christmas Eve, just after lunch – not that I ate much of it – I was so fogged up with misery I didn't have the capacity to explain how I'd been feeling in his brief absence, or how I felt now that he was back. And he didn't seem to have the words, either.

We just somehow fell into an embrace, and then, still without talking, into bed. There was something so final about it. Even snatching at pleasure, there was pain we couldn't smother, and afterwards we lay in a tangle under my duvet, heads touching and hearts splintering. I knew something horrible might be around the corner. I was simply trying to delay it.

'Do you want to go for a walk?' he suggested, waking me up from a restless doze where I'd lost all sense of time. 'I feel like I need to keep moving while we talk. I don't want to sit around.'

Dusk was already falling as we left the annexe and headed out into Swallowtail Lane. It didn't matter who saw us together now, not that it should have mattered before. Pebblestow lay spread out below in all its Yuletide glory; windows beginning to glow or glimmer; the lights strung above Market Square blinking frenetically. But it was ages since I'd felt this drained of Christmas spirit, as if it could be any other season, rather than the one I'd loved most as a child. Walking hand in hand with Wilf, I knew this Christmas Eve had the potential to be either the best or one of the worst. It was the not knowing which, that made it so tragic.

As we neared the fringe of the village and hedgerow gave way to rough stone walls, he spoke at last, almost tripping over his words.

'Cara, listen. I viewed a flat. In Bristol. My friend Aaron found it. He knew I might be interested.'

My hand peeled away from Wilf's. This was the first time I'd even heard his friend's name. It made the announcement more real, more immediate.

'It's everything I could want, for the foreseeable,' he continued. 'Ten minutes on foot from the tutoring centre; although I'll be buying a car, for longer journeys. Ground floor. Two bedrooms. There's even a small garden: half-paved, half-lawn. And it's—'

'Close to all local amenities?' I found my voice, too, but hated the serrated edge to it. 'Sounds perfect for you.'

'Cara…' He stopped walking, but resumed when I failed to stop. 'When I went to look at it yesterday, I wasn't just picturing it for me. I was viewing it as a potential place for us.'

Now it was my turn to stop. 'What?'

He turned to face me, fumbling with the zip of his coat, pulling it up to his densely stubbled chin. 'This could be a new start. God knows, we both seem to need it. We'd have to move fast, though, if we want it. It's not cheap, but it's in a prime location—'

'Did you sign anything?'

His brows pulled together. 'No. Of course not. How could I? I needed to speak to you first.'

'But still. This isn't so far off from what Greg did. Planning out my life. Do you know what it makes me, Wilf, if I let you get away with stuff I wouldn't have tolerated from him?'

'I'm not… This is an *option*. That's all.'

'If I'm so important to the decision, why did you go on your own?'

'Because…'

'What?' I pressed.

'You needed time to think. Without me getting in the way. JoJo landed a bombshell on you.'

'It was news, but it wasn't a "bombshell" I couldn't have got over, relatively fast. You didn't have to disappear the way you did. And it would have been better coming from you, anyway, at an earlier stage.'

'Because it changes things? Me, having

ADHD, changes everything…?'

I couldn't believe the insinuation behind this. 'Yeah, naturally,' I drawled. 'That's why we spent all afternoon in bed – because I don't want to know you any more, and I obviously think so much less of you now. Hell, *Wilf,*' I scowled, 'is that what you think of me? That I wouldn't be able to deal with it, or wouldn't want to? Is that why you didn't tell me sooner? You accused JoJo of being scared, but you're just as frightened of rejection, too.'

He sighed, his breath feathery, hovering ghost-like in front of his face. 'I was psyching myself up to tell you everything. It's what I wanted to talk about; we just never had the chance. My sister got there first.'

I didn't like the way he said 'sister'. With bitterness. It set off alarm bells.

'You've been hurt before,' I said, fighting to think coherently. 'And let down by people who should have had your back. Zoe, for a start. But this was never going to be a dealbreaker for me. I don't care about the ADHD. Well, no, that's wrong, I *do* care. It's the way your brain is wired, or constructed. It's part of who you are. And I'm ready to hear more, and help any way I can. I've been reading up about it—'

'You have?'

'It's what anyone would do – isn't it? Find out more about something, if it'll help someone they care about. And I know I won't get it right a lot of the time, but I'm…' He was looking at me oddly, half-smiling. 'What?'

'Zoe never bothered. None of my girlfriends made the effort. Too much of a stigma. I was just supposed to take my meds and stop banging on about it.'

'But that makes no sense. Medication alone isn't enough, according to what I've read. It doesn't necessarily help with impulsivity or…' So many things were slotting into place. 'Is that why you thought this might not last? Because it was too sudden, too fast, and maybe just one of those shiny things you'd chased in the past?'

His curls flopped forward as he bowed his head. 'It's a lot to take in, Cara. And I can't say it doesn't still freak me out. But I'm old enough to know when it's different from other times. When it feels *righter* than anything else. I don't want to be like my dad, doing stupid shit to the people he loved. I promised myself I never would.'

'And you haven't.' I moved nearer, peering up into his face, close enough to see a miniscule muscle working in his jaw. 'But you can't just race off and look at flats for us. I mean… we're nowhere near ready to play house like that. And Pebblestow's my home. That's why I couldn't bear leaving it last time. I'm not saying I'll never live anywhere else, just that I don't want to right now. I've got friends here, a job I like. There's even an art course I've found, an hour away by bus. It's part-time, so I can still work. It's just something I wouldn't mind trying. Working with textiles. Not just yarn but fabric. Perdita—'

'There are great colleges around Bristol. I had a quick look online while I was at Aaron's. You could apply as soon as you've had a browse. You could even visit them, if we both go down after New Year. And you can start studying full-time in September; you don't have to restrict yourself to part-time. There'd be nothing stopping you getting a casual job like you have now, either, in the short-term. Or you could just carry on selling the clothes you design, or your upcycled stuff.'

'And what? You'll support us both, if it comes to it?' I stepped back. 'I could go all that way, Wilf… uproot my life here… with no guarantee of being accepted anywhere I might want to study, or finding a job I like as much. And I'd be gambling everything on a relationship that's barely begun. I just…' My voice was hoarser by the second. 'I don't understand the rush.'

He curled his hand, pressing it against his head. 'Right. Okay. I've messed up again. Bristol might as well be the moon, as far as you're concerned.' He stepped back, too, hesitating; then walked away, further into the village.

'It's far enough,' I snapped at his retreating back, pulling a sheepish face seconds later as a family walked past, hunched together against the chill in the air, carrying gift-bags with whirls of red ribbon dangling from the handles. A Mum, Dad, two small kids. I stared after them, and a wrench in my chest told me all I needed to know.

I hurried after Wilf. 'Wait... Please...'

As the churchyard loomed, with the stone wall encircling it, he relented and slowed down.

'Wilf, is working with your friend really what you want to do?' There was an urgency in my tone now. A fresh determination. 'Only, not that long ago, you didn't seem so sure.'

He shoved his hands in his pockets. 'Yes. No. I don't know. But it's something concrete, rather than just...' He shrugged.

'What about the publishing idea? The one we spoke about the other day?'

'I don't know anything about running a business. I'd be on my own. It's a nice pipedream, but —'

'Just think. You could lend a voice to people who need help getting theirs heard. You might do some real good, too, Wilf. In a different way from teaching. Reach people, like JoJo could, if she's open about everything.'

'Yes, but... I wouldn't know where to start. How to go about it...'

'So? You'd learn. If it's something you feel passionate about, wouldn't you be able to hyperfocus and learn faster than most people? Maybe you have friends, or know people from college, who work in publishing now. Even if they're based in Canada, they might be able to give you advice, if you reached out to them.'

He turned and started walking again, but

slower. Glancing over his shoulder, he held out his hand, coaxing me to follow.

'The problem is, Cara… I'm not sure I'm strong enough to stick around *here*. I've never actually lived with JoJo before. We were always close, but we weren't brought up in the same house, like average siblings. And I know she's been over to Toronto for two or three weeks at a time, but it's not the same as living under her roof, by her rules. Being dictated to.'

'But you're not going to live under her roof forever. No one's saying that. This is just temporary. I don't want to live in the annexe the rest of my life, either. Running away to Bristol doesn't have to be the only solution, though. My parents ran, but they had worse than JoJo to contend with. She only disapproves because she thinks this might end badly.'

He opened his mouth, then closed it again, his brow hooding his eyes.

We walked on in silence, reaching the edge of Market Square. Everything was shut for the holidays now, but the leaded panes were still lit up in their cheerful finery, and a few people mingled in the square around the Christmas tree.

'I've not got much of a filter,' Wilf blurted out, as if illustrating his point; pulling us to a stop again in front of a shop window. 'And I hate that. I'm trying to say the right things here. I don't want to sound like I'm giving you an ultimatum. My sister's against us because she knows the dynamics would likely change if you and I got together properly. She's scared of losing you, Cara. She relies on you too much.'

'But...'

'I don't want you to have to put up with that bullshit any more. I've only had to deal with her in small doses. And right now... I'm finding it hard to forgive her. For a lot of stuff. Like how she didn't put Quentin off, or warn you about him. That could have been...' Wilf's wide shoulders sagged, and seemed narrower for it. 'As far as I'm concerned, it feels like she might have gone too far this time.'

Maybe she had. I was angry with JoJo for countless reasons, yet her skin seemed to be stretched thinner than mine right now. So transparent, I could see each of her vulnerabilities laid bare, and how she felt about Wilf and me was one of them. We couldn't pretend it wasn't.

I stared into the shop window without focusing on anything except what I had to say. 'But... is this the right time for you to make a stand? The pressure she's been under, taking JoJo Pem to the next level – it's obviously been too much. And her public life isn't just a stream of adoring devotees, she has to contend with the trolling, too. Plus this thing with Des...'

'Des knows he needs to step up. Negotiate more.' Wilf stood close again, his breath in my hair; it was only then that I noticed I'd forgotten to wear a hat. 'JoJo isn't your responsibility.'

'But she's yours, Wilf. And by default, if we become an item, she's mine, too. And even if we aren't together...' a sharp jab between my ribs at the thought... 'JoJo helped me once. More than once. She's in a bad place right now, and I couldn't turn my back on her without worrying it might trigger something worse.'

'Cara—'

'I can't just leave her there and go off and be happy, Wilf.'

Silence.

As I blinked and focused, I saw we were directly in front of the toy shop. An old-fashioned display crowded the bow window; painted wooden toys, of all shapes and sizes, competing for attention. My eyes paused on a giant nutcracker doll, music from the 'Dance of the Sugar Plum Fairy' instantly filling my head. And then, as if serendipity was guiding it, my gaze fell on something smaller next to it.

With an inward gasp, I turned away from Wilf, pressing my gloved hands to the glass.

Chapter 30

My breath misted the window. I had to step back again for a clearer view.

A carousel. Red and green and gold. Candy canes rising up from snow-white horses with shimmering, dark blue saddles. And a small wooden figure, top half black, bottom half mulberry, tiny arm raised as if waving to me.

'My wish,' I murmured, and felt a warmth stir through me. Wilf came up behind and rested his hands on my shoulders. For a moment, a trick of the light, our reflections in the glass made us look old and wizened. I blinked, and the illusion was gone. I'd looked so different from the Cara I saw in the mirror every day… yet oddly familiar. A mirage. A fantasy. Projecting myself on to Perdita the way she'd projected herself on to me.

'What wish?' asked Wilf, softly.

I hadn't told another living soul. But I found myself telling him, drawing short at the substance of the wish itself, with the excuse it might not come true if I spoke it out loud. Days ago,

I couldn't see how it ever could. Tonight I was wondering if, gradually, without my realising, it already was.

'The carousel looked like that one.' I pointed through the glass. 'And it's just like my snow-globe, although that's plastic.' I told Wilf the story behind that, too. 'Do you believe in this sort of stuff – the universe trying to tell you something?' I wasn't sure I wanted him to answer.

'My mum would have liked me to say yes. She said coincidences happened when you needed to take note, and listen, because the universe couldn't get through to you any other way.' He gestured to the toy shop window. 'And these sort might, perhaps. But not the ones where you google how to stop your trainers from stinking, and days later you're still assaulted by adverts for antibacterial insoles. Mum couldn't quite grasp the difference.'

I grunted. 'Fair enough.'

'If I want to believe in anything' – he urged me gently to face him – 'it's where this could go.'

It wasn't going anywhere if we couldn't agree on one fundamental thing.

Run or stay.

How had Perdita even known I'd have to make this choice? Was it because she'd faced it herself? I couldn't say her advice wasn't influencing me, but it was also the honourable thing to do. It was time for compromise, and healing, however trite that sounded. I wouldn't turn into my grandmother, Sophia Constanza. Stubborn and bitter and too weak to change.

You're stronger than that, Cara.

Regardless of how patched up I might be, the threads that held me together had somehow never felt tighter.

'Wilf, I know where I'm *not* going. And that's down south, even if that's what you decide is best for you. I don't want this to sound like an ultimatum, either, but it probably will. Helping JoJo… it's going to have to be a collective effort. And I can't leave Belle and Vicki, either. They think they're so grown up, but I know what it's like to see your mum disintegrate in front of your eyes.'

'Cara…'

'For years, my one real wish was that my mum could be happy, Wilf. And other than my dad, I didn't have family I could fall back on. I know I'm not technically related to the girls, but I've loved them for so long. They were put in my care; and you were right, I never gave up that responsibility. I thought they didn't need me, but they do. And they're going to need me more if JoJo gets worse before she gets better.'

His chest rose and fell in a sigh that seemed to lose itself in his throat. Wilf stared past me, distractedly fiddling with my hair. 'You're too good for me, Cara Mia,' he muttered at last. 'I've stopped being able to measure how much JoJo cares. All I see is how she controls. And she needs strong people around her, to cut through the crap. I think you might be one of them. I don't think you're going to let her get away with half as much.'

I could sense what was coming. It was already cleaving me in two. 'Wilf...'

'I'm not there yet, Cara. There's a lot I'm going to need to figure out. And I'm not sure how I can do it if I stick around here.'

'It's a small place,' I admitted forlornly. 'A small life. Pebblestow doesn't suit everyone.'

'Life doesn't have to be small here. I'm just not used to the UK, in general, after being away so long. And this village – I confess it's the most... rural place I've ever lived. I'm not saying I hate it, far from it; that isn't why I think I need to leave.'

'I know.' I nodded. 'It's complicated. But you've got a point. You have to consider yourself in all this, too. Your own health. If you think being around JoJo for too long might have a negative impact on you... then maybe you're right to go.'

It killed me to say it, to set him free like that, but if it was the best thing for him, what else could I do? I'd been so caught up worrying about JoJo, and my own conscience, I hadn't fully put myself in his position. He was the best judge of how much he could handle.

'So... I take the easy way out, and you don't?' His voice had such a crack to it. The most plaintive, fragile thing I'd heard come out of his mouth.

'I don't think this is in any way easy for you, Wilf.'

A ricochet of laughter, as a group emerged from the narrow side street of Lovelorn Alley and headed across the square, where the glow of the Tarnished Key beckoned in the still, calm night. Not even the faintest whisper of a breeze. Even though there was talk of a white Christmas in the county, no one was really convinced of it, except for those young enough to believe in Santa.

Here I was, though, believing in something far more abstract. A wish I'd made a few weeks ago. But all the wishes in the world weren't going to save Wilf and me today. We'd reached another impasse.

It might well be the better option for him was to leave Pebblestow, while the best thing for me was to stay. Maybe we were the right people for each other at the wrong moment in time. Or maybe Perdita had turned me into a soppy old mare.

'Cara,' he said raspily, 'I'm sorry.'

'So am I.'

It was a break-up, of sorts, although I couldn't have pinpointed when we'd formally – or even informally – got together. Our lives had collided, against our will at first, it seemed, and it felt now as if I'd known him far longer. An entire lifetime, in some weird and incomprehensible way.

'Damn,' he said, and swiped at his eyes.

That simple gesture set me off, too.

The worst Christmas Eve, second only to the year I'd lost my parents and endured my first December without them.

We stood locked in an embrace for an endless moment, before we both pulled back, coordinated in our distress.

'You're still going to spend tomorrow with the family?' he asked, forehead pleated in concern. 'Everyone wants you there.'

I shrugged, because I honestly didn't know. 'I'm not sure…'

'You don't have to play the martyr and spend it alone. Des and the girls are helping more this year. So they claim.'

'About time, I suppose. But that isn't the reason.'

'I don't have to be there… if that's what's stopping you.'

'Yes, you do, Wilf. JoJo will only blame me if you're not, and that won't make the day any easier. Anyway, I don't have to be on my own. Sallie's invited me to hers.' I looked towards the pub again. 'And they're all meeting at the Tarnished Key this evening, as usual. I think I want to join them. They're probably already there; they always start early.'

Wilf followed my gaze. 'Oh… Right.'

'I don't want to be alone, I think I need my friends around me.'

'I can understand that.'

But I hesitated. 'You could come, too?'

'That would go down well. You and I, at crisis point, dragging the mood down. They'd love me.'

'Well, Nushrat already does. And I know the others would, too, if they got to know you.'

'I can't. I should get back to the house… Make an effort to show my face.'

'That's fine.' I gave him a frail smile. 'It was just a suggestion.'

'How are you getting home afterwards?'

'They walk me back. Don't look like that; they've done it loads of times. You can't get a taxi around here for love nor money on Christmas Eve.'

'You've got good friends in Pebblestow, Cara.'

'They care. Even if they get it wrong sometimes; but that's only human.'

'I can see why you wouldn't want to leave them.'

More laughter erupted in the square. A couple in their forties this time, walking arm in arm towards the pub. I recognised them both. One of our local GPs and her husband of twenty-odd years. Known at the surgery as the chatty one, she'd rabbited on about her wedding anniversary one time, as I'd sat in the consultation hot seat, her eyes continually darting to the lovely new bracelet her husband had given her.

My heart splintered a little more.

'I'll walk you across,' Wilf said.

I turned, and he fell into step beside me. We didn't speak now; there didn't seem much left to say. At the entrance to the pub, as festive music and conversation and high spirits spilled out in a puddle of amber light, Wilf stopped.

'Have a good night, Cara.'

I didn't dare talk, so I just nodded. Perhaps this wasn't such a great idea. In the past, I would have needed to be swept up by noise and alcohol and other people's lives. In a similar way, the jumble of humanity gathered together tonight, and their communal joy and laughter, might displace the penetrating ache inside me, and for a short time I might be able to forget. As if it was that easy...

I already knew as I stepped inside, that I wouldn't find what I needed in a bottle of cheap house wine, the cordiality of strangers and acquaintances, or even the empathy of my closest friends. Not this time.

This time I didn't want to forget *anything*.

I pivoted in the porch and ran back out. 'Wait —'

He jolted to a halt, looking round.

'Wilf... that day... in the games room – what was it you said to me, in Italian?'

He frowned and shook his head. 'I can't remember.'

'Yes, you can. Please don't lie.'

'I said you'd be the death of me.'

'Really?'

'Or that I fancied extra parmesan on my gnocchi. I don't know, for sure. It's been a while since I had to speak it.'

I laughed helplessly. Painfully.

'It was insensitive. I didn't want to tell you.' Wilf shuffled his Doc Martens. 'Cara… why aren't you in the pub?'

'Because I've never been good at just ripping the band-aid off. I'm more into prolonging the agony.'

'So…?'

'So, let's both go back to the house.' I laced my hand through his. 'I think I should show my face, too.'

We walked slowly back across the square, while I texted Sallie to tell her I was otherwise engaged and wouldn't make it to the Tarnished Key. If they'd spotted me walking in and straight out again, one of them would have followed to check what was going on.

As Wilf and I passed the church, I relived the day I'd come here with Perdita, and pictured the honey-coloured, hallowed space flickering to life later for Midnight Mass. Maybe one year I'd get around to going. I missed singing carols like I used to in school. And I imagined the church full of elderly people; couples and families; a few beer-fuelled strays from the pub; and children with sleepy, lolling heads, who would probably spring to life the instant they got home, eager for the tinkle of sleighbells and a glimpse of Rudolph.

Wilf glanced down at me. 'Cara, nothing's different… is it? From before? What we said…?'

'Not this time.' I gripped his hand tighter, dreading the day I'd finally have to let go. 'But however long we've got, I promise with all my heart – we'll be as happy as we can be.'

Chapter 31

I woke to his kiss the following morning, gossamer-soft on my cheek. Wilf hadn't stayed over. I'd gone back to the annexe alone after a subdued, but argument-free dinner prepared by Belle and Vicki. By the sound of it, there'd been a few disputes beforehand as they'd clashed in the kitchen, but by the time we'd all sat down at the lavishly decorated table, the strains of Michael Bublé's Christmas hits playing softly over the Bose speakers, the sisters were wreathed in smiles and best of friends again.

Over a comforting gratin of fresh and smoked salmon, potatoes and dill, with the most delectable crust, Des had showered well-deserved compliments on his daughters, and cast regular solicitous glances at his wife. JoJo had been quiet; scarily beautiful in her neutral linens, offset with lustrous black pearls. She'd looked across the table at Wilf and me, as if trying to suss out what was going on. But we hadn't given much away. When we'd first turned up at the house, Vicki had impishly called me Aunty Cara, but after Des murmured something in her ear neither sister had teased us again.

As the night had drawn to a close, I'd discreetly given Wilf a spare key to the hovel. The first time I'd done that with anyone I'd dated. Even Sid hadn't had the honour of possessing one (and if he had, I would have changed the locks ages ago).

'What time is it?' I slurred now, rubbing my eyes as Wilf perched on the bed.

'Not that early. Everyone's up next door. I wanted to wish you a Merry Christmas.'

'Well, thanks. Same to you. Could I get a few more minutes kip, though? Or alternatively, a really strong coffee?'

He emitted a rumbly chuckle that made me smile, even through my laziness. 'I'll give you ten minutes, max.'

I burrowed into my pillow. But what felt like only seconds later, Wilf was back.

'My sister the barista made this for you.' He wafted something in front of my nose.

My olfactory nerve tingled. 'Cappuccino…?' I pulled myself upright, as he set down the holly and ivy adorned mug on the bedside table.

Wilf smiled, but it was tight. 'I didn't mean that to rhyme. But JoJo is on her best behaviour, so I'm trying not to be too cynical. At least for the next twelve hours. I'm medicated for the day. I think I can comply.'

'Don't joke.' I frowned.

'Why not? I'm allowed to, aren't I? Of all people.'

'You don't have to be all doom and gloom. But I don't want you to be blasé about it with me, either. Don't shut me out, Wilf. I need to see every side of this.'

'I'm not shutting you out.' He stood up, paced the room. 'You don't have a Christmas tree. Why not?'

'Where would I fit it in, for a start? And you're being evasive.'

'I'm not, I'm just... We're doing *happy* – remember?' His face was drawn. 'It's what you promised. So I'm making the most of today.'

'Is that why you're wearing that shirt? It's very... "romantic male lead."'

He glanced down at the flannel shirt, with red, black and white checks. 'Belle and Vicki gave it to me this morning. They insisted I wear it. At least it fits. You should see what they're making Loki wear.'

'Ha! Santa hat and scarf? Same as every year. Don't worry, the hat doesn't last.' With an ungracious snort, I dragged my legs over the side of the bed. 'Got to love your nieces.'

'Do I?' His lips twitched.

I took a tentative sip of the cappuccino, as expertly made as ever, before taming my hair back with a scrunchie in a low pony-tail. 'Okay, let's see.' I bent to rummage under the bed. 'Here you go, then. Happy Christmas. Sorry it's such a rubbish gift.'

I was about to say I'd do better next year. But…

I'd been awake till around two, mulling over our options. After all, my parents had managed a long-distance relationship, in the beginning, and Bristol was just down the road compared to Italy. Yet I couldn't see how it would work in our case without negativity creeping in. It would niggle me that he wasn't here to help, however sincerely I understood why. And he'd probably grow to resent that I hadn't chosen him over his family. As for solutions beyond the obvious: they'd only become more unworkable and farfetched, until my brain had spun from the effort.

Wilf sat on the bed and unwrapped the wallet and keyring set, nodding politely. 'My wallet's splitting, so this is good timing. And the keyring will come in useful…' He tailed off. We both seemed to realise what it would be useful for. The key to the hovel would probably only be a temporary addition.

'It's a "meh" gift,' I said quickly, not wanting to think about faraway ground-floor flats, waiting to be occupied. 'But I got it before we were even together. Men are hard to buy for imaginatively, in my experience. And they don't usually appreciate my floral crochet creations.'

'Women aren't much easier, if you don't know where to start. I'd thought of getting you jewellery; a necklace or bracelet. I was standing in front of a shop in Bristol when…' Wilf unfolded himself, and picked up a crudely wrapped, flat package I hadn't noticed before, from the coffee table. He sat back down and held on to it as he spoke, as if hesitant to hand it over. 'I've never seen you wear jewellery, though, so I don't know if you prefer silver or gold, or you just don't like bling the way JoJo does. Anyway, there was a window display in the shop next door, and I couldn't help getting distracted. My eyes kept homing in on this, and after seeing you in that red dress at the party…' He paused. 'You should wear more colour, Cara. It suits you. I think you might be hiding when you don't.'

'Hiding?'

'From the world. Or from life.' Wilf glanced towards the clothes rail. 'The things you sell, the way you've decorated in here… Everything matches your personality. I just don't think you can see it.'

Oh hell, what had he bought me? Something I was going to have to pretend to love, by the sound of it. And his words unsettled me, about the hiding part, because there was too much truth in them.

'Okay, then, so what did you get me?'

'It's nothing big, although it wasn't all that cheap.'

I rolled my eyes. 'You're not supposed to say that.'

'No. I know, but… it's more symbolic than anything else. Anyway, here.'

He handed me the gift with reluctance, and I tore a small section to start with, but there was a layer of tissue paper I was going to have to get through, too. I paused for a moment, speculating if it was a flamboyant silk scarf or shawl or something along those lines, then galvanised myself into action again. If it was, I didn't necessarily have to wear it; I could simply drape it from my headboard with my others.

Oh, just get on with it, Cara. Stop faffing. I primed myself, ready to smile. As the layers of paper fell away, my lips spread upwards automatically. And then the smile froze, as if it didn't know what else to do with itself.

I blinked down at the vibrant pink beret. Newer, and slightly brighter for it, than the one I'd touched at Perdita's days ago, but the same shape and texture and detailing.

'You hate it… don't you?' said Wilf, after an infinite silence. I looked up again, opening and closing my mouth, but no sound came out. He frowned. 'Cara, what's wrong? Is it that bad?'

'It's not bad at all,' I said quietly. 'But who told you?'

'Who told me what?'

'About Perdita wearing one of these?'

It was Wilf's turn to open and close his mouth. He shrugged, spreading his hands at his sides, palms facing upwards. 'No one. No one told me.'

'And you never saw her? Around the village?' I was gabbling now. 'She always wore a beret like this. You wouldn't have even realised it was Perdita. She would have been just some random person to you. *Think*, Wilf.'

'As far as I'm aware, I've never seen anyone wearing one of these around Pebblestow. Like I said, it was in the window display beside the jeweller's near where Aaron lives. I don't know why, but it just drew me. I could picture you wearing it.'

I jumped up, stood in front of the mirror in my comfiest, well-worn PJs, and falteringly slipped the beret on my head. With my hair pulled back, only a few stray curls hung wispily around my face. They were dark, almost black, but if I imagined them pure white...

And I saw it again, like the reflection in the toy shop window.

Oh... My... God.

'It suits you,' Wilf was saying, and I fought to listen to him, not the roaring in my ears. 'I'm sorry you think it's an old lady's type of hat. Personally, I think it can suit any age. Cara, are you okay? You're starting to freak me out—'

'Perdita's husband gave it to her,' I cut in softly, almost reverently. 'Well, they weren't actually married at that point. The beret was his first gift to her. They hadn't been together that long.'

Wilf was silent a moment. 'Perdita's husband… the publisher?'

I stared at his reflection behind me in the mirror, as I nodded. 'Indie publisher. I don't know his name. She never actually said.'

'Oh… Right.' I watched as Wilf blinked at the wrapping paper I'd left scattered over the bed.

A compulsion swelled within me, burning like acid. 'I need to go up to Riverside,' I said. 'Their house. It's the other side of the village."

Wilf looked up again. 'As in… right now? I thought Perdita had already left?'

'She has, and it's a holiday home, there might be people in there for Christmas.'

'So, why…?'

'I have to try to make sense of this, and I've got a *feeling* – a strong one, Wilf – that the house holds the answer. I don't think any of this is just a huge coincidence any more. I really don't.' Shakily, I swung to face him. 'Will you come with me?'

Creases lined his brow, half-covered by chestnut curls. He pushed his hair back. 'We'll borrow a car, it'll be quicker.'

'Could you get the keys while I throw some clothes on? I'm not going in my PJs.'

Ten minutes later, we were driving through the village. A sudden flurry of snowflakes danced across the windscreen. Wilf peered upwards, over the steering wheel. 'The forecasters got it right, for once…'

I stared at the tiny stars of billowing snow, mesmerised, even as my heart thudded faster. I was in jeans, jumper, coat and boots now; the beret at a jaunty angle, as if nothing would induce me to take it off. There were hardly any cars on the roads. I made Wilf slow down, though, when we neared the top of the north road. The gap in the high hedgerow seemed even tighter as I pointed and Wilf flipped the indicator.

'Are you telling me Perdita used to walk up and down this hill?'

'Sometimes,' I said. 'But I gave her lifts, when I could. It must have taken her forever on foot. I don't know how she did it…'

The narrow lane, hemmed in by hedgerow, widened as usual on to the expanse of gravel, but the sign on the low wall looked grubbier than I remembered, surrounded by a tangle of weeds that almost obscured the 'R'. My heart thumped harder, determined to leap out of my chest. The house loomed ahead, an almost fairy-tale forlornness to it, with the ivy – so neatly clipped every other time I'd visited – overwhelming the front, as if trying to shield it from prying eyes.

Every window was boarded up.

Without speaking, Wilf parked close to the stone steps, his knuckles pearly white as they gripped the steering wheel. The front door was covered with plywood, too; in shadow under a rotting timber porch that hadn't existed on the Riverside I was familiar with.

Instead of an answer, I had a hundred more questions.

'Cara…' My name scraped hoarsely out of Wilf's throat. 'What's going on?'

'I don't know,' I said breathlessly, fumbling with the handle, pushing open the passenger door.

Wilf didn't move. 'No one's lived here in ages.'

'I can see that. It wasn't anything like this when I used to visit Perdita.'

'Did anyone ever come up here with you?'

'No, I was always on my own. Well, Perdita was around, but…' I pulled up my collar against the bite in the air, and frowned at him through the open door, realising what he was implying. 'You… you think I made her up?'

'That's not what I'm saying.' He was still hoarse. 'I just…'

'She used to come to the café. Sallie spoke to her. Perdita was a fan of her mince pies.'

Just as much as I was.

'I – I don't understand.' He pushed open his own door, at last. 'Are you sure this is the right place?'

'Of course I'm sure. How many other Riversides do you think there are up here?'

'I saw the sign. It's just… I don't get it.'

'Neither do I.' I dug my nails into my palms, as if trying to wake myself up if I was dreaming. 'There's no sense in any of this, Wilf, but I need to see round the back.'

He nodded hesitantly. We picked our way along the mossy, crazy-paved path on the left-hand side, stepping over an excess of weeds as we neared the rear of the property. The view down the slope to the river, and the hills rolling into the distance, greeted us instantly. No enclosed garden. No wall at the bottom, with a gate. Only the jetty, jutting out into the water.

The garden was wild and abandoned, reinforcing the fairy-tale effect. Bare-branched trees reared up from the long grass, the borders on either side straggly and overgrown.

The back of the house was as boarded up as the front. As I approached the window that had once drawn in the pale December sunshine, I knew the kitchen beyond would look nothing like the one I'd loved to spend time in as I'd luxuriated in the warmth of being welcome there, and wanted. I pressed a hand lightly to the wood and tried to picture the room as I'd known it... Yet, as the snow started to fall more fiercely, I couldn't. For some reason, it was hazy, as if the memory had burrowed too deep to ever see light again. All that was left was the way it had made me feel.

I looked towards Wilf, who was standing motionless a little way down the garden, gazing into the valley, up to his shins in the grass. I followed where he'd trampled, and he stirred, looking down at me. Pale-faced. Eyes glittering with something I couldn't place, the green flecks in the hazel more conspicuous than ever.

'The view's spectacular...'

A smile tugged at my mouth. 'I know.'

We turned together to look back at the house. Structurally it looked sound. I remembered vaguely what Perdita had told me. A dispute over inheritance. A property falling into neglect.

'I don't think it's ready for its ending yet.' There was a dent in Wilf's brow as he spoke. Instinctively I knew he was trying to imagine Riverside in its glory days. 'I don't know why it's empty and alone now, but it shouldn't be.'

I leaned against him, threading my arm through his. 'I don't think it's alone any more. I think it knows we're here.'

'Cara – how can it feel so much like...'

'*Home*?'

He pulled me closer to him, as if craving my warmth. 'What else did Perdita tell you?'

'I don't know why it's so fuzzy in my head now, but I know she said her husband bought it, partly as an investment. I think they took years to restore it. But it was so beautiful, Wilf. I remember that much. The most glorious family home.'

'Family?'

'Children and grandchildren. I don't know the specifics; Perdita was never that clear. There's no use asking, and... do we really need to know?'

I turned again, looking towards the river, the sight smudged now by a curtain of snow, the weight of something sad pressing on me. But whatever it was, it seemed so far in the future that the weight grew lighter until it was nothing more than a flimsy cloak, covering me without pinning me down.

'I still don't understand,' Wilf said, and shook his head. 'But somehow… I don't care.'

We stared at each other, dazed, disoriented, and then skirted the house, skimming the brick walls proprietorially, taking our time even as the weather worsened. At the front, Wilf pulled at a frond of ivy hanging over the plywood covering the door, spotting something white pinned to the board behind it that we hadn't noticed before.

An envelope.

His hand shook as he passed it to me.

Just two words on the front.

'Dearest Cara'

My own hands were shaking, too, as I opened it to find a large square Christmas card. I gasped audibly at the painting of a carousel, set against snow. Red and green and gold. White horses. Midnight-blue saddles.

Inside, there were just a few lines written in the same handwriting as the note that had accompanied the dress. Handwriting very like mine, I realised now, but spidery and weak, as if the hand that penned it was about to crumble away and vanish.

'From one Cara to another,

The greatest delight of my life was knowing you.

My darling girl, your wings are strong enough now, so use them wisely and well. You're not lost any more. And neither am I.

"The privilege of a lifetime is to become who you truly are."

— Carl Gustav Jung

With love,

C. M. B.'

I read it twice, then handed it to Wilf, who was waiting for me at the bottom of the stone steps to the gravel drive. I paused at the top. His hand still trembling, he read the card and returned it for me to slide back in the envelope. Inhaling a deep gulp of cold crystal air to cleanse my lungs, I tucked it into the largest of my coat pockets.

'Wilf.' I met his gaze, as earnest as I'd ever been. 'At the risk of sounding bossy and demanding and controlling, I want you to stay here, in Pebblestow. I don't want you to go to Bristol. You're not meant to leave, I'm sure of it. Every moment of this is worth fighting for. *We're* worth fighting for.'

'Cara—'

'Hear me out. Please. I realise this is totally unbelievable, but I *know* you're strong enough to stay. I know you can do this. I know because, somehow, you've done it before. We both have.'

I'd barely finished talking before I was crushed against his chest.

I let him hold me, and held him in return for as long as he needed. Whatever emotions were wreaking havoc on me were possibly amplified in Wilf. I'd read that about his condition. And besides, I felt as much at home in his embrace as I had in the kitchen here at Riverside.

He pulled away, the snow falling even faster now, as he stepped back down on to the gravel. His words rushed, breathless, confused. 'Cara, your wish – on the carousel… the one you told me about yesterday…'

'You want to know what it was?' He nodded intently, and I told him, because I didn't think I could jinx something that had already come true. 'Well, it was simple really. And complicated, I suppose, at the same time. I just wanted to like myself.'

Wilf took a moment to absorb this. 'You wanted to like yourself?' He stroked his thumb across my cheek, wiping away a tear I hadn't noticed I'd shed.

I was tall enough on the top step to be able to look him straight in the eyes without either of us having to tilt our heads; equals in every sense.

'Isn't that what we all need? To value ourselves more? And I don't mean in a big-headed, I'm-so-much-wonderfuller-than-anyone-else sort of way. I don't mean that at all.'

Wilf stared at me in silence, blinking snowflakes from his lashes, and then I was spinning in his arms, my feet dangling for a few heady seconds, and his kiss met mine with so much relief and joy and possibility wrapped within it, that I never wanted it to end. Except, of course, it did. And that was fine in its own way, too. Because *everything* from this moment on would be better for having come here this Christmas morning, in a swirl of snow, to discover where we belonged.

'I wish I could have met Perdita,' Wilf muttered into my hair, almost knocking off the precious pink beret as he squeezed me again.

I grabbed at the beret, and laughed. 'Oh, you will, one day, Wilf Brooks. I'll make sure of it. And something tells me you're going to absolutely *adore* her.'

Want to read more from Lottie Cardew?

Return to Pebblestow in

One Last Dream for December

∞∞∞

Thank you so much for reading this book, I sincerely hope you enjoyed it. If you did, why not consider rating it, or leaving a review, to help others find it too. It would make a big difference to a little author!

Warmest wishes,
Lottie xx

Acknowledgements

Like Perdita, I have a lot to be grateful for and I never stop saying thank you. So I want to start with my family, for their continued support, especially my husband for his lockdown cups of tea and coffee, not to mention lunch on a tray.

Also my friends in Novelistas Ink (particularly fellow villager, Louise Marley) – the best cheerleaders in the business! – and the writer and book-blogger friends who encourage us to keep smiling and storytelling.

Last but not least, I want to thank my more-than-probable ADHD, for picking up on a shiny new idea and running with it, when my autistic-self wanted to hide under a pillow and cry.

About the Author

Lottie Cardew was born during the Great Lockdown of early 2021, and writes uplifting, heartstring-tugging romcoms. She lives in North Wales, subdues the other members of Novelistas Ink if they misbehave, and is an advocate for diversity in fiction. Lottie is diagnosed autistic with suspected ADHD. Her home is overrun by husband, not-very-small children, and a ball of fluff masquerading as a Pomeranian, so Lottie frequently takes refuge at her desk.

Twitter: @MsLottieCardew
Facebook: Lottie Cardew - Author
Instagram: @bossynovelista

Printed in Great Britain
by Amazon